Chandru Bhojwani

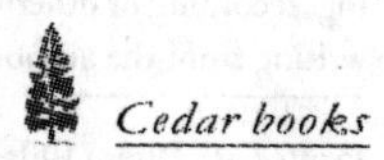

*Published by:*
Cedar books

*An Imprint of*
**Pustak Mahal®**, Delhi

J-3/16, Daryaganj, New Delhi-110002
☎ 23276539, 23272783, 23272784 • *Fax:* 011-23260518
*E-mail:* info@pustakmahal.com • *Website:* www.pustakmahal.com

***Sale Centre***

10-B, Netaji Subhash Marg, Daryaganj, New Delhi-110002
☎ 23268292, 23268293, 23279900 • *Fax:* 011-23280567
*E-mail:* rapidexdelhi@indiatimes.com

**Hind Pustak Bhawan**
6686, Khari Baoli, Delhi-110006
☎ 23944314, 23911979

***Branches***

**Bengaluru:** ☎ 080-22234025 • *Telefax:* 080-22240209
*E-mail:* pustak@airtelmail.in • pustak@sancharnet.in
**Mumbai:** ☎ 022-22010941, 022-22053387
*E-mail:* rapidex@bom5.vsnl.net.in
**Patna:** ☎ 0612-3294193 • *Telefax:* 0612-2302719
*E-mail:* rapidexptn@rediffmail.com
**Hyderabad:** *Telefax:* 040-24737290
*E-mail:* pustakmahalhyd@yahoo.co.in



**First Edition: 2009**

**Second Edition:** 2011

ISBN 978-81-223-1091-7

**Disclaimer** : The novel is entirely a work of fiction. The names, characters and incidents portrayed in it are the work of the author's imagination. Any resemblance to actual persons, living or dead, events or localities is entirely coincidental.



*Printed at* : Param Offsetters, Okhla, New Delhi-110020

# This Book is Dedicated to

***Saju, Indur and Dev Bhojwani***

*Where I've reached in life couldn't have been achieved without the three of you. A lifetime of thanks wouldn't be enough to express my gratitude and appreciation for the life, love and support you have provided me with. You have been my guiding light during my darkest moments, my crutch when I was at my weakest, and my best friends who continue to share in my joy and success. This book is dedicated to you. Love you always.*

# Thanks to

**Heena Bhojwani**

Thank you for your unwavering support and belief. I really am blessed to be able to share this amazing milestone and journey with you.

**Sherna Khambatta**

You were the catalyst that motivated me to overcome the last obstacle and I thank you for that. Without your belief and tireless effort, I wouldn't have accomplished what I have. Thank you.

**Deepa Asnani**

I thank you for being by my side at every step of my journey. Your friendship, support and sacrifice have been priceless. Know that you were instrumental. We did it!!!

**Malti Bhojwani**

Your positive support and constant visualisation finally manifested. Thank you for being that pillar of encouragement and always believing and supporting.

**Amit Butani**

Thank you for your help and constant effort. It is an honour to call you a friend.

**Madhuri Hemandas**

Duri, thanks for your support, your feedback and being on call whenever I've needed.

**Sonia Vaswani**

Thank you for being a constant in my life. Your untiring support and never ending willingness to help are invaluable. You truly are an inspiration.

**Tarun Gulrajani**

Jigga, thank you for being my side always and for your continuous support. NBL

**Aarti Mahtani**

You have always been a pillar of support and your loyalty as a friend knows no limits. Thank you for your support and your friendship.

**Vick Chugani**

Not only have you always been a voice of encouragement but your belief in me and my future is truly poetic. Thank you.

I'd also like to thank,

Prakash Thawani, Hansa Thawani, Sumit Thawani, Suhin Thawani, Rachana Mirpuri, Kanchan Sakhrani, Pooja Samtani, Vishal Daryanani, Leena Kewlani, Navin Belani, Leena Kinger, Peter McClusky, Nadia Munwar, Puja Sujanani, Bobby Ray Sharma, Radhika Desai, KB.Singh, KP.Singh, Sunita Masigani, Roshni Sahijwani, Lena Gidwani, Nitya Khemlani, Kate Fitzgerald, Vini Kewelramani, Reshma Kalwani, Rohit Gupta, Bharti Lalwani, Kalpana Behara, Susan Abraham, Shana Ninan, Mauie Hernando, Kavita Daswani, Anil Vaswani, Avisha Mukhey, Kavita Chugani, Sandee Harilela, Arun Bharwani, Anjali Sakhrani, Nandini Bhaskaran, Aneesha Gaba, Sid Mehta, Shalvi Mangaokar, Sakhi Shah, Malaika Mahtaney, Inder Singh, Shweta Ganesh Kumar, Sam Vaswani, Misha Mathew, Kaveri Lalchand, Akansha Agrawal, Gautami Tripathy, Roshmi Sinha, ArtFlipping, Oye Times, The YSA, Beyond Sindh, Sub Prime Media and Pustak Mahal.

Thank you all for the help, making my dream a reality!

## Author's Note

Devastated by Preeti's betrayal, the protagonist Om collapses in emotional and physical exhaustion, and with that, begins his arduous battle for peace and solace. Plagued by nostalgia and restless nights, Om inadvertently slips into a world of alcoholism. Struggling to maintain his job as a columnist in New York, he turns to his support system in Mona and his best friend Arun, only to watch their lives unravel while he attempts to recover. In essence, *The Journey of Om* is every person's story.

Having experienced an episode similar to that of Om's and learning how common it was in almost every circle and age group, I felt inspired to write this story. During that time, I witnessed how almost everyone suffered through their own magnified anguish, which no one could fully comprehend unless they've shared a similar fate. And yet, in spite of that knowledge, the kindest and most caring of us can be as hypocritical and selfish as the next person. Over time, I discovered that somehow, there always seemed to be a connection between the main players in our life at that very moment and eventually, a balance always ensues.

I wanted to capture that constant cycle of life with events that were personally hellacious and yet, an everyday occurrence. Hence, in essence, *The Journey of Om* is in fact, everyone's story. In spite of being a light and enjoyable read, the plot is layered and complex when deliberated on. It captures numerous facets of life from loss and betrayal to hope and justice. I believe a story that moves readers to tears, allows people to feel that the words on the page are their own and illustrates they aren't alone while allowing them to feel understood, deserves to be shared.

*The Journey of Om* is such a story.

– *Chandru Bhojwani*

# Chapter 1

Cold, almost ice cold, and yet it felt refreshing. The soothing water passed over my blistered feet, revitalising them. Judging by the heat and the position of the sun, it was noon. I had been running for over an hour.

My breathing, finally, calmed as I gazed at the water flowing in front of me. The current had me hypnotised and my eyes remained fixated on the stones that lay at the bottom of the crystal stream. A flurry of thoughts came rushing; as I tried to make sense of them, I began to slouch and felt the remaining few ounces of energy seep out of me.

Sure, things hadn't been going smooth in our relationship, but I had been trying to make it work. Between meeting deadlines at the magazine and trying to get the mortgage for the flat, I barely had time to breathe. When I did make time, she was always occupied with a birthday, anniversary, or some ladies lunch. Finally, it all made sense. I couldn't believe how blind I had been. If I had just paid a little more attention and raised my head once in a while, it would have been as clear to me as the stream I was peering into.

I had all the pieces in place for our special day together. The plan was to arrive at Preeti's and first surprise her with breakfast in bed. A basket of warm croissants along with scrambled eggs and a Vanilla

Latte. I was then going to take her cycling in the park followed by a champagne brunch for just the two of us. It was going to be a simple day, filled with romance and quality time.

They must've heard me climbing up the stairs since he was already standing by the bed, hastily pulling up his underwear. I don't remember what crossed my mind at that instant. I was blank and yet a crushing array of emotions passed through me. I remember feeling enough rage to pounce on him and tear his limbs apart. The crashing tray snapped me out of my bewilderment and when my gaze hit the floor, I saw the juice and coffee gush over her beige shag carpet. I stood there and stared, not knowing what to say or even think. I remember her saying something to me but I couldn't make out what it was.

The stinging on my hand brought me out of my hypnotic state. I saw the little vampire feasting on me, and with one crushing strike, sent him to his doom. If only I could have done to Ravi what I had done to the mosquito. The reality was that it was not as much his fault as it was hers. I had always believed that it was human nature to prey on what others possessed, so much so that not coveting what belonged to others was the tenth commandment. But, Preeti allowed it to happen.

I lost count of how many minutes or hours I had spent sitting by the stream, but after a while, I had lost all feeling in my feet. I wasn't sure if it was the water or the pain that had left me numb all over. It was time to head off but not home, not yet. I began to walk around, staring at the moist green grass beneath my feet. Suddenly, I had nothing to do.

Eventually, I'd have to go home but sitting there alone within those four walls would drive me insane. I had to concentrate on getting control of my mind. I focused on my surroundings – the gentle breeze brushing my hair, the quiet rush of the stream and the open air. That's when it struck me – the car! I had left the car in her driveway. Was he still there? Had she called me? Had she noticed my car parked outside? Thoughts began to race faster. That was it. I would never go back to that house again. I was alone. It was over. A deep dark sadness enveloped me and I collapsed onto the grass in sheer emotional exhaustion. The weight in my chest grew heavier as the lump in my throat increased in girth. A whirlwind of emotions swept through me. Too many to count, let alone describe, but two emotions were consistent, sorrow and rage.

I had met Ravi at our weekly basketball game. He was just another one of the guys. Preeti would come and watch us play; a habit of hers I treasured. I never knew if she came because she knew how much I liked having her there, or because she enjoyed watching the game. That was also where they first met. How many times must I have played with him, unaware of the reality that continued to transpire around me? Who else knew? My head was spinning and I felt nauseous. I had been such a naïve fool.

The skies began to darken and I realised that hours had passed while I sat drowning in my misery. Standing up, I walked to the curb and hailed a cab. The car would have to be left for another day.

❖❖❖

## Chapter 2

It was early November and I was still settling in. I had moved from London to Manhattan a month ago and hardly knew anyone. Evenings and weekends were usually spent watching movies and sports in my Upper Eastside studio apartment. One Friday night, an acquaintance invited me to a fashion show with a colleague of his. I accepted without deliberation, oblivious of the magnitude to which the events of that night would affect my life.

The thought of sexy models strutting their scantily clad bodies down a runway had us eagerly pacing down West 52$^{nd}$ Street. Once we arrived, however, I learned there was no fashion show, but instead we had entered a '*Desi* party'. As expected, when entering an event full of Indians, heads turned and stared. Our broad smiles transformed into shock. Breaking away from the others, I headed straight to the bar for refuge.

My eyes darted around and scouted the venue as the red-vested bartender poured my drink. Generic crimson wallpaper clung to the walls and the air was thick with the aroma of Indian cuisine. In the corner, a buffet was laid out with oily appetisers and paper plates, while stained curtains had been draped over folded tables. No one seemed to notice or care though, as they were content with jumping around to the latest Bollywood tunes on the makeshift wooden dance floor.

Drinks in hand, we stood and watched people dance. A few sips into my rum and coke, I turned around and noticed the wall of men standing behind us, also surveying the dance floor. It was like being placed amidst a disturbing Stanley Kubrick movie in which a group of onlookers were observing an orgy. A horrific thought crossed my mind:

"*I've just arrived in New York and I'm already a loser!*"

However, the voyeurism continued as I sat between the other two at a table. Soon realising that neither of them was going to make the slightest effort to socialise and were instead content to let the night slip by, I shook my head in disgust and downed my liquor. Excusing myself, I found my way out of the male human sandwich in which I had been the meat, and fled to the restroom.

With the name 'Armitage Shanks' staring back at me, I established that I had to shed my shy personality and make a conscious effort to mingle. It was an ideal opportunity to make a fresh start, and I couldn't afford to be complacent. Turning towards the sink, I began conversing with the only other person in the restroom.

"Do you come here often?" Realising what I had just said, I quickly injected, "Err, I mean to these events?"

"No, not really. Just once in a while."

The bathroom banter continued as Dheeraj and I headed back to the solitary bar. Fortunately, he didn't think I was trying to pick him up, nor was he the type to hang around a men's room waiting to be picked up while humming 'I want your sex'.

Dheeraj had arrived alone that evening, but back at the bar, we ran into some of his friends. Of the four girls to whom I was introduced, I only recalled the names of the first two. Later, I decided to invite the seated pieces of bread to join us. As we stood together, I asked Dheeraj to introduce his friends, but he said he didn't know the other two girls, so I boldly circled around to the semi-strangers.

"Hi, sorry, I didn't get your name."

"Preeti, and you are?"

"Om."

"Nice to meet you again," she smiled. "You have a bit of an accent, where are you from?"

"London. I just moved here last month."

"Wow, that's a big change. What are you doing here?" she asked as she sipped her drink.

"I have a column in a lifestyle magazine. You may have heard of it, it's called 'Asian Life'."

"Sorry, I haven't. But then again, I don't really get much time to read."

"Oh really?" I leaned in closer to her ear, "So, what is it that you do?"

"I'm in Med School."

"Whoa!" I looked at my watch, "Isn't it past your bed time?"

She smiled.

We chatted for a while and when we finally raised our heads, everyone had dispersed. Our friends had gone in their separate directions while we stood there in our own little world. We looked at each other and continued talking.

As the evening progressed, we had been together for most of it. 'Sapphire Tonics' kept the mood relaxed as our conversation flowed. She hinted that the song playing was her favourite and with that cue, I pulled her to the dance floor. Soon after, the DJ played the timeless 'Too close' by Next. Taking the mood to the next level, I inched closer towards her and she reciprocated. We melted into the song and into each other. It was then I realised, not every part of me was under my control. I attempted to back away as subtly as possible, but as soon as I did, I feared that maybe others around could see what I did not want her to feel. I tried not to be too close, nor too far, while staying composed and maintaining my rhythm. At the time, it had felt like a feat worthy of Cirque du Soleil!

Making our way to the rest of the group, I couldn't help but smile and feel like the man of the hour. Eventually, the rest of the sandwich went home and I mingled with my newfound friends. Towards the end of that evening, Preeti came up from behind and wrapped her arms around me, holding me close, it was as if this was the way we had always been.

❖❖❖

# Chapter 3

The reflection in the mirror said it all. Dark circles around bloodshot eyes; the result of a restless night with few intermittent naps. It was the first day, and it was going to be a long one. I contemplated skipping work but knew all too  well, it would only make things worse. After all, an idle mind is Preeti's playground, I thought to myself. All I could do now was keep busy and get through this, get through to the other side.

I resembled a rabid dog as foam trickled down the side of my mouth and dripped down in to the white sink. That's when I heard barking in my head and figured it was the first step to insanity. They came once again, the muddled thoughts about Preeti; I remembered the beautiful moments we shared, the priceless memories we had created and cherished. I remembered the multiple clichéd candlelit dinners, the 2am knock on her door in the rain because I just couldn't wait to see her. I remembered her walking up behind me, leaning in and gently resting her head on my back while I shaved in the mornings. I always smiled when I rang the doorbell and heard her anxiously scurry to the door. Then like a wrecking ball, the image of Ravi and Preeti came out of nowhere, shattering my memories. My grip on the basin tightened as I shut my eyes and leaned over. The hollow pain rushed in with increasing intensity, pulsing and throbbing. I bit hard on the toothbrush, ripping out the bristles.

I stared at the numbers blinking at the same single beat. I wanted to hear the messages. I wanted to know if she had called and what she said. I wanted to hear her cry and beg for forgiveness. But what if she hadn't called? How much would that hurt? If she did call, how much would her message hurt? What if her message was in line with us splitting up and she wanted her things? I was going insane! I plugged the phone back in and walked away, leaving the machine blinking.

As the distance to her home shortened, the pace of my heart quickened. Would she be standing outside? Probably not, it was far too early in the morning to be up. The fact that it took me almost twenty minutes to get a cab was evidence of that. Part of me wanted to see her, and yet, I hoped I wouldn't. The battle between my heart and mind was going to ruin me. This confusion between logic and desire was devouring my soul. As the internal struggle intensified, I tried to boil it down to the hard facts:

Do you have feelings for her?

Yes.

Do you miss her?

Yes.

Do you want to be with her?

No!

Could you be with her?

"Fuck no!" I whispered, as my hand turned into a fist, digging my nails into the palm.

"What was that?" asked the driver, "I couldn't quite hear you."

"No, nothing. It was nothing."

This was always the part I hated about break-ups, the recovery. It takes far too long, the extreme and unpredictable mood swings sparked off by insignificant reminders. Then, there are the moments of weakness, when we want nothing more than to be with the person. We justify calling the person, knowing that doing so only makes it harder, after which, we are faced with the gaping void we try to fill. We seek companionship and security and give way to vulnerable desperation. As a result, we jump from person to person, only to realise in the quiet moments that the void remains. The cycle continues, and we're trapped in a descending spiral.

As we approached her house, I saw no one outside. In spite of my unrealistic expectations, I couldn't keep the awful feeling of disappointment at bay. I stood at the end of the pebble path flanked by luscious grass, and stared at the wooden door, desperately hoping that it would fly open and she'd run to me teary eyed and arms spread wide.

"Fucking Bollywood," I chuckled as I turned away from the porch.

Walking towards my car, I recalled her spontaneous reaction when she had first seen it. Initially she didn't like the inferno red pearl colour, but it gradually grew on her. She had wanted me to lease a BMW or a Lexus, but after taking a spin or two in the Dodge Charger, she was smitten.

I caught a whiff of her familiar jasmine scent while pulling the door shut. Her presence must have always been there, but today was when I first noticed it. I took a deep breath to inhale it completely. I felt like a smoker taking his first drag after months of deprivation. Eyes shut, I allowed the scent to fuel the memories that flickered in my mind. Preeti's aroma filled my lungs, invoking a deep desire for her. With that came the sinking feeling of depression, one I knew I'd experience often.

I saw a cream coloured envelope pinned under the left wiper. I reached out to grab it and it simply read 'Om'. There was no 'dear' or any other term of endearment. I traced my forefinger over her handwriting. As pretty as it was, it felt so empty and yet heavy. I wanted to tear it open and read the note, but I was scared. I looked up, but there was no one by the window. The next emotion, anger, was on its way.

I flung the envelope onto the passenger seat and slammed the accelerator to the floor. The tires screeched, undoubtedly leaving skid marks on the tarmac. The scent in the car now fed the feelings of betrayal and humiliation that I suffered. For whom I once only wished joy and happiness, I now desired pain and misfortune. How rapidly emotions could swing from one extreme to another! How suddenly had I been forced to cross that thin line between love and hate! I wanted vengeance, I wanted her to get hurt, to suffer and most importantly, I wanted her to regret.

# Chapter 4

A week had passed and I only wished for the torment to be over already. I had been holding on to brief moments of peace and grappled for any form of diversion, however, her name constantly reverberated in my mind. The deep echo haunted me at every turn, and eventually, it took on an almost majestic quality. I heard it being whispered in my mind over and over and over.

With the sudden abundance of time and nothing to do, I desperately needed to occupy my mind. Writing my column had become a struggle and it was only a matter of time before my emergency stash of articles ran out.

As expected, the news spread like wild fire, although I hadn't been questioned much about what transpired. Friends chose to sensibly tiptoe around the subject. I hadn't seen Ravi or Preeti yet, but the inevitability hovered over me. I didn't know how I was going to deal with facing them, but I would have to cross that bridge when the time came. I was sure the possibility of seeing me, the awkwardness, embarrassment, or the feeling of discomfort that would arise if we met, would leave her unperturbed. The thought probably never even crossed her mind.

Preeti had this uncanny ability to 'block' things out and I hated it. I despised that I had to experience the agony and stress while she seemed unaffected. I recalled an incident when we had a long and heated argument that had left me feeling terribly depressed. She on the other hand had a night out with her friends and ended up calling me at 4am, drunk.

The next morning we fought again and when I expressed how awful I had felt after the fight, she said, "Om, you know I can block things out, and yes, I *did* block you out! I'm not going to feel guilty about going out and having fun with my friends. I don't want to feel like crap because of you. If you chose to stay at home and be depressed, well that's idiotic of you."

It wasn't always perfect, but then nothing ever is. We did have good times and enjoyed each other a lot, but our fights used to be rough. She would always express herself with a few curt words and left it at that. Whenever I probed, her response was "I have nothing more to say, I'm going back to my place," and with that, Preeti would be gone. She would continue with her day while I struggled to function as a normal human being. If only I could block her out.

The longing for companionship and closeness consumed me. I also wanted my revenge and knew that if I would let myself get intimate with someone, I'd fulfil both urges. But that would be temporary and rebounding. I had to be smart and simply hold out. It was time to detox.

During the sleepless nights my mind wandered, reminiscing and touching upon painful memories. Before she fell asleep, she used to lay her head on my chest. I would have to wait for her to roll over before I could stretch and sleep on my stomach. In the mornings, the first one to wake up would cuddle the other. I had become used to having her being beside me.

The thought of calling her crossed my mind again, like it had a thousand times, but then I'd picture her and Ravi. She'd be moaning his name in ecstasy. With eyes firmly shut, I shook my head hoping to rid myself of the horrifying vision.

I focused my mind towards positive and constructive thoughts.It was during one of those anguish-filled sleepless nights that I woke up a-la 'Jerry Maguire' and started writing a 'Recovery' plan:

**Objective:** Get over Preeti quickly, efficiently and with as little pain as possible. We all know emotional pain is a lot worse than physical and there is only one healing factor. It's our best friend and worst enemy: TIME.

*Step 1:* Acceptance

This step is essential to achieve recovery. The subject needs to ACCEPT, for which certain amount of time is needed. Focusing on getting over it immediately will lead to frustration, anxiety and worsen the depression. Instead, it is important to understand that there *is* a finish line.

*Step 2:* Emotional Spring Clean

Get rid of everything the ex has ever given you. Anything of sentimental value must be disposed off. It is imperative for the subject to remain strong and be focused at this point, and not to be weakened by random reminders.

*Step 3:* The Calculation

How long should the recovery take?

If the subject had an idea about the duration, they could prepare themselves for the long haul. Four to six months is a fair estimate for one to completely clean one's system out.

*Step 4:* Occupied

Stay busy, meet old friends and make new ones. Exercising is recommended. It is important not to have the break up festering in one's mind.

*Step 5:* Communication Lock Down

This rule cannot be emphasised enough. There has to be no communication with the ex. Do whatever it takes to minimise the chance of talking or meeting with them asmuch as possible.

*Step 6:* The 'Bonus'

In this day and age, 'Bonus Booty' is common after the relationship is over. Although this may satisfy an itch, it only hinders the recovery process and brings up semi-fresh emotional wounds.

After spending half the night rewording, fussing and dwelling over the plan, it was finally printed. As time went by I would add to this, build on it and one day perhaps even have it published.

Although the 'plan' made sense and did help, there were times when I couldn't help but sink into thoughts of her, into thoughts of us. I couldn't help but wonder how things would be if I had taken advantage of every minute we had. Every misspent moment came back to haunt me. I missed her scent, her touch, her soft skin, her hair and her lips. The ache returned, but I accepted it with a soft and heavy sigh. I knew these were steps I needed to walk through. At every moment of weakness, I peered into my soul and recognised my flaws and accepted them.

I could throw away everything that reminded me of her, but I couldn't rid myself of the strongest and most intense tie to Preeti, her memory. I slumped lower in my chair and covered my face with my hands.

*I missed her.*

# Chapter 5

For the next couple of days, Preeti and I kept in touch over the phone. She asked what I had planned for my $28^{th}$ birthday and suggested spending it together. I still remember the chilly Thursday in November, four days after we had met for the first time at the India Palace party. I wore a dark brown suit with a tanned shirt and looked quite dapper. I hoped she would think the same.

As I waited anxiously outside her building I tried to recall the last time I had been on a date. It was then that it hit me. I didn't clearly remember what she looked like! It had been fairly dark at the party, not to mention I had been drinking. What if she didn't look like what I pictured? At that very moment, I saw her petite frame walk through the glass lobby doors and I noticed her big, captivating smile. Her long straight hair bounced as she descended the stairs in her black knee high leather boots. She turned to me and reached up to give me a hug, simultaneously putting all my fears to rest.

While we waited for the doors to open for the recording of the David Letterman show, our hands met and our fingers interlocked. We both felt a feverish nervousness and excitement. After the show, we proceeded to a bar and it was there, she began to open up and share what was important to her. She expressed her goals, her family and the loss of those close to her. She allowed herself to be vulnerable with me as tears rolled down her soft cheeks.

New Yorkers strolled in and out of the drab tavern but left us alone in our little world at the end of the bar. We continued to talk and laugh about different topics and time raced by as she enjoyed her 'Bombay Gin' and 'Tonic'. At one point I had stopped paying attention to what she was saying and focused on summoning up enough courage. Then in an instant, while she was in mid-sentence, I leaned forward and kissed her briefly on the lips. When I pulled away, we were faced with a few moments of stunned silence. Apologising I told her I couldn't help it. She smiled and leaned in.

That evening, we found ourselves at Scharmanns, a spacious lounge with wooden floors on West Broadway in downtown Soho. The mood was perfect; dim lighting, candles, a thin crowd and numerous vacant sofas waiting for our arrival. The exchange of affection continued as we were lost in one another. Her indescribable kiss had me captivated, and yearning for more. Never had a kiss felt so good, so hypnotic, so right. I'd later discover that I'd never tire of her kiss and its magic never faded. The passion between us would only intensify with time.

The waitress hesitantly interrupted our romance by placing our dinner on the table in front of us. Preeti leaned forward sticking her fork into the steaming ravioli, brought it to her lips and blew. She turned and smiled, as she fed me the first bite. The flames flickered all around us, and I thought to myself, 'She's the one'.

# *Chapter 6*

*Nobody said it was easy,*
*No one ever said it would be this hard*

– Coldplay

The naked flames danced gracefully around me as the pain flowed through my veins. The grief and sorrow enveloped me and I descended into it without resistance. Coldplay strummed their beat as their melancholic lyrics rang so very true.

The candles began to die one by one. They had served their purpose for that brief moment in time and finally reached their destiny. The sands of time continued to slip on by. The merlot mixed with my blood and the bitterness ran through me.

I reminisced about our nights together, nights when I lay next to her and watched her sleep. I used to place a gentle kiss on her cheek, before I went back to sleep, and pulled the comforter over her. Every day she woke up unaware of the affection she received during her slumber.

There would be more instances where I'd find myself plunged into past memories. Some will be worse, some bleak and some will feel never ending. It is in the dark of night that I'd stand alone and confront my demons. I'd have to keep reminding myself that this would all end with time, our friend and enemy.

The last candle flickered in the darkness and once that passed on, I would only have the half bottle of wine and music for company. I yearned for sleep, a peaceful night. I hated going to bed simply because I knew that sleep never came. It passed over my roof to those around, but never visited me anymore. How I longed for it to call on me!

I often wondered what she was doing, but that only led to venomous thoughts. She was probably out and about, gallivanting around the city with him. They must be laughing and kissing without any remorse for their actions.

The pain of the visions seared through my veins and almost felt physical. Unable to shake it, I hoped in vain that the big swigs of wine would counteract the growing ache. It ripped through without mercy. My mind unable to stop the stream of graphic visions flashing rapidly, and with each image the pain intensified.

I walked across the littered wooden floor to the answering machine and stared. The messages from that fateful day still remained. I could feel the pounding of my heart all over my body. I had been here many times before in the past few days. In moments of weakness I had even pressed 'play' only to press 'stop' immediately afterwards. My palms were sweaty and the confusion in my mind drove me insane. I had a desperate yearning to listen to the message, hoping I'd hear her voice begging me to forgive her, to come back and that she regretted her mistake, to hear her cry and hurt as much as I had. On the other hand I was scared, scared that there wouldn't be a message from her, that she was unaffected. The thought of that was too painful to bear.

I continued to throw away everything Preeti gave me until all that remained was the letter she had left on the windshield of my car. I sat by the fire and placed it on the mahogany coffee table. After staring at it for a while, I picked it up and inched closer towards opening it. My mind wrestled with the decision, arguing that I could handle it, that I was over it, justifying that I owed it to myself. The other part of me didn't want to take the risk. I finally decided and there was no turning back. My eyes fixated on the paper and the emotions that ran through were indescribable. My grip on the wine bottle tightened. The pain came back with all the graphic visions in tow. I could feel myself living through it again and again. My body began to stiffen and an array of confusion, anger and despair blanketed me as I watched the flames consume the letter. I would never know what she had written to me, never.

Standing up, I walked to the answering machine dropping the empty wine bottle on the way, and in one single motion I pushed the button.

'Messages have been deleted.'

# Chapter 7

The warm, sweet brew slid down my throat warming my chest. The weather had turned nippy and the Tazo *chai* was perfect, especially since I wasn't appropriately dressed. The first time I had tried the *chai*, I felt it had a distinct *masala* flavour to it. Others argued that it was cinnamon but whatever it was, it took me back to my childhood days in India.

I recalled having lived close to the Arabian Sea in Cuffe Parade, and having my school nearby. I stayed with my grandmother in a small two-bedroom apartment on the 5th floor. The bathrooms were without a bathtub so when we showered, everything got wet. The only view we had was of the other buildings surrounding us and when the winds changed, the flat was consumed with the stench of the fish market behind the building.

In the afternoons, the commoners used to wheel a couple of rides over close to our apartment building. There was a Ferris wheel and the other was a ride that rotated too, but horizontally. The carriages on both were rickety, but it still amused all the neighborhood children. The Ferris wheel was my favourite and I remembered thinking it was humungous. The fare for each ride was relatively cheap but then again, money was a big deal to a child in those days.

On one occasion, my mother had stepped out and I was desperate to ride the wheel. My grandmother had refused to give me the money and decided to turn in for her usual afternoon nap. Still, I was adamant about riding the Ferris wheel. Propping myself up on a stool in the minute kitchen, I reached into one of the higher cupboards and pulled out a packet of Maggi noodles. Sneaking out of the flat, I ventured down to one of the food venders close to the building. It wasn't much of a grocery store; in fact it was a small green wooden shed with a door and a cut out window in front. Raising myself on tiptoes and after steadying myself on the countertop, I attempted to get the owner's attention.

With oiled hair and a worn blue shirt, he leaned closer into me and nodded his head upwards in a gesture to ask me what I wanted. I handed him the packet of flavoured noodles and asked him for my money back. He closely examined the packet for a few seconds and handed it back to me, saying that I hadn't purchased it from him. I insisted that I had. I was going to have my Ferris wheel ride by any means. Once again, he leaned in only to tell me that he didn't sell that particular flavour I was attempting to obtain a refund on. After a few more minutes of fruitless bickering, he was victorious and I walked back home. With my head down and shoulder slumped, I plodded past the Ferris wheel ride with the packet of noodles in my hand and continued onward to my building.

Whenever I return to Mumbai and walk past probably the very same rainbow coloured Ferris wheel, I realise how little I must have been at that age since the wheel was fairly small. My biggest problem then was getting 50 *paisa* to indulge in the highlight of my day. Life was so much simpler back then. As a child, the concerns that dominate our life are so insignificant and if I knew then what I know now, I'd have held on to that childhood a little longer.

The breeze knocked the paper cup over, spilling the remaining *chai*. The drops raced towards the edge of the uneven table until a sudden gust of wind swerved them sideways. As I studied the drops inching towards the edge of the metallic tabletop, I thought to myself, Nature often sends some form of resistance when we reach for our goal. It's ironic how we find meaning in the most insignificant facets of life.

Almost three weeks had passed and I felt a brief vacation was on the cards, especially with the cold weather coming in. Perhaps a trip to cousin Mona, would do the trick. Friends were constantly attempting to introduce me to single women; an act of kindness, which was becoming increasingly irritating. But, the healing was gradually showing the effect. My plan was working and would continue to do so as long as I adhered to its rules. The last thing I needed was diversions.

Suddenly a scent wafted past me. It was Preeti's perfume. I turned around immediately. In that split second of the turn, a million thoughts crossed my mind, but the most prominent one was that she had found me and wanted forgiveness. She had come back because she wanted to be with me. My heart quickened instantly. In the next second, I discovered that no one was behind me. My eyes kept darting around, searching, hoping that she was there but I knew better.

Leaning back into my chair, the excitement wore off as quickly as it had risen. Memories began to flood my mind as my pulse calmed. Preeti was still a part of me and although things were gradually improving, it would take a long time to flush her out. We had something magical and as much as I hated to admit it, I did love her.

Letting out a sigh, I dropped my head. The loneliness and grief enveloped me once again, but it wasn't new anymore. I stood up and dropped the cup in the trash. I looked around behind me once more and although I hoped otherwise, I knew she wasn't there. Putting my hands in my pockets, I began my walk home. Looking down I noticed the glimmer of the million shards of glass embedded in the New York pavement.

"I need to get out of here," I murmured under my breath.

❖❖❖

# Chapter 8

Her perfume was intoxicating. I was hypnotised by her glossy pink lips as she spoke. Her attention was focused on the screen while her long, slim feminine fingers typed away on the black keys. Without looking at me, she regurgitated the usual spiel for the thousandth time.

"Sir? Excuse me, sir!"

Blinking rapidly, I took a small step back.

"Yes? Sorry, I was somewhere else," I stammered.

"Did you pack these bags yourself? Have they been under your supervision at all times…" she muttered on.

I nodded and repeatedly said 'yes'. Whenever I was asked the routine questions at the airport, I wondered, who would admit that they hadn't packed their bags themselves or were actually carrying a weapon of some sort? Certainly not anyone planning to carry out an attack during the flight.

"Have you got any hand luggage, sir? Please place it on the belt to be weighed."

I had never understood why, but when women wore power clothing, it served as an aphrodisiac for me. A well-groomed woman, in a power suit, and black stilettos; her long, voluminous, wavy hair swaying as she walks by, her perfume leaving a trail behind. Few things grabbed my attention more.

Unfortunately Jeanette wasn't as captivated by me as I was with her. One always hears stories about men scoring with airhostesses and joining the mile high club, but they're never about someone we directly know. Even if someone we know claimed to such fortunate circumstances, we would more readily believe them to be a liar.

Mona had once predicted that female staff would always attend to me. She stated my boyish charms had the power of putting them under a spell. So, I had hoped to be checked in by Jeanette since she was one of the few women at the counters. I noticed from afar that she didn't wear a wedding band, and thus, became the primary target.

Leaning over the counter I attempted to make conversation by asking her about the flight, the possibility of an upgrade, if she had ever been to Los Angeles, but I got nothing, just direct responses. She had probably heard the routine so many times that now it was nothing more than white noise. I convinced myself that being snubbed was a result of poor material rather than her sensing my state of 'recovery'. It is said that women can smell desperation on a man like cheap cologne, and talking about your ex is a dead giveaway.

I'd have to let Mona know about my unsuccessful experience, which in turn would discount her theory, though, Mona would probably accuse Jeanette of being a lesbian. Perhaps I had lost my *mojo.* Then again, I never thought I had it.

"Everything is in order, sir, and I have given you a window seat next to the emergency exit for extra leg room. Is there anything else I can do for you?" she asked with a smile.

I always enjoyed travelling and visiting friends in other places, I just hated the actual travel part of it. Even six hours was an ordeal for me. The unusual odour only found on aircrafts, the turbulent take off and landing and not to mention the atrocious garbage the airlines try to pass off as food. If only they drugged their passengers.

Fastening my seat belt, I pulled out the latest issue of 'GQ' along with my iPod. If I was lucky, the next six hours would fly by and I would be able to sleep peacefully. Popping on my headphones, I pressed play and rested my head on the pillow against the window.

❖❖❖

## Chapter 9

The mood was perfect; dim lights, champagne on ice, black silk sheets on the sofa and Buddha Bar playing in the background. Walking in slowly, I slid my brown leather bag off my shoulder on to the cool marble floor. Aromatic candles filled the air with jasmine which tantalised my senses. Taking in my surroundings, I looked around, but saw no one. I proceeded to sit on the plush white sofa which had been covered with rose petals. Reaching for one of the chocolate covered strawberries on the table, I picked up the note next to the ice bucket.

"Take a sip…"

I sat back and admired the effort that went into creating the vibe as I bit in to a sweet, succulent strawberry.

The sound emerged from behind me and as I began to turn, I felt a hand on the top of my head forcing me to look straight. She smelt like rain after a long summer day which had me spellbound. She leaned over.

"Shhh… don't move," she whispered in the back of my ear. Her warm breath sent tingles through my body.

She lifted her hand off the top of my head and although I was extremely tempted, I didn't turn. She caressed my neck with something silky. I barely caught a glimpse of the black fabric before it swiftly rose blanketing my eyes and sending me into complete darkness.

The lack of control and uncertainty of what was to come combined with her soft touch, her sensual voice and titillating scent were incredibly thrilling. I couldn't see anything and I didn't want to. I wanted to enjoy this slow and deliberate moment exactly as it was intended.

Her heavy breath brushed the back of my neck and ear. She softly nibbled on my lobe with her lips and began to moisten it with her tongue. Her hands came around to my chest and her fingers began to unbutton my pink shirt. I tried to raise my hand, wanting to hold the back of her head and bring her close, but she stopped me. Pushing my arms down, she held them against the sofa. Slowly she began kissing my neck with her soft, moist lips, giving me goose bumps everywhere. Her hair brushed my face and I tried to inhale as much of her scent in one breath. I wanted so much more right there and then. I wanted to rip off my blindfold and bring her around in front of me, to hold her close to my chest and kiss her deeply, but this was so much more fun.

"I want you. I'm going to have you," she declared in a soft, sensual whisper.

Her breath was hot and her voice soft and deep. She kept everything agonisingly slow. Her lips moved close to my ear once again and she began dragging her nails up my bare chest. Biting my ear she whispered, "I'm going to make you mine tonight."

Suddenly she was gone. My neck and ear were left moist and my shirt unbuttoned. Confused, I sat up with the intention of removing the blindfold when I heard a soft roar. Baffled, I tried to figure out what the noise was. I then smelt the burning wood and heard the crackle from the fireplace.

Suddenly I felt a cold, hard material push up against my chest and then a sharper point a few inches below. She had placed her foot on my chest and pushed me back hard with her stiletto.

"Behave!" she commanded.

Leaning over, she started kissing my neck again. I tried to lean forward to kiss her lips, but she backed away. I wanted to taste her, to feel the fullness of her lips against mine.

"Patience..." was her response.

She continued kissing my neck and slowly moved lower down my naked chest, gently biting my nipples sending my mind reeling. I raised my hands once again, but she was prepared and grabbed them.

"Don't make me tie you," she threatened.

I was forced against the backrest of the sofa again. I wasn't sure how much more of this I could take. My trousers were beginning to feel claustrophobic. As she slowly straddled me, she reached for my hands and placed them on her tight and juicy buttocks. I gently caressed her through her silky gown. Thoroughly aroused, I unconsciously began to lick my lips and grind my pelvis.

I continued to explore her body with my hands and she allowed it. The fact that I was given that freedom and little bit of control only excited me further. I ran my hands over her warm, naked, smooth thighs on either side of me, quarantining me, keeping me close to her. I once again stroked her soft buttocks, which felt like sheer perfection. My hands explored higher, into the dips of her slim waist, the curve of her smooth arched back and finally on her relaxed shoulders. She shrugged off the gown and I began to explore the rest of her naked flesh. Suddenly leaning forward, she kissed me. The soft, warm lips left my spine tingling. Immediately I held her tight so that she couldn't escape. Once I knew she wasn't going to tease me again, my hands reached for her face so I could enjoy her kiss longer. I couldn't play her games anymore. I wanted her. I had to take control. She didn't resist and continued to kiss me, softly biting at my lip and flicking her tongue, but she never let me have control.

Briskly running her long fingers through my hair, she pulled me close and brought her lips to my ear. I could feel and hear her heavy breath on my neck and ear. She whispered, "I love the way your body feels below mine, so take your time. You won't forget tonight."

She softly pulled my hair back, leaned forward, bit my ear lobe and whispered, "I'll make you scream my name."

Kissing her eagerly, I ran one hand through her hair. My other hand began to caress her soft behind while she grinded in rhythm with me. She slowly began to untie my blindfold. The anticipation was killing me. I wanted to see her, I wanted to devour her. She loosened it, but I couldn't wait anymore. I reached up and ripped it off.

"Ladies and gentlemen, we are approaching Los Angeles and have begun our descent. Could you kindly raise your tray tables and return your seat backs to the upright position? The captain has turned on the fasten seat belt sign. We are aware that you had several other carriers to fly with and would like to thank you for choosing us and we hope you've enjoyed flying with us. Cabin crew, prepare for landing."

My eyes popped open instantly. Within a second I realised where I was and snatched the pillow from the window placing it on my lap. Turning toward the grey-haired elderly lady sitting on my left, I noticed her staring at me through her large, plastic spectacles. I smiled at her weakly, but she didn't reciprocate. Instead she huffed, shook her head and turned away.

"It's been too long," I sighed as I looked out through the window, continuing to hold the pillow on my lap.

❖❖❖

# Chapter 10

Cousin Mona was all smiles and hugs. Thrilled to see me, she hopped about with excitement, paying no attention to the people around her. A large chested, 34-year-old woman who stood 6' without heels, bouncing up and down at an airport, attracted more attention than one could imagine.

Cousin Mona wasn't always my 'cousin'. When we first met during one of my vacations to the States, we hit it off, instantly. She was besotted with my Michael Jackson impersonation and after seeing my moonwalk, she was a fan for life. Eventually, we had gotten so close that potential suitors were put off, assuming Mona and I were a couple. Convincing people we were only friends was an arduous task in itself, after which we had to explain *why* we weren't romantically interested in one another. We knew we had to figure out a solution without distancing ourselves as friends or 'blocking' one another. Mona decided she'd refer to me as her cousin or *Rakhi* brother. Understandably, that led to its own set of problems.

During our visit to India, when Mona and I were exiting a play with a few friends, Mona was ahead of me talking to Anil and I was walking alongside his sister, Meeta. She asked how I knew Mona and I promptly responded that she was my cousin. Later Mona informed me that when Anil had asked her the same question, she referred to me as her *Rakhi* brother. Initially we were anxious about the suspicions we would raise among the real siblings, but after briefly staring at one another in horror, we couldn't stop laughing. Since that day we agreed on remaining 'cousins'.

Embracing me, she gave me a tight squeeze. I realised how emotionally weak I'd become. Although I was happy to see Mona, the love she gave me with that hug made me aware of the sadness within. I had become extremely sensitive to my surroundings. One word or scent could send me spiralling in to an ocean of depression. I had an aching for love and seeing Mona made that very apparent. Still, being in Los Angeles with her was the right thing.

I never understood why Mona wasn't hitched yet. She was pretty, smart, hard working, loving, caring, considerate, giving and compassionate. Add to that, the height which almost guaranteed kids that could one day play in the NBA. Then again, the height often worked against her, which was a shame. Still, she had guys swooning over her and not just single guys, but married men with kids too. However, being a home wrecker was never really her forté. In spite of all her admirers, no one had enchanted her as yet. The other thing about Mona I never understood was why she insisted on reading rubbish like "The Rules" of how to get and keep a man, which was written by a couple of frustrated women.

"How was the flight?"

The expression of the wholesome grandmother watching me as I savoured my provocative fantasy flashed in front of me.

"Err, it was alright, just slept," I responded.

"Come on, Om, nothing in your life is straightforward or simple, you always have some sort of drama going on. Tell me, did you meet any cuties?" she asked beaming at me.

Granny may have been cute once upon a time, but I wasn't around in the days of black and white TV.

"No, nothing like that, I just slept," I answered.

Mona was right, nothing in my life was simple. I recall one night after a South Asian conference, when a large group of friends congregated in my hotel room in San Diego for a nightcap. Eventually, the conversation reached a point where we shared our stories of heartbreak, and after each story, the room sighed and expressed their sympathy with 'oooohs' and 'aaawwws'. Eventually, all the eyes turned towards me, and they waited. There I was sitting with a bunch of single women and my good friend Raj in our personal session of Oprah. Sighing, I began to regale them with one of my tragic affairs. I had many to pick from, but decided on something recent.

I was attending a wedding reception in Los Angeles and the story began with me standing at the buffet line. I had noticed the queue consisted of only men at which point, an attractive young hussy came and stood beside me, armed with a plate in hand. I turned to her with a weak line which was something to the effect of, "Ah, so we finally have a woman in our line."

Dressed in a grand wine-coloured *sari* with heavy embroidery and beadwork, she was radiant. Smiling, she walked around me to the food on my right.

"Let me guess, you're vegetarian?" I continued.

"Yes."

"I thought it was odd that you skipped all the meat."

"Yes, well I have been vegetarian for a while now because of my mum." She remarked as she pinned her long brown locks behind her ear and leaned over to pick up some *naan* bread.

"I'm guessing it was a bet and when the time was up, you were hooked?"

"Yep," she smiled.

"Smart mother," I acknowledged.

We continued to chat till the food display came to an end and we began walking away with our plates. All of a sudden, she started to walk across me indicating that we weren't going in the same direction. She pointed out the table in the large ballroom where she was to be seated, at which point I left her with a cordial "See you later", and headed to my friends. Back at my table, I was abused by friends who went on and on about my idiotic mistake of not sitting and dining with her.

During the rest of the evening, I had made several attempts to manoeuvre myself in her path, but met with little success. I saw her make her way out of the ballroom. Equipped with my friend's mobile phone, I raced out and stood in the hallway pretending to make a phone call, waiting for her to return. Hopefully we would be able to resume our conversation. When she did return, she wasn't alone and I chickened out. What did I expect her to do? Wait beside me while I finish my pseudo phone call? Another failed attempt. I decided to put plan B in effect. I decided to stand by the dessert trolley with the hope that she would wander over to chat. Fifteen minutes later, I was a fool with his hands in his pockets next to a dessert trolley. My friends still continued to hound me about how cute she was, how well she danced and how well she probably cooked! Leaning in, they told me how one day they could have referred to her as their *'Bhabhi'*.

Later that evening when I was shaking my 'money-maker' to the beats of Punjabi MC, I saw her stray from her group on the dance floor. She stood sideways a few feet from me, which gave me a perfect view of her profile. Her *sari* only accentuated the slopes of her curvaceous, mermaid-like body. She tilted her head back and her flowing hair fell playfully as she laughed. This was my chance to swoop in and say something. I left my little entourage and began walking towards her.

The few steps of the vacant dance floor between the two of us felt like the Grand Canyon. I was almost certain that every eye in the ballroom was on me. Those few steps hurled me out of my comfort zone. I adjusted my yellow Versace tie and wiped my brow dry before returning the handkerchief to my back pocket. Making sure the black suit sat perfectly, I fastened the top button and embarked on my courageous journey. As the distance between us shortened something unexpected happened. I hadn't accounted for this. She began to move away, almost turning her back to me. I began to panic. The canyon just got bigger. The audience must have been split between laughter and curiosity about what I would do next. I wanted to turn around and rush back into my element, but I couldn't. She hadn't seen me coming or at least I hope she hadn't. I quickened my pace and continued forward. Two quick steps and I arrived just before she completely turned her back toward me.

"Wow you guys really can party," is what dribbled out of my mouth.

"Sorry?" She turned towards me with a raised eyebrow.

"I mean, you know, you guys are really enjoying and partying." Would the gibberish ever stop?

Luckily she smiled, which usually was a good sign. Her sister came over and introduced herself, after which she gave me the third degree. Within the first minute she uncovered my name, age, residence and education.

Anita and I resumed our conversation as I started to adapt to my new environment. Her chocolate brown eyes had me in a trance and she giggled like a cute schoolgirl when I joked. There were awkward moments of silence when our eyes were transfixed and we smiled clumsily. We spent the rest of the reception evening together as we danced, met each other's friends and discussed the party taking place the following night. She wasn't sure if she would attend, but I informed her that it would be thoroughly enjoyable. Little did I know that during the whole time her mother was sitting behind us observing all my antics. Still, after she left, I felt quite chuffed. Being a shy guy, I had to deal with a lot of missed opportunities and regret. That wasn't going to be the case tonight.

The next night at the Garden of Eden, I noticed Anita at the back of the club as soon as I walked in. I figured I'd play it cool and not greet her until later. Instead I walked around the club bordered with mirrored walls creating the illusion of being a bigger space. Large crystal chandeliers dropped from the ceiling and reflected the disco and laser lights which accompanied the thumping music. Waiters smartly dressed in black scuttled around offering hors d'oeuvres and standard cocktails to the guests. Over a hundred attractively clad twenty something's had graced the night and were anticipating an exciting night of fun and frolic.

Spotting Mona near to the entrance, I made my way over and greeted her. Donning a figure hugging, black and purple silk qipao, she looked positively fabulous. I joked, laughed and shared a shot with her, all the while keeping an eye on Anita until eventually, whilst mingling, our paths met. Sporting a model's height and a lovely innocent face, she was blessed with the curves of a Bollywood siren, and wavy brown locks that begged for fingers to be run through it. Her smile was as dazzling as it was genuine. Placing her hand on my chest, she leaned in and kissed my cheek as she said hello.

"So, are you going to bust out with all your moves here tonight?" I asked her with my hand still on her waist from our greeting.

"I will, if you dance with me," she smiled.

I was 'IN'! I could almost hear Gerado's 'Rico Suave' in the back of my head. All that was left to do was pop my collar.

"No, no, you don't want to dance with an old guy like me."

The conversation began to strain as the DJ increased the volume. I couldn't fully gather what she was saying, but I managed to get the gist of it.

"Why, how old are you?" she asked.

I thought it rather odd that she would ask me, since her sister had obtained every bit of information from me the night before. Hadn't they discussed me yet, especially since I was hitting on her in plain sight?

"I'm twenty five."

"Oh hush, that's not old," she said as she affectionately slapped my chest.

In her patent black stilettos, she stood eye to eye with me at 5'10". Sipping my vodka tonic, I took a moment to admire her in the brandy strapless satin dress that seductively caressed her voluptuous figure. Her long, graceful neck was complimented by a set of flawless, naked shoulders. She had hit the balance between sexy and conservative perfectly. Anita was a vision, and she was with me.

Everything was going swimmingly. She laughed at every joke and we took every opportunity to touch each other flirtatiously. The interest was definitely mutual. We continued to converse about various subjects. I told her what I did for a living as I contemplated the appropriate time to ask her out on a date.

"Yes, but regardless of what's on the card and what my job description is, the fact is I am my boss's bitch. I do whatever I'm told," I said with a smile and she responded with a laugh.

"No, come on, I bet you do a great job."

"Well, it's not all bad. Travelling on the company dime is always a joy."

"I'm sure," she acknowledged.

"So, what is it that you do?" I asked.

"I'm in high school."

All of a sudden there was a pause and the air in the San Diego hotel room was filled with dead silence. Then, with an almost uncanny, perfect synchronicity, the group erupted with laughter and my friends, who had been hanging on every word, rolled off the bed and on to the floor clutching their guts. Eventually the hysterics subsided and they invited me to continue.

I remember the feeling of instant horror when Anita told me her age. My face must have turned pale white. I almost broke the glass in my hand from the shock. My mind went completely blank and I had nothing to say. What was I supposed to talk about? Sesame Street? The Muppet Show? Pokemon? I took a much needed sip of my beverage in an attempt to buy myself some time to think, but I noticed there wasn't enough vodka in my tonic. There probably wasn't enough alcohol in the whole club at that particular moment. I wanted to run, but I couldn't, I didn't want to offend the young girl, the very, very young girl. I tried to maintain my composure as long as possible, but she must have seen right through me. I finally got away with the excuse that a friend of mine was sitting alone.

My friends from the reception the previous night asked me what had happened. I regurgitated the saga as my head lay between my hands. They broke out in laughter while my mind was swirling with thoughts of being in prison with a big hairy guy named Bubba who would make me his 'bitch'. Anita left around 1am and I never saw her again.

That night wasn't a complete loss in any way. In fact it was at that party that Mona and I bonded. Until that party, it was almost as if she didn't exist. By the end of the evening, we were wishing it never ended. From then on, our camaraderie continued to grow and it was as if we had been friends for life.

I threw my bags in the trunk of the cream coloured Camry and fastened my belt as I sat down.

"How's work going? I read your article yesterday, very funny." Mona slipped her Gucci shades on and turned to me, "Have I told you how much I love your writing?"

"Yes, but feel free to tell me some more," I smiled.

"Well, I love it," she giggled. "When are you going to write this book you talked about?"

"No clue. Anyway, what's the plan for tonight, fatty?" I asked.

"Okay, I am dropping you to the hotel, freshen up and I will be back to pick you up in a couple of hours. We are meeting everyone else tonight," she instructed.

"Mona, I don't know if I am up for a big gathering," I whined.

"Bullshit, we are going to party hard tonight. Also, if you are up for it, you may meet some cuties."

Ignoring the statement, I peered out the window over the Los Angeles skyline.

"How's the rest of the gang back home?" Mona broke the silence. "When are Arun and Rakhi going to tie the knot? Oh, what about Jim?" she bounced in her seat as a wave of excitement surged through her. "Is he still having those wild escapades you tell me about? He's probably one of the funniest guys I've met."

"Truthfully Mona, I've been laying low these days."

"Well, we're going to change that tonight, hon. It's going to be just like old times!" she rubbed my hand soothingly. "Alright, the hotel's coming up, check it out." She pointed out the windscreen at a palatial five star hotel.

Mona had a ton of great qualities and one of the best perks about our friendship was the fact that she could hook me up at a fabulous hotel in Beverly Hills for $50 a night.

## *Chapter 11*

We pulled into Mona's driveway at 2.30 in the morning after a brief night of clubbing. I never could get used to the fact that clubs and bars closed at such an absurd hour in California. Back in New York we only made our way out close to midnight!

"So, did you have fun?" She asked exiting the Camry.

"It was alright, good to see the old faces and all you know."

"Well, what did you think of Yasmine? Cute right?"

"I don't know, I don't really know her." By now, Mona knew that was my polite way of saying I wasn't interested.

"But why, Om? She's really cute and a great person," she turned towards me almost exasperated.

"Let it be, Mona, I really don't want to get into this."

She agreed and headed straight in to the immaculately clean kitchen. Following her in, I noticed everything had its own place. In the middle stood a large island with a smooth, black granite top that matched the kitchen counters and cupboards. In contrast, the floor was a white marble as were the leather seats on the stool.

"Black and white kitchen, ey? I think you take your Michael Jackson obsession a bit too far, Mona."

"Very funny! So, how are you holding up? You seem alright," she said as she brewed the Columbian coffee.

"It hasn't been easy," I sighed. "It gets really hard at night, you know. Sometimes I escape and don't think about it, but the smallest things can just trigger all the sadness."

"I know, honey, I know. You know it just takes time. I promise everything is going to be okay. She didn't deserve you and I know one day you will find someone who will give you everything you ever dreamed of."

"You know, I hate it when people say that. How do you *know*?" Irritated, I felt my brow furrow. "How do you know everything is going to be okay? I mean how can you be certain? You don't know. Sure I'll get over her, but what in the world makes you think one day I'll be swimming in an ocean of joy?" Drops of saliva flew across the air with my seething response.

"Don't get upset. You are a great guy with a lot to give. It's only a matter of time. I know, in my heart..."

"What about you?" I interrupted. "You're a great girl, Mona, with a lot to give, but here you are."

Mona looked down at her mug as she stirred the coffee silently. The picture perfect kitchen was soundless for the next few minutes. I felt terrible for snapping at her and what I had said, but I couldn't take it back. Mona had often shared her dreams of having a family, being a loving wife and mother with me and I knew she too carried a great deal of sorrow. She too had cried on my shoulder hoping one day she would find the answers to her questions.

"You know what's screwed up?" I asked softly.

"What?"

"People's perception of romance," I stated. "Hollywood and Bollywood skew our image of romance, love and relationships.

It's never how it's portrayed on the silver screen and most of us figure that out the hard way. There are some people who can make stuff like that happen, but they are far and few in between."

"Well, what do you want, Om?" she asked still jaded.

"I want the passion, the desire, the magic. I know it can happen and I know I can make it happen. I can even tell you the things I did for Preeti…"

"No, please don't," interrupted Mona. "Last time you told me what you did for your girlfriends, you almost brought me to tears, I don't want to know, please!"

"Why do you women react like that?"

"Om, it's depressing to hear about guys like you when there are so many women who don't even receive flowers from their boyfriends. Listening to your stories makes it apparent to us what we never had."

"Alright fine, but then you know how I am, you know the stuff I do and can do. Well, I want that reciprocated. I want someone to show me how much I mean to them, to fight for me, to have the courage to make things happen for us and not be scared of others. I want someone to give back, to appreciate, to realise. I don't want to feel alone anymore. I want to share my life and have someone who wants to share hers with me."

"I want the same things for you, Om, and you'll get it."

I stood up from the kitchen table shaking my head out of frustration.

"I'm sorry, but I just know and feel it," she continued.

"I know you do, but I can't help but think it's all just bullshit. None of it makes sense. I am just tired of being hurt and going through all this. You give your best and try to make things work and at the end you just get shafted. You remember Seema, the girl I dated in London? Well, her family didn't treat me right. They didn't respect me or give me any importance. What made it worse was Seema simply watched it happen and never did anything about it. She admitted what her family did was wrong, but didn't say anything and just let it fester. She was weak and they all took me for granted and at the end of the day I was the one insulted and hurt after giving it my all."

I could feel the anger surging within me and an increase in my body temperature from the whole experience.

"Alright Om, well what about, Mala? Did she not tell you that when she and her sister were younger, they were only interested in the high flyers, the guys who had memberships at clubs and fast cars, but a couple of years later she realised how many good guys she turned away for the 'bling bling' life and that she regrets it? Did she not imply that she regrets not having something work out with you? Did she not say that Preeti would regret this?"

Pulling off my sweater I walked to the window over the sink and threw it open.

"Fine, Mala said that and okay fine, people regret, but where does that get me, Mona? All these women regretting now doesn't help me. It doesn't change anything and it doesn't change the now!"

As I took a sip of the coffee, I stared out of the window into the darkness. We both remained silent and the only sound was Mona's spoon clinking against her mug.

"Has she called?" Her voice was barely audible.

"I don't know."

"What do you mean you don't know?"

"I didn't listen to any of my messages."

"Don't you want to know what she has to say?"

"What's the point? It will only make it harder. I just want to get over her as soon as possible and move on."

Once again, we sipped our drinks engulfed in silence.

"She left me a letter," I murmured under my breath.

"Really?" expressed Mona with surprise. "You never told me this. What did it say?"

There was a brief pause while our eyes met and Mona stared at me anxiously. I looked out of the window again and said, "I don't know."

"What? What do you mean you don't know?"

"I burned it."

"WHAT!" she screamed.

She covered her mouth and glanced towards the stairs hoping she hadn't woken up her family.

"What?" she said in a softer tone. "She gave you a letter and you burned it? Be serious, did you really burn it?"

"Yes."

"So you don't know what it said?"

"No."

"Om, sometimes I don't know what goes into that head of yours."

"That makes two of us," I smiled.

Mona smiled back and shook her head. We remained in the kitchen in comfortable silence, thinking and contemplating. I looked down at the half empty mug and as I fiddled with the handle, I sighed.

"I feel so alone, Mona."

"I know."

"With all that has happened in the past and all the relationships, I just feel emotionally exhausted."

She remained quiet.

"It feels as though my life is one of loneliness and sadness peppered with specks of joy here and there."

"You know what I think, right?" asked Mona.

"Yes, you think that I'm being melodramatic, but I do feel that way sometimes. You know I'm a fighter, but at times I just feel so weak and defeated, that I just want to give up."

"Om, everyone goes through it. Some people go through a lot worse."

"I know," I sighed under my breath. "I'm just tired, Mona."

She stood beside me and held my hand.

"I just feel alone, Mona."

# Chapter 12

**D**ear ?,

*This is a rather strange letter to write since I don't know who you are let alone where you are. In fact I don't know if anyone will ever get to read this letter but I just needed... someone.*

*I'm in Los Angeles right now visiting Mona and should be heading back home within the next few days. I was hoping that coming out here would help me get my head straightened, but then again, I know better. No matter where I go, I can't escape my problems. I can't escape my thoughts.*

*It's 5am and I can't sleep, in fact I don't remember the last time I had a peaceful night's rest. I can't stop thinking, feeling, thinking, feeling. I toss and turn in bed, while my mind drifts through the harrowing past. I am unable to rid myself of the feelings; no matter what I do, it hovers above and within me. It feels like a heavy and yet hollow weight in my chest and mind. The loneliness is constant and I can't escape it. Its intensity fluctuates throughout the day, but it's always there. I'm going insane, all the pain and loneliness is eating me up alive. This letter doesn't even make sense; it feels like I am writing gibberish!*

*I recently broke up with my girlfriend after I caught her cheating and since then I've been going through a whirlwind of emotions. At times, I miss her and remember the sweet memories we shared, and at other times, I am consumed with anger and hatred. Detailed visuals of them together penetrate my mind and I have to shut my eyes and vigorously shake my head hoping to get the graphic pictures out of my head. The image of them together in ecstasy, enjoying one another intimately, her loving every moment without any concern for me just haunts me.*

*Never do I have peace of mind; I'm in a constant state of confusion. I need help and I have nowhere to turn. Even if I did, I don't know how they could help. I feel so alone, I want to rid myself of the disappointment, the sadness, the loneliness, the anxiety. I'm so tired of feeling this way, so very tired. I can't and don't want to go through this any more; I've been hurt far too many times. I am tired of being the nice guy, always being the one who puts in more, always fighting to make it work and turn dreams into reality.*

*I am scared of being with anyone else now. I don't think I can handle it emotionally. I can't deal with the uncertainty, the risk of disappointment, the insecurity. I don't want to visit this place again; I don't want to touch this world of pain any more. The risk of coming back to this world and feeling again frightens me so very much.*

*I used to dream of being with you, sharing my life with you. Whenever I went through tough times, I used to escape by dreaming of our future. I had hoped that I would have met you and been with you by now. At times I thought I had met you, but I was obviously wrong. I had magnificent dreams and believed that when I would suffer hardships in the future, I wouldn't be alone. Now when I look ahead and begin to escape into a dream of you, it shatters and reality comes crashing in.*

*How I have longed to be with you! There were times I wondered if I had already met you or perhaps we saw each other in a crowded street. In fact there have been moments when I stood in the frozen food aisle at the supermarket and wondered if it was there that I was going to meet you. I have dreamt up a number of possible scenarios, but you are still a mystery.*

*Although we've never met, I've missed you. I have wished to have you by my side. I always felt that you would be the remedy to my loneliness. Even if I didn't want to talk, you'd sit next to me and rub my back to let me know you were there. When I wanted to be alone, you wouldn't leave me. I dreamt that you would never give up on me.*

*There I was, giving myself hope and dreams, which in the long run have just brought me hurt. I don't even know if you exist any more. I feel as though life and fate have played a cruel joke on me. The truth of it all is that I am alone and have always been that way. There isn't a pot of gold at the end of the rainbow. There is nothing around the next corner, but another corner. Once you get over the sand dune, all you have is another one to walk over. There is no end. You are all alone in this abyss.*

*If all that is true, why am I writing this? Well, maybe it is that final, little flicker of hope, which too will fade. At least then I won't be kidding myself any more.*

*I'm so confused, so alone, so tired. God, I need help… but I know it's not coming. Nothing's coming and yet, I don't know you and still miss you.*

*Om.*

❖❖❖

## Chapter 13

Visiting Los Angeles had been an enjoyable break and spending time with Mona was always pleasant. She'd been a good friend and was always there whenever I needed her. Still, there was only this much she could do. It was up to me to face and conquer my demons.

"Sir, could you please not stand there?" instructed the security guard.

Hopping away from the metal counter, I dropped the shoe on to the floor. As I wriggled my left foot in to the black leather slip-on, I felt a sharp pain. Years had passed and my ankle still felt sore. I could never forget the night which began with Dino and I trash talking at a bar in Soho about who was better at basketball. At 4.30 in the morning we drove back to my apartment building and got ready to duel. Dino was stone cold sober while I was as merry as they come. I was thrilled to play especially since I believed that I was going to be unstoppable. I wouldn't be inhibited and would just let my natural game flow. How cocky we are after a few pints!

I swung the door open to the deserted gym and let Dino walk in first before flipping the switch. As the lights flickered and slowly illuminated the gym, his eyes darted back and forth processing his surroundings. Impressed with the building's amenities, he turned and nodded at me with a smile. Dino inspected the high-end equipment before walking on to the edge of the court and threw the ball towards the fibreglass board.

We stepped on the court and as always, I didn't stretch or warm up. I wanted to start playing immediately. The game began and my confidence was riding high. It was time to school Dino and make him another statistic. A few minutes into the competition, reality came thumping and I began to struggle. I was a step slower than Dino and he just kept knocking down his shots. My jumpers refused to drop and with each miss, my confidence withered. Even my go-to moves, my bread and butter plays weren't working. I was the one being schooled. I was struggling to breathe as the booze was taking its toll, but I kept going.

I remembered standing in between the free throw line and the top of the key. Dino was guarding me as tight as he possibly could and refused to give an inch. I held the ball low and then jumped straight up with my eyes focused on the rim. I raised my hands and got the shot off, while Dino tried to contest the jumper. I knew immediately it was another one of my many bricks. As I began to descend, I watched the ball float towards the front of the rim, never taking my eyes off it. I had to get the rebound. Following your shot was simple basketball fundamentals and had become instinct.

The next few seconds were a blur. I found myself screaming and cursing as I lay on the floor. While coming down, I had landed on Dino's foot, rolling my left foot inwards, and sprained my ankle. The pain was excruciating. An ankle sprain is one of the biggest fears of anyone who plays basketball. It's painful to watch and even hearing about it makes people wince. In a matter of a split second, the foot rolls inward and all your weight comes down on your ankle pushing it closer to the floor, almost turning your foot 90 degrees away from the joint, and then it bounces back, if you're lucky.

I tried to walk it off so I could keep on playing but I was done. The next day, instead of attending to it, I had been out and about the city, limping and undoubtedly causing more damage to the ankle. By the time I arrived home, my whole left leg was in pain. The orthopaedist saw the swollen, black, blue and purple ankle, and was certain that it was broken. However, the x-ray revealed that I had torn every single ligament all the way around my ankle and had almost dislocated it. He seemed to think I was 'lucky'.

The rematch with Dino took place a few months later where we both were sober. I walked away with a confident win and a frustrated Dino. Unfortunately my ankle never healed properly. If only I had allowed the ankle to recover, if only I had taken more care of it, if only I was more patient. If I had done what the doctor and physiotherapist instructed, I could have full movement in my ankle and wouldn't have to ice it all the time. If only I had patience, my life would probably be a lot different today.

"We will be seating rows 20 to 30 now, please have your boarding pass ready."

Ten minutes remained until departure and the seat next to me, covered in cheap blue fabric, was still empty. I was relieved that I didn't have another granny sitting next to me, and the fact that I might have a spare seat almost had me giddy. A vacant seat next to you can make all the difference to your travelling experience, especially when you sit in coach. Ten more minutes and it would all be mine. I began placing all the essentials, such as the book I wouldn't read, the magazine that I would flick through, and my iPod, on to the free seat.

The airhostess, also dressed in what appeared to be cheap blue fabric, walked down the aisle making sure that everyone had their belts fastened and seats in the 'upright' position. I never understood why we had to bring our seats forward. What difference did pushing it back two inches during take-off and landing make? It's bad enough flying in economy with the crying babies and the oversized passengers beside you who overflow into your seat, can't we have two inches just to make it tolerable? Yet, the airline is adamant about making our flying experience that much more uncomfortable by insisting we put our seats forward. Either way, as soon as flights take off, I always put my seat back immediately.

We were close to take off and I assumed my usual position of putting my head on the pillow which was placed against the window. Sade's 'Lovers Rock' blared through my headphones as I shut my eyes ignoring the performance by the airhostess, and hoped that I only woke up once we had landed.

## Chapter 14

The brief escape had come to an end and I had arrived back to reality. Everything I had left behind still remained the same except for the fact that I had more bills to pay. Nonetheless, I felt as though I had brought something back with me. A second wind if you will. I felt stronger, focused and determined. Although I still had a soft spot for Preeti, it was only a matter of time before that too would disappear.

On the drive back home, I realised how much I had changed. I am able to block her out more and the weight in my chest had become lighter. I had obtained a certain level of peace, or perhaps it was control. Sure at times I walked with my head down, wallowing in self pity, but I knew even then, I didn't want to hear from her let alone talk to her. I knew that it would all end soon enough. I had faced the storm of recovery before, and even though it wasn't easy, knowing how it would unfold provided some peace.

Dropping my bags, I hopped over the pile of bills on the hardwood floor and desperately ran to the bathroom to relieve myself. Urination is perhaps one of the most under appreciated sensations. After enduring your bladder reaching its bursting limits, and doing anything and everything including crossing your legs in order not to wet yourself, we don't truly appreciate the liberation that comes from releasing oneself. The sigh of relief and joy that escapes from our lungs while our body relaxes, followed by our amazement at the length of time we relieve ourselves. We then begin to wonder if we are breaking some record and if the Guinness Book has a category for the 'Longest time a person has urinated constantly'. Do women think this way?

Washing my hands in the basin, I raised my head and stared at the image in the mirror. The once rabid reflection was now healthier. The combination of time, a vacation and Mona had done the soul some good. The former miserable reflection managed to crack a smile when it realised it was now on the path to contentment.

After sifting through my mail and throwing the junk in the bin, I placed all the bills on the cherry wood, hand-carved cocktail table which adorned the middle of the seating area. Switching on the 40″ LCD television, I lay back on the cream futon and let ESPN update me with the world of sports.

Looking through my personal mail, I reflected on the value of a handwritten letter. In this day and age, letters had reached new highs, thanks to advancements in the world of communication. With emails, texts, blackberry messenger and what not, everything was instant. Most of the communication was electronic and cold. To write with one's own hand, put the letter in an envelope, stick a stamp on it and mail it carried with it such significance and worth.

The pensive silence of the apartment was interrupted by a sudden ring.

"Hello?"

"What time did you get in? Didn't I tell you to call me when you get home?" bellowed Mona.

"Damn it woman, I *just* got in!"

"Do *not* bullshit me, Om! It's not right, I've been waiting for your call," she continued.

"Listen, let me call you back, I have a call waiting," I pleaded.

"Humph, BYE! Make sure you call, I want to talk to you about something."

I clicked over to the other call.

"Hello?"

"Om, when did you get back? I've been calling you."

"Hey Arun! How you doing? Sorry man, I just got back this very minute. I haven't even checked my messages."

"Alright, no problem, listen we got a game going on in an hour, you up for it?" he inquired.

I paused for a second, "Sure, why not? Count me in, I'll see you there."

"Wait! Hello? Om?"

"Yep?"

Arun paused for a moment before softly saying, "Dude, I just wanted you to know that Ravi is probably going to be there too."

We shared an awkward silence until Arun snapped us out of it.

"Om, you there, bro?"

I tried to sound as composed as possible but I knew my voice didn't convey the desired tone.

"It's all good, thanks man. I'll see you there." I said hurriedly.

Replacing the handset on the receiver, I sat back and shut my eyes. Arun had caught me off guard and although he was just looking out for me, it all came rushing back. I was, once again, thrust into the world of anxiety and confusion. I rubbed my temples as thoughts raced through my mind a mile a minute. I had to go, I couldn't back out. This was something I had to face.

I knew from experience that I couldn't stay at home and allow myself to be consumed by my emotions. I jumped in to the shower and began my ritual before the game. I'd have to call Mona back later, she'd understand once I explained. ❖❖❖

# Chapter 15

The nylon danced as the orange rubber sphere spun through, sending the white net reeling upwards. The basketball bounced on the wooden floor and its sound echoed throughout the desolate gym. I hadn't been back to the gym in over two months. There was a sole reason why I had stepped away from my weekly game, Ravi. Today was the day I faced one of my demons and I was ready to slay the bastard.

To want what you can't have, to covet what belongs to another is in the nature of man. Today, rappers and so-called R 'n' B artists are always singing about possessing another man's woman. It's as if there is a shortage of females in the world. To walk away with what belonged to another is the age-old tale dating back to when Paris stole Helen. Little did he know that it would lead to the Battle of Troy, the destruction of his kingdom and family as well as the death and humiliation of his brother, Hector. Ravi must have felt invincible after coming into my life, stealing what was mine and having me out of the picture. I did nothing that day. I simply walked out, never to return. He paid no price; there were no repercussions or consequences. He walked in and captured my kingdom without a fight and raised his arms in victory feeling like a God.

I knew no one would be at the court when I left home but I couldn't stay at home. The guys would start to trickle in soon enough and were going to ask me where I had been, but today wasn't about catching up; it was about taking back what was mine. It was about waging a war. He could keep Preeti, but I needed to salvage a piece of myself by facing him. He entered my life and stole what was mine. By just walking away, I lost something. I couldn't put my finger on it, but I knew something was missing. Perhaps it was self-respect, ego, pride or my masculinity. I just knew I had to face him, especially because I was scared.

He would be surprised to see me, but then again, I was already nervous. My hands were clammy and left moist handprints on the ball. Adrenaline pumped through my veins. Each time the beige gym door swung open, I held my breath, scared to turn around and yet eager to face him, to face my fear.

Finally he walked through, laughing and joking. He hadn't seen me at first and continued to smile as he jested with Sean. Raising his head, he met my gaze. A cold shudder passed through me. Ravi stood a good three inches taller than me and had a bit of burly build. He slowed down and almost stopped. The last thing he expected to see was me. He probably believed I was out of his life for ever.

Anger filled me instantly. I slammed the ball in my hands and was ready at that moment to rip him apart. The rest of the guys stopped shooting around and turned towards Ravi and then towards me. They knew this wasn't going to be an ordinary game, but they also knew not to get involved.

"Let's play," my voice was stone cold.

❖❖❖

## Chapter 16

The cell phone vibrated precariously close towards the edge of the bench. Arun rushed towards it as soon as he heard the Mission Impossible ring tone blare through the gym.

"Hello?"

"Hey baby, are you still playing?" asked Rakhi.

"No, no, we just got done. We're just shooting around right now. What are you doing?"

"Nothing, I'm just waiting for you. How was the game, baby?"

"You have no idea, it was crazy. Om came to play today," Arun covered the phone with his hand hoping no one could hear him.

"What?" Rakhi interrupted. "I thought he was out of town, when did he get back?"

"Today, just today, but get this, Ravi was here too!"

"No way!" Rakhi gasped, "What happened?"

"I'll tell you when I get home."

"No, no, tell me now," she pleaded.

"I can't, not now. Don't worry, I'll leave now."

Rakhi waited anxiously in Arun's flat and attempted to kill the time by cleaning up his modest one bedroom flat. Rakhi always enjoyed coming to Chelsea, especially since most of the residents were homosexuals, she always felt safe. However, she hated having to climb three flights to his door. Pushing aside the Ikea coffee table, Rakhi continued to sweep the crumbs off the $20 mosaic rug that lay in the middle of the living room.

She heard the key slide into the lock and leapt for the door. She knew how much Arun loved coming back to his place and having her there. She hoped that one day soon, it would be a permanent arrangement. Running to the door, she pulled it open and startled him. Arun didn't even have a chance to remove his keys, which rattled violently as they dangled off the lock.

"Well?" she demanded.

Strutting in, he pecked Rakhi. After dropping his bag on the tiled floor, Arun sat on the mahogany leather couch and stretched his legs on the coffee table. Rakhi watched every move and then slammed the door.

"This isn't funny, Arun. I'm in no mood for this crap. Unless you tell me this very minute what happened, you and your hands are going to be really close friends for quite some time. And take your bloody feet of the table!" she commanded.

"Okay, okay, calm down, woman," Arun retracted his legs and sat up straight.

Rakhi sat beside him and looked at him in keen anticipation. Arun turned and looked down at her. Slowly standing up, he walked to the other side of the coffee table.

"What are you doing? Where are you going?" questioned Rakhi.

"Shhh."

Clearing his throat Arun picked up a fork from the Formica dining table, which was only big enough for two. Facing Rakhi, he raised the fork inches from his mouth and smiled.

"Welcome to ESPN Sports Centre, I'm your host Arun Gulramani, covering the most hyped game of the decade."

Rakhi giggled and placed her hand over her mouth. She always loved his 'ESPN' commentary.

"Two bitter rivals came face to face today to fight for one simple trophy, honour! Sports fans expected a battle of epic proportions on the hardwood floor and they weren't disappointed. Before the game commenced, Om declared he would be guarding his nemesis, Ravi Desai. The rage in his eyes said it all and once we tipped off, it was evident in his defense. Those who weren't aware at first soon discovered that more lay on this game than simply winning.

"Om refused to let a sliver of light pass through in between Ravi and himself. When in the post, Om fought for position with great vigour, but the bigger and bulkier Ravi took up the challenge and made it hard for Om to dominate him. In the early stages, Om kept throwing bricks, most likely because of the adrenaline rush. The score was tied and both Om and Ravi remained scoreless at the end of the break. Teammates continued to play the game but could sense the tension building.

"In the second half, Om seemed to have calmed down a bit and managed to nail two sweet jumpers from the baseline, while Ravi seemed apprehensive about guarding him tight. Emotions erupted when Om blocked Ravi's lay up and screamed in his face. Ravi reacted immediately, 'What the fuck is your problem, man?' 'What? What did you say, bitch?' Om responded. Their faces were inches away from one another."

Rakhi gasped, "Oh my God!" and sat back covering her mouth with her hand.

'You got a problem?' Ravi stepped closer narrowing the already tiny gap. Om stared while the players around began to inch closer towards the two.

'I didn't think so,' Ravi let out a little smile as he peered down into Om's eyes. That was all Om needed.

'BASTARD!' Om exploded. He raised his arm and clenched his fist. Ravi began to raise his arms to protect himself. Om started to swing and his eyes widened."

Arun stared at Rakhi who had covered her mouth in shock, eagerly expecting to hear what ensued. Arun said nothing and just watched her.

"Well? What happened? What happened next? Tell me. Why did you stop?" questioned Rakhi.

Arun smiled and brought the fork to his lips again and said, "We'll be right back after these messages."

Rakhi screamed and threw the pillow at him. Arun laughed. She ran towards him and he sprinted behind the worn sofa.

"You're such a prick, Arun!" she threw a sofa cushion which missed Arun and bounced off the faded green wall.

"Hey, watch the evil eye on the wall. It's glass, you know?" he hissed.

"I didn't hit it, so relax. Now tell me!"

"Get me a beer and I'll tell you the rest," Arun smiled.

"I can't believe you! You're so obnoxious!"

She continued to chase him around the apartment and Arun continued to laugh.

"Okay, okay, stop, I'll tell you the rest, go sit down."

Rakhi pushed him out of the way and got comfortable on the couch again.

"Om's wielding fist swung towards Ravi, when suddenly out of nowhere a couple of players grabbed Om while another stepped in between the two. Om threw one of the guys aside and charged towards Ravi once again while another player still hung on to him. Ravi, on the other hand, didn't move and stayed back. Finally, the team calmed Om down and suggested not continuing the game. However, Om interjected and insisted on playing, assuring the rest of the group that there wouldn't be a fight. The guys were reluctant in letting Om guard Ravi again, but after Om's persistence and Ravi's insistence on letting him, the guys gave in. The game began with Om on defense. He walked up to Ravi and said, 'I am going to fuck you up!' 'Bring it on, bitch,' countered Ravi."

Arun rushed towards Rakhi and sat next to her while her eyes were fixed on him.

"You won't believe what happened next, I have never seen Om play like that. He was tired, we could all see it, but the guy was just unbelievable. Every time he got the ball, he made everyone clear out, so he could play Ravi one on one. The guys didn't even bother arguing with him. Each time, he told Ravi what he was about to do and each time he schooled Ravi. He would then stare at him as he walked away backwards. It was so intense I can't even begin to describe it. He drained threes, drove to the hoop and did everything at will. When Ravi got the ball, Om just destroyed him. He blocked a bunch of his shots, rebounded over him, stole the ball and just took him out of the game. After a while, Ravi gave up. Then, we needed three more points to win. Om dribbled the ball up past the half way point and slowed down. Ravi was waiting for him near the three-point line. Om dribbled right up to him and crouched down, dribbling the ball in his right hand. Ravi tried to steal the ball a couple of times but Om brushed his arm away. He then dribbled it through his legs, from right to left and then brought it back to his right. Everyone watched. Om was staring right into Ravi's eyes and Ravi was looking at the ball. Om then faked to his right and immediately brought the ball back to his left, faking Ravi to the right, and when Ravi tried to get back to Om, he twisted his ankle something awful. He may have even broken it. Baby, it was the sickest crossover I have ever seen! The guys were just 'Ooos and aaahhhs'. Ravi just fell into a heap and Om rose up and shot. BOOM! Nothing but net! As soon as he landed he screamed 'GAME!' He looked over to Ravi and called him a 'Bitch' and then just walked away. The rest of us crowded around Ravi to see if he was okay. Later, I found out Om was throwing up outside because he pushed himself so hard. On the other side, Ravi was on his way to the hospital. Baby, that game was just out of this world!"

"Oh my God," Rakhi whispered wide-eyed.

"Yeah, you should have been there Rakhi, it was ridiculous."

"How's Om doing?"

"I don't know, but I told him I'd meet him for a drink later."

"Later when?" she frowned.

"When you go back home for dinner baby, don't worry."

"Good, because I didn't wait for you just to see you leave."

"I know, chill. Now give me some booty, you know how horny I get after playing ball," Arun instructed while leaning in to kiss her.

Rakhi giggled and lay back returning the kiss.

## *Chapter 17*

My eyes wandered back and forth, searching the top shelf for my preferred poison. Since I had tasted the Captain's special blend, I denounced all other spirits, well almost all. Each person is tailored for a particular drink, and Captain Morgan's spiced rum was my venom.

"Hey player, what time did you get here?" Arun threw his jacket on the back of the barstool. "Sorry I'm late, the parents called."

"No worries, how are they?" I extended my hand.

"Same old, asking when I'm coming back to Charlotte to visit. I think they're trying to get me to move back."

"Is it working?"

"Hell no!" he chortled. "Rakhi's here, you're here, why the hell did you think I moved here in the first place?"

"I thought you moved here for the Knicks!"

"Please! I think they'd be playing better if they brought Ewing and L.J. back out of retirement!" Arun shook his head in disgust. "Isiah really fucked up that team."

"I hear that!"

"You really love this place, don't you?" Arun asked looking around.

"Dude, it's Sliver. Beautiful women, great music and all that booze, how can I *not* love it?!"

When I had first stepped into Sliver in downtown Soho, I was smitten and it instantly became my favourite watering hole. A small, yet hip, joint with a beautiful aquarium built into the wall above the trendy and comfortable sofas. During summer nights, they opened up their French doors and the luminous aqua blue was visible from the street. Customers couldn't help but move to the beat of the music as the drinks kept coming and the live DJ on Saturday always spun the newest tracks.

"How much bloody money do you make at that damn magazine to keep coming to this place?" asked Arun as he sat down.

"The stock market's been good to me, buddy," I smiled.

"Lucky guy! Anyway, before I forget, dinner and dessert at Divya's next week, Tuesday. Don't bother trying to get out of it, we're all going!" rubbing his hands together, Arun looked around the bar, searching, "So, where is she?"

"I haven't seen her yet," I responded.

As soon as the words slid out of my mouth, we both turned towards the entrance. Each graceful step was poetry in motion. We were entranced by every movement of this Goddess-like creature. The stiletto heels with dark, tanned leather straps just above her ankle complimented her olive skin and accentuated her sexy, long legs. Her hips swung ever so gently from side to side with every step she climbed. The frilly edge of her skirt bounced in jubilation with every stride. She raised her head as she walked in and her radiant and innocent smile was a sight to behold. She had tied her hair back, but a few strands fell loose at the sides. If perfection did exist in this world, Maria had to be it.

"Hello boys, been waiting long?" she stood behind us and placed her warm hands on our shoulders.

Within seconds, the natural scent of sandalwood that seemed to exude from her body blanketed us.

"Just got here, lover," Arun said with a cheesy grin. He never could stop himself from flirting with Maria.

She smiled and walked towards the back of the bar greeting the regulars along the way. We watched her walk away until she was out of sight. We both exhaled like little schoolgirls with a crush.

"Damn! Is it me or does she get finer every time we see her?"

"I need a drink," was all I could muster.

"Amen! Joe," Arun bellowed at the bartender, "Get me a double black & coke and a double Captain & coke."

"Make it a single," I interjected.

"Screw that! Make it a double, Joe," there was no point arguing.

"How's Rakhi?"

"Man, she's good. She was waiting for me at my place after ball. I can't tell you how great it feels to go home to her after the game. Just knowing she's there makes me want to run home," Arun grinned as he placed his hand on my shoulder.

"Yeah, I know the feeling."

I couldn't help but reminisce about coming home to Preeti. The rapid pitter-patter of her bare feet, the quick unlocking of the bolt, her bright smile as she yelped "Hi!" The deep, hollow pain returned. I exhaled trying to release the tension form my body.

Wasting no time when the drinks arrived, I grabbed the glass and took a long swig. The rum and coke were in perfect blend as the warmth of the alcohol spread through my body and allowed me to escape my memory.

"Damn, no 'cheers' or anything?" Arun raised his glass.

"Sorry, just thirsty."

"I bet, especially after today's game. Man, you schooled that boy. I can't remember the last time I saw you play like that."

"Yeah, it was a good game," I murmured, hoping we could talk about anything that didn't connect to Preeti.

"What's wrong? I thought after what you did to him, you'd be bouncing off the walls."

Arun waited for a response but I continued to sip on my drink, looking at my reflection through the bottles on the shelves.

"Come on, I'm one of your closest friends. If you don't bitch to me, who are you going to bitch to?" he broke out his trademark cheesy grin.

I let out a loud sigh and my body slumped. Instantly, I winced in pain as my back tightened up. Random parts of my body always cramped after each game but I still refused to stretch.

"I don't know. When I saw him, I just wanted to tear him apart. I thought facing him would help and it did, but when I got home I was just depressed."

"Depressed? Dude, you kicked his ass!" Arun was shocked, "Why in the world were you depressed?"

I looked straight ahead and took another sip. Arun waited patiently as his eyes were transfixed on me.

"It just brought everything back."

Arun opened his mouth and was about to say something, but then realised there was nothing he could say that would change how I felt. He knew that I had to go through this and deal with it on my own. He squeezed my shoulder, patted my back and then turned to face the bottles.

"Lately I've just been feeling alone."

"I'm here for you, Rakhi's there too and you've always got Mona, Jim and all your other friends. How can you feel alone?"

"You don't get it. It's not that kind of alone."

"Well, tell me, what it is then, Om? How will I understand if you don't explain it to me?"

"I can't explain it, Arun. The trip to L.A. helped, but then seeing Ravi just fucked everything up. Now I can't help but feel like all that progress has been undone and I'm back where I started."

"So what are my two favourite customers drinking on this lovely evening?" Maria breezed in and interrupted our morose conversation.

Arun turned to her and said, "Well, what would you have me drink, darling?"

She giggled, "Don't you ever stop? Anyway, how's your girlfriend?"

"Girlfriend? What girlfriend? I'm saving myself for you!" Arun put his arm around Maria's waist and drew her closer.

"Does she know you flirt with other women like that?" asked Maria.

Arun sat back and laughed. He knew if Rakhi got a word of this he'd have to deal with the silent treatment for at least five days.

"And what's wrong with you, handsome? You're awfully quiet today."

"Don't mind me, it's just been a long day," I responded as I twirled the glass on the marble coaster.

"Ooohh, sounds serious."

Arun's mobile phone sent vibrations throughout the bar slab. He saw the caller ID and smiled, "I'll be right back. It's the wifey."

Arun grabbed his jacket and headed for the door.

"Anyway, how have you been, Maria?"

"You know, busy with school and work. Same shit different day."

"I'll drink to that," I raised my glass to her and followed the gesture by knocking back all that remained.

"Easy there, tiger, what are you celebrating?" Her warm, dazzling smile could brighten up anyone's life.

"Celebrating?" I asked and paused. "Celebrating liberation, I suppose."

"Liberation? From what?" her thin eyebrows arched with curiosity.

"Liberation from the shackles of my demons, demons of the past."

"Wow, that's too deep and philosophical for me," she cringed.

I smiled back and watched as she poured the golden rum into the glass. The liquid seductively caressed the blocks of ice before it began to drown them. Within an instant, the higher blocks collapsed to the bottom of the glass, almost as if succumbing to the magnetic allure of the rum.

"And what will you be drinking?" I asked.

"Whatever you want to buy me, big spender."

"Pick your poison, any poison."

"A tequila shot then, and one for you, too."

"Tequila it is," I confirmed, slapping my hand on the bar.

"Should I pour one for Aaron?" After numerous attempts, Maria gave up and pronounced his name the only way she knew how.

"No, let him be. He'll come back and catch up."

The stubby shot glasses stared at me. Maria had filled the Tequila to the brim and the surface shimmered from all the vibrations around us. I hadn't eaten, and the vomiting session after the game left my stomach empty. I could feel the alcohol getting to me.

"Where is the salt and lime?" I looked around.

"No, no, no, my dear Om, we drink it straight up," she winked and I was sold.

"Right, straight up," I mumbled.

We raised the glasses.

"Cheers!" I brought the glass towards my mouth.

"No wait!" Maria placed her hand gently on top of the glass, "A proper toast, Om."

I paused for a second and smiled. We raised our glasses and I said with a smirk, "May the best of yesterday be the worst of tomorrow," and without losing a beat I gulped the tequila only to shake my head violently as I exhaled.

Maria placed her glass on the bar, "Thanks for the drink honey, but you really need a new toast," she smiled and walked away to attend another customer.

"Man, I'd like a bite of that peach!" Arun whispered in to my ear without taking his eyes off her.

"What did your *woman* say, Arun?"

"Dude, I'm just looking, I'm not doing anything. Anyway, she just said she missed me."

"Poor girl."

"Full of jokes today, aren't you? Wait and watch, Om, I'm going to marry that girl. Crack all your jokes now but you'll see."

"You're going to marry her? Poor girl," I smiled.

"Between you and me, I can't argue there. I am the lucky one," he raised his glass.

We both burst out laughing.

"So what about you, when you going to settle down? I'm sure your mother's on your ass."

"No clue man, no clue at all," was my response.

"What is that you want from marriage?"

"Once again, no clue."

"Come on, you must have an idea. What is it that you want, sex on demand? Leather, whips, chains? Someone to cook, clean and pamper you? Toe sucking? How about some furry handcuffs, I have a pair, you know?" he leaned forward with great interest.

"Arun," I placed my drink on the bar, turned and said, "You *had* to have been a crack baby."

We laughed heartily once again and reached for our drinks.

## *Chapter 18*

The ringing tore through my skull like a blunt, rusty saw. Reaching across the bed, I grasped for the phone.

"Hello?" I slurred.

"I thought you were going to call me back!" roared Mona.

I instantly pulled the phone back as her voice still echoed in my head. I cautiously brought the phone back to my ear praying that the screaming was over.

"Hey fatty, what's going on? What time is it?"

"You said you'd call back, what happened?"

"It's a long story," I grimaced once I was aware of the pungent morning breath.

"Well, I'm waiting," and she did exactly that.

"I went to play ball."

"And?"

"Ravi was there."

"NO WAY," she gasped and instantly forgot about my treachery.

"Don't shout, damn it!" I moaned. "My head's killing me!"

"Okay, sorry, sorry. So, what happened? Everything okay?"

"Nothing happened, we played and he got hurt and left," I was in no mood to go into details.

"Did you hurt him?"

I paused for a moment.

"No."

"Om, did you?" she questioned sternly.

"No Mona, I did nothing."

"Why didn't you call me after the game?"

"I met Arun for a drink at Sliver."

"Great, how's he doing?"

I sat up and swallowed, hoping to moisten my parched throat. Reaching for the water bottle on the floor, I noticed that I managed to survive the night without using the trashcan Arun so thoughtfully left beside my bed.

"He's alright, I guess," I almost whispered.

"What's wrong, darling?"

"Nothing, just feeling tired," I lied.

"You know love, you need to make an effort, you need to go out and do things. It's important to stay busy."

"I know and believe me I have tried, but I always want to come back home. I just want to be left alone. When I'm out I itch to get back."

"What happened to you, Om? You were so much better when you left LA and all of a sudden you're like this," her voice now filled with concern.

"It happens at times, I regress. It's the loneliness I guess."

"But how? How did this happen all of a sudden?"

The pain in my chest intensified and I remained quiet as I tried to maintain my composure.

"Hello? Om? You there?"

"Yes."

"Well?" she persisted.

"It was seeing Ravi."

"Why? What did he do? Did he say something?"

"It just brought back memories," I paused for a moment, "I just started to think about Preeti."

"Om," Mona sighed, "What are we going to do with you?"

"Anyway, please let's talk about something else. What are you up to?"

"Well, there is something I want to talk to you about. First, promise that you won't get angry with me."

"Fine, what is it?"

"Well, there is this guy that I was sort of introduced to and we've been chatting and getting to know each other. We've reached a certain point and now I'm flying to meet him."

"What?" I yelled as I jumped forward, only to slowly lean back again in pain.

"Hon, I didn't say anything because of everything you were going through and also nothing was certain. I didn't want to make a big deal or anything. You're the first person outside of my family that I have told. Don't be mad, please."

"Fine, fine. So what's the story?" I asked.

"Well, I was introduced to him a few months ago by a mutual friend and we started chatting online."

"Wait, you haven't met him yet?"

"No, we just chatted on the computer and on the phone."

I started laughing, to Mona's annoyance.

"Mona, do you have a cyber-lover?" I sniggered.

"I don't know why I bother telling you anything."

"Honey, just a piece of advice, cyber-sex isn't always safe, you can still contract a virus," my laughter continued.

"That's it, I'm going!"

"Alright, fine, I'm sorry. Go on."

"Okay, so we've been chatting, and Om, I can't begin to tell you how great he makes me feel. We connect in so many ways. He makes me laugh and we talk for hours on end."

"Where is the 'Cyber-Man' from?" Throwing aside the goose down comforter, I slipped out of bed and drew open the blinds.

"Hong Kong," she said with almost a whisper.

"Wow, you really know how to pick 'em. Couldn't find anyone local?"

"I don't know what to tell you, I didn't expect it to turn out like this. Anyway, I told mum about it and I think I am going to fly out there and meet him."

My heart sank. Although I was happy for her, knowing that she wasn't going to be around made everything harder, especially today.

"When are you going?"

"I haven't decided but I think in a week or two."

"What's his name?"

"Sunil, Sunil Ramchandani," she squeaked with excitement.

"So is he 'The One'?"

"I don't know, Om, but I really like this guy."

I started to feel worse and needed to get off the phone before I soured Mona's joy.

"I'm really happy for you hon, but you really should have told me." I tried to say the right thing, but she was right in keeping it from me while I was visiting.

"I know, I'm sorry but to bring this up, with what all you were going through just didn't seem right. For what it's worth he knows everything about you."

"How did he take it?" I asked, returning to the bed.

"Well he thought it was odd how we are so close, and seemed a little bothered but that passed quickly. Now, he asks about you and how you're doing all the time."

"Well, I'm happy for you fatty, let me know when you're off. But for now, I need to go take a leak and get some Tylenol."

"You'll never change, Om, call me later."

Returning the phone to its cradle, I leaned forward at the edge of the bed and placed my clammy face in the palm of my hands. As soon as I closed my eyes, my head began spinning. A long night of boozing especially on an empty stomach, always came with a heavy price tag. They say the best solution is a beer, but I chose instead to sleep it off. I slipped back under the covers, escaping from my thoughts and hangover.

❖❖❖

# *Chapter 19*

She swivelled the black leather chair around until we faced one another. Monica slowly placed the draft she was reading onto the freshly polished mahogany desk. The pristine office was complemented further by the giant windows that looked on to the Empire state building. With a fridge, 50' LCD television and a mini putting green, Monica had inherited an office of pure luxury.

As she raised her eyes to meet mine, she interlocked her fingers, cleared her throat and said, "I'm sorry, what do you mean by 'you can't write'?"

"I don't know, I just haven't been able to write."

Leaning back she smiled and revealed her stained teeth probably from a lifetime of smoking. Upon closer inspection I discovered they matched the colour of her blouse, dark yellow.

"I don't understand what you mean by you can't write. You're a writer, it's what you do!" stressed Monica.

"I understand that, but I haven't been able to write anything for months, I've…"

"Months? What the hell do you mean months?" interrupted Monica, "What about the articles you've been submitting?"

"They're from my stock."

Confused, Monica leaned forward.

"Stock?"

"Well, I have a bunch of articles I had written in case of emergencies so that I don't miss a deadline, backups you know?"

"So this latest piece you submitted about recovering from a break up?"

She threw the current issue with precision towards me, and it landed inches away from the table's edge.

"Well, I did write that but it was the only thing I could write about. I've been trying to think about other topics but..."

"I don't care," she interrupted again, flaying her hands around.

Leaning back in her chair, she continued to stare at me, her mouth agape. A hundred thoughts ran through my mind as I searched for something to say to break the awkward silence, and yet, my gut told me to hold off and wait for her.

Finally, having regained her composure, she leaned forward once again, "Om, let me be frank with you. I don't give a crap about your column, it's not really my cup of tea. The readers seem to like it and that's great. When management hired me, they brought me in to turn this sinking magazine around, to make it sell like it used to, better than it used to."

Wheeling her chair back, Monica stood up and walked around her desk as she peered down at me, "How do you expect me to do that if my writers don't write? Anyway, what is it that you need?"

I remained quiet, unsure of what to say.

"Well?" she asked again as she leaned forward.

"I think I need to take some time off,"

She stopped all movement for that instant before exhaling and standing upright. She looked at her feet and smiled her putrid yellow smile.

"Didn't you just take some time off, Om?"

"Yes well, I need some more time just to clear my head."

Monica turned her head to the left and gazed out into the main office for a moment, and then in an instant she jumped forward slamming her hands down on the arm rest on either side of me. Her face was no more than six inches away. I jolted my head back as far as it would go.

"What the fuck do you think I'm running here, Club Med? You best get your shit together and give me my articles. I don't care what you do. Smoke some weed, sleep with a hooker or tie up your boyfriend and spank him! I have enough crap on my plate and don't need to deal with this shit! I'm here to save this magazine, not hold your fucking hand while you take a piss!"

She didn't blink and her piercing stare impressed upon my soul. I caught myself holding my breath and reminded myself to breathe. She took a step back and stood upright again, and as she straightened her blouse she looked to her left again, in case someone was watching.

"You have till tomorrow to figure out what you're going to do, or I'll replace your column with another fucking agony aunt," she turned around and began to walk around the desk toward her chair, "Lord knows people like to read about the misery of others," she reached into her purse and pulled out a pack of cigarettes, "And you can be the first person to write in complaining about being unemployed."

She slammed the door leaving me alone in the room.

I let out a sigh of relief and collapsed in my chair. After staring at the magazine, I picked it up and started to flick through the pages.

Truth was I wasn't a fan of the publication either, but it provided me an avenue to vent and a monthly pay cheque.

As always, I arrived at my column and began to read the only piece that interested me in all of the pages.

## The Break Up

*We've all received the email, which aptly illustrates that people come into our life for a reason, season or a lifetime. Nothing can be truer when it comes to relationships. We meet, date, and fall in love with that special someone. As time progresses, and feelings blossom, we dream and plan ten years in advance with excitement. Then, as we get used to one another and the 'honeymoon phase' starts to wind down, annoyances creep in to the relationship. Traits that we once found cute, like how she snorts when she laughs or how his unibrow looks, are no longer charming. She storms out of the loo complaining about his annoying habit of squeezing the toothpaste in the middle. He's fed up with having to miss the trailers, and leaves her behind at home with her movie ticket, while she's changing her outfit again, this time to match the shoes. The fights increase, and all of a sudden you're both staring at one another, wondering how it got so bad so fast. Then, the inevitable, painful, and always questionable breakup ensues. Boyz II Men said it best, 'It's so hard to say goodbye to yesterday'.*

*Once we pass that tearful crossroad where we had to make that gut-wrenching decision, we face arguably the worst stage of the break up; the recovery! Unfortunately, this process is unavoidable, and the only cure is time! C.S. Lewis stated, 'The future is something which everyone reaches at the rate of sixty minutes an hour'. No matter what we do, there are no quick fixes to this type of recovery. Sure, we escape by indulging in vices such as smoking, drinking, drugs and rebounding into another relationship too soon, but that only delays the recovery process and could very well lead to other issues. Nevertheless, letting off some steam can be quite therapeutic. The point is to enjoy everything in moderation while setting aside time to heal.*

*On the arduous journey of recovery, there are numerous speed bumps. The first step is acceptance. Accept that it's over and it's time to move on. Accept that it's not going to be easy and you won't recover overnight. Give yourself a realistic deadline for when you'll be back to yourself and remain focused. If need be, stand up in a room full of people, introduce yourself and state that you've been dumped. You may receive peculiar glares as opposed to a round of applause, but hey, at least you just accepted it.*

*Ideally, one should discard all that holds sentimental value, such as the photographs, lingerie, perfume, handcuffs and that naughty version of trivial pursuit you hide in the closet. If ridding yourself of such memorabilia proves to be too difficult, keep it out of sight! The last thing you want in those two weeks into your rehabilitation is to stumble upon that nauseating Hallmark card that reads 'I love you more today than yesterday, but less than tomorrow,' and feel that horrible pang causing you to reach out for some moisturised Kleenex tissues. Hence, it's imperative to dispose of that Mix CD he/she made you with all those winning power ballads by pop heartthrobs such as Michael Bolton and Kenny G.*

*Accept that your immediate life is filled with 'spoilers' as you'll be facing numerous reminders of your partner throughout the day. For instance, you can't enjoy Scrubs (your favourite TV show) because he's a chemist. You may no longer be able to enjoy a Dhokla because it reminds you of his/her Gujarati heritage. Perhaps because he was one of the millions that loved Ray, you won't (well, not for the moment anyway). She forced you to part with your collection of Spice Girls CDs because she modelled herself after Scary Spice. Yes, it is unfair that facets of your everyday life have been spoiled by them, and mundane surroundings take you back to the most painful memory. Accept it and find solace in the fact that it is* ***temporary****.*

*Your friends and colleagues will never admit it to you, but you will behave pitifully. At work, you will tirelessly click the 'send/receive' icon on your Outlook hoping to receive an email from him/her. You may find yourself checking your cell phone repeatedly, hoping to miraculously receive a text message or a missed call from them, in spite of your phone never ringing! When it does ring, your heart will probably skip a beat or four. Whatever you do, for God's sake, do NOT fall into the realm of 'blank calling' them… that's just another kind of pathetic!*

*If you can entirely avoid contact, it's a bonus! Learning that they are enjoying life while you weep into your pillow, as Bill Withers sings 'Ain't no sunshine (when she's gone)' won't help anyone, especially those that have to live with you. You will come across buffoons that will enlighten you with the fact that they recently saw your 'ex' at the local 'hooters'. You could either put these senseless individuals in their place by giving them a piece of your mind, or alternatively nod and avoid them for the simple reason that they are morons!*

*During this morose recovery period, some prefer to wail away in the dark confines of their room while listening to 'Tere Bina Bhi Kya Jeena…O Sathi ree' on repeat. Others choose a more productive route of keeping themselves busy with activities and exercise. It isn't easy to escape your thoughts, especially when there are unexpected reminders in your daily routine that make you painfully nostalgic. However, each second when you aren't thinking about the ex is a second away from the anguish. Also, the endorphins released from a good work-out not only uplifts your mood, but is likely to garner you some attention from the other proverbial fish in the sea.*

*The ultimate question, 'How do I make the pain go away? God why hast thou forsaken me, please take the pain away!' still remains. As we've already established, it will take time and there is no avoiding that; however, how much time is in the individual's control. Not keeping in touch with the ex, discarding sentimental items, and keeping yourself busy helps a great deal.*

*Sitting at home bawling to Brian McKnight does not, nor does calling and hanging up when you hear their voice. In fact, that could lead to a restraining order, if anything. Whatever you do, do not inflict the torture upon yourself of watching chick flicks. This will only hinder the stages of recovery. Instead, indulge in some feel-good retail therapy, or find an escape by going out and meeting new people, which may allow the wound to ebb a little quicker. No one is ever in the mood to step out for a night on the town when they have the blues, yet such efforts are necessary, and whether you acknowledge it or not, it does help as you realise there is more out there than just the ex.*

*Some may feel turning to religion and spirituality allows them answers and stability. When you are really in the pits, just take heed from Ms. Gloria Gaynor's timeless classic, 'I will survive'. If all else fails, set an effigy of theirs ablaze. Then, call a shrink!*

*Whatever path one follows, it is necessary to maintain a positive attitude and a focus to recover. Eventually, the weight will subside and it won't be as much of an effort as you get back to being the normal you. Scrubs will be funny again, you'll enjoy a nice greasy Dhokla while watching Raymond, and maybe, just maybe, you'll realise how sad you were for being a fan of the Spice Girls! Whatever the case, tomorrow is another day and as Bill Withers so eloquently put it, 'It's going to be a lovely day, lovely day'.*

*Alternatively you can adhere to the phrase; 'The easiest way to get over someone, is to get under someone else!' Might I add there is a 'vacant' sign beneath me, any takers?*

*The Mind of Om*

# Chapter 20

Divya placed the box on the glass centre table and stepped back with a grin of excitement. She bounced her tiny frame on her tiptoes as she slipped her hands into the pockets of her fitted Seven jeans.

"Well? What do you guys think?"

Arun seemed curious while Rakhi's expression only spelt shock.

"Where the hell did you get an Ouija board from? Is that how you pronounce it?" Pooja reached out and pulled the box towards her.

"I got it from a toy shop!" Divya jumped up and clapped her hands in eagerness.

"Toy stores sell that? You've got to be kidding me!" Rakhi was still wide-eyed, "That's so scary, how can they sell that in a kid's store?"

"Babe chill, it's made by the same guys that make monopoly," Arun placed his arm around Rakhi.

"So are you guys up for it?" Divya asked once again raised on her tiptoes.

I picked myself up off the plush maroon carpet and sat back on the beige sofa.

"You can count me out."

"Om, what the hell? Dude, you've got to be shitting me!" barked Arun, "It's just a flipping game. Even Rakhi's going to play."

"What do you mean by '*even Rakhi*'? Anyway, I haven't decided if I *am* going to play!" Rakhi snapped.

"What?" Arun pulled away from Rakhi, "See what you did, Om?"

"C'mon guys, it's no big deal and I really want to play. How about you, Pooja?" Divya pleaded.

"Sure, I'll try anything once," shrugged Pooja.

"There you go girl, put it there," Arun raised his hand into the air anticipating Pooja to slap it until Rakhi pulled him back to the floor.

"C'mon Om, why are you being such a kill-joy?" Divya sat beside me and grabbed my hand, "Please, for me!"

"Trust me, I have a good reason for not playing," I leaned forward letting go of Divya's hand and reached for the bottle of merlot on the table.

"Well, we're listening," Pooja crossed her arms and stared at me through her bottle thick lenses.

I leaned back with the glass and asked, "You sure you guys want to hear this?"

"Damn right, I want to know why you're being such a pussy!" Arun smiled.

Divya stood up and moved around to the other side of the Parsifal coffee table, and sat opposite me. Pooja tied her curly brown hair back and rested her head against the large armrest of the sofa and Rakhi cuddled with Arun. They all sat on the carpeted floor and looked up at me, anxiously awaiting my reasoning.

"Alright fine. You asked for it, but before I begin I want you to remember one thing carefully. When I sleep, I *always* sleep on my stomach. Never do I sleep on my back, *never*! Keep that tidbit of information in mind."

I placed the wine glass on the side table and leaned forward. The vanilla scented candles in the room flickered and at that moment Rakhi turned towards Arun and held him tighter. Their eyes were focused on me as I brought my hands together and interlocked my fingers.

"While I was at university in London, I lived in a small one bedroom flat on Edgware Road. Around 11pm one night, a couple of my friends, Zubin and Sheila, dropped by and Sheila had brought over an Ouija board, just like this one. I was always curious about the paranormal and when I was studying in Bristol, we had even tried to make an Ouija board with a glass and a sheet of paper. Nothing ever came of it. Anyway, Sheila began to explain the rules to me. The most important was never to play with the Ouija alone. Always ensure at least two people have their fingers on the counter at all times and *never* remove your finger before you've exited. If one person removes their finger before exiting, the spirit you are in contact with possesses the person whose finger is left on the counter. You may not leave the board until the spirit allows you to leave; hence you have to ask its permission. As you leave you have to repeat 'good-bye' and exit. If the spirit doesn't let you leave, you ask it until it does allow you. The other thing most people do is ask if the spirit is good or evil. Sheila also warned never to talk about God and *especially* not to ask when you're going to die."

Rakhi buried her head into Arun's chest. "I don't want to hear anymore," she mumbled.

"Anyway, so after explaining all the rules Sheila said she wasn't going to play and would watch Zubin and myself. So we unpacked the game and did as Sheila instructed. As soon as we contacted a spirit, we asked if it was good. The counter moved to 'No'. I turned to Zubin and he asked, 'Are you an evil spirit?' The counter began to move across the board to 'Yes'. At that point, I was terribly scared and immediately asked if we could leave, but the spirit refused. Zubin on the other hand was entertained. He began asking numerous questions, testing the spirit to gauge if it was legit. After he paused, I asked to leave once again, but the spirit refused. Zubin then asked if it wasn't allowing us to leave because of one of us, and the counter moved across to the 'Yes'. Zubin asked if it was him and after getting the answer he wanted, he asked if it was me and once again the counter landed on 'Yes'. I was petrified at that point, and we both kept asking if we could leave but the spirit wouldn't let us. My eyes were fixed on the board and I just hoped that it would give in. Suddenly, Zubin said 'fuck this!' and pulled his fingers away leaving my finger alone on the counter. A cold chill ran through me in that very instant and time seemed to stand still. I stopped breathing.

"I remember screaming at Zubin afterwards, asking him how he could do that. For the next twenty minutes, fear consumed every inch of me. I hadn't a clue about what to do next. Zubin suggested I should stay at his flat and with very little deliberation, I accepted. Standing at the door with bag in hand, I was ready to leave and then suddenly, I stopped. I looked at Zubin and Sheila and told them I couldn't leave. I explained that I'd have to come back here eventually, so I may as well stay. They left shortly after and even though I was frightened, I eventually managed to get some sleep. Everything was fine and the Ouija experience wasn't at the forefront of my mind anymore, until the dream.

"It was two nights after we had played with the board. I had watched a movie and went to sleep a little after midnight. When I woke up, I found myself lying in my bathtub on my back with my arms crossed. As I lay there in the darkness, I looked around and discovered the bathroom layout was a mirror reflection of what was the original blueprint. The tub, sink and door were on the opposite side of where they should've been. I was confused. I looked around and could see the silver faucets in front of me. All of a sudden, my torso leapt forward and I was sitting upright. I had no control of my body. Then, something gathered strength from within. My mouth dropped wide open. A deep, hollow laughter bellowed from the pit of my stomach. And then came the thunderous roar and the voice announced, '*I'M POSSESED*'. I turned in the tub and shrieked towards the door, screaming for my brother to help me, but he didn't live with me. The evil laughter ricocheted off the walls as I screamed in vain. My eyes were focused on the silver towel rail on the back of the door which started to swirl round and round. As water swirls down a sink, I came out of my dream. My eyes thrust open and I was in my bedroom, enveloped in darkness. I was shivering and covered in a cold sweat. I then realised, I was lying on my back, with my arms crossed!"

Rakhi shrieked causing everyone to jump including Arun. Everyone but Rakhi stared at me as I sat back and sipped the wine.

"Fuck! I need to change my shorts," Arun looked away.

"Om, don't bullshit me, is that a true story?" asked Divya who had pulled up her knees to her chest and wrapped herself tight with her arms.

"I shit you not, true story," I smiled.

"That's it, I'm not playing that fucking game," proclaimed Pooja, "And I'm not going to the toilet alone."

"I think I'm going to return the game tomorrow," Divya picked up the box and locked it in the large wooden entertainment unit behind her.

Everyone sat silent, lost in thought until Pooja broke the silence.

"Do you guys ever feel a presence around?"

Rakhi jolted forward, "Shut up Pooja, that's not funny!"

"No I'm being serious, sometimes when I'm lying in bed at night, I feel like I'm not alone. Like there is something else in the room with me. I reach for my '*Gurubaba*' pendant, hold it tight and chant '*Om-nama-shivay*' until I fall asleep."

"Alright," Arun raised his voice, "Enough of this nonsense, no more scary talk. I'm getting freaked out too."

He turned to me, "Dude, what's wrong with you, can't you dream of having two women at the same time like normal guys? Chant 'ménage a trois' before going to sleep!"

Rakhi immediately pulled away and stared at Arun, at which point he realised the implication of what he said.

"No baby, it's not like that. I dream of having two of you!" he smiled and reached out to bring her close. Instead she looked disgusted and punched him before storming off towards the kitchen.

"Baby," Arun pursued, "See what you made me do?" he pointed his finger at me before following Rakhi.

"So are you saying you're possessed?" enquired Pooja softly.

I shrugged my shoulders and poured myself another tall glass of the wine.

"Rakhi, turn on the bloody lights!" Divya screamed.

❖❖❖

## *Chapter 21*

Of all the eateries in New York, no one could ever understand why Rakhi had an obsession with Chevy's. The four of us used to eat there often, especially since the 42nd & 8th avenue location was next to two movie theatres.

"Hey, if it isn't our favourite customers, a bit earlier than usual, aren't you?" asked the uniformed waitress.

"Well, Om here was free for lunch so we thought we'd drop by and grab a bite!" replied Rakhi.

"Nice. Where are your partners in crime?"

Rakhi paused and looked at me, uncertain of what to say. They weren't the best of friends, but Preeti and Rakhi had built up a rapport with one another. Both being a size 6, they even shared clothes and accessories on occasion; however that relationship came to an awkward end after the treachery. Still, Rakhi seemed unsure of how to approach me about break up.

"They're at work," my eyes didn't leave the menu.

"I wish I could get away for lunch too," she smiled, "You guys want your regular drink orders?"

"No, no, I have to get back to work, just get me some water please, how about you, Om?"

"Whatever you have on tap, thanks."

"Alright, I'll be right back," the waitress chimed and made her way toward the bar.

"Isn't it insane, we come here so often that the waiters know us by our first names?"

"I think its pretty cool, makes it feel like we have some influence," I smiled.

Rakhi giggled and placed her hand over her mouth.

"Om, it's been ages since you and I have hung out like this."

"Well, you're always with that stumpy idiotic boyfriend of yours, what can I do."

"Very funny, he's not stumpy, just vertically challenged," she chuckled, "But seriously, it has been a long time. How have you been? How was Los Angeles?"

"I'll tell you this, it was good to get away and spend time with Mona."

"How is she?"

"She's good. I spoke to her last night and she told me she's headed to Hong Kong this week."

She tilted her head and looked puzzled.

"Hong Kong, how come?"

I had said too much. If Mona took as long as she did to tell me, she obviously didn't want anyone to know.

"To handle some family work, I think," I lied.

"Wow, at least some of us are enjoying life. You know I always thought you two had a thing for each other."

I couldn't help but laugh.

"Mona and I? No way. Anyway, you aren't the first person to think that."

"No! I didn't think so," she sipped her water, "Anyway, I think it's time we hooked you up with someone."

"That's quite alright, I don't need a *maite-vari* just yet."

"Very funny, how about Pooja? She's cute."

"She is cute but still, I don't think so."

"It's because she's stubborn, isn't it?"

"Pooja? Stubborn?" my confusion was apparent.

"Oh my God, you don't know? That woman was born with a stubborn gene embedded in every orifice!" she pushed her glass aside and inched forward, "I'll tell you but you didn't hear it from me."

Rakhi had me very curious and I leaned in shrinking the gap between us.

"I have never met anyone so stubborn. When she was about four or five years old, she was flying to London or somewhere with her mother. Anyway, it was 4am and they were in transit and Pooja's mum kept telling her to eat a cracker, but she refused. Eventually her mum just broke off a piece off and stuffed it in her mouth and sat back. Pooja sat quietly after that. Didn't move a muscle nor say a word. Time passed by and not a peep. All of a sudden, her mother notices some gooey liquid dribbling out of the side of her mouth! Pooja didn't even take a bite of the cracker and it had melted in her mouth!"

I spat the beer out on to the table as I coughed and laughed at the visual. Rakhi jumped back and laughed into her hand.

"Om, calm down."

"I'm sorry, I didn't expect that. It's just so funny to picture a little Pooja doing that," I responded as I regained my composure.

"Oh, you have no idea. This girl is all about rebelling! When she was younger and her mum used to potty train her, she used to wait till the training was done and *then* stand up and pee on the floor, just to rebel," Rakhi cackled and sent me into a laughing fit.

"That's really cute," I exhaled as I tried to catch my breath.

"So Om, can you deal with a stubborn and rebellious 5'1" woman?"

"Can anyone?" I smiled.

"Okay, how about Divya, she's a great girl."

"I don't doubt that, I just don't really know either of them and don't really feel a click. Besides, I think Divya is a little spooked after the Ouija board story I told her."

"Please don't remind me, I couldn't sleep. I kept calling Arun the whole night!" shaking her head Rakhi reached for her glass, "But I'm sure she'll get over it and you can get to know her, right? So, what do you think?"

A devious smile crept across my face and I tried to mask it by covering my mouth before Rakhi could notice.

"Om, why do you have that devilish grin? What are you not telling me?"

"Well, the thing is," I knew Rakhi well enough to know resistance was futile.

"She, well, how can I say this?" I stammered.

"Om, just spit it out!" Rakhi commanded.

"She's hairy alright, she's just too hairy!"

"So? We all are, you dummy! And she waxes," she snapped back.

"I know, but I once saw her with a moustache and a little undergrowth in her pits and now..."

"So, we all get that," she interrupted, "And we shave or wax. It's not permanent, Om."

"I know, but I can't get that visual out of my mind! It's like I'm scarred now and I can't see beyond that."

"That's so immature, Om," she folded her arms, "I really expected more from you."

"Hey, don't blame me. Most guys are turned off by it."

"What rubbish!" she looked away in disgust.

"Seriously, I wrote an article about this and other turn-offs."

"Om, I've read all your work and never came across any such article, so please don't make up stuff."

"It's in my reserve stash of articles, my backup, in case I ever have a deadline I can't meet."

After a short period of silence, Rakhi placed her elbows on the table and leaned forward with curiosity and asked, "Well, what are the others?"

"Other what?"

"Turn-offs!"

"Oh!" I let out a chuckle, "Well, when a girl has bad BO, that's another thing that's hard one to forget about. That awful scent haunts your memory, so to speak."

"You're so dramatic, Om!"

"Then you have gold diggers and social climbers. It's as though they have no substance and their goal is only for self-gain."

"Any others?" Rakhi nodded.

"Clingy women, you know the sort that call twelve times in the space of ten minutes when she knows you're playing ball with your boys or something. Then there is the type that plays games."

"Please! Women don't play games. Men are the players."

"Whatever!" I shook my head. "That's why there are books like 'The Rules' floating around telling woman how they can trap and keep a man."

"Really?" she said with genuine surprise.

"Yeah, they've mentioned all the tricks of how to keep a man on his toes and so on."

"Wow, when can I read this article?"

"The way I'm going, probably soon," I chuckled.

"Okay, so forget Divya, but there must be someone. I really miss our double dates."

Silence dawned upon us. Rakhi had caught me off guard and my eyes were glued to hers. I could see she realised what she had said and didn't know how to react. I turned to my left, looking through the window at the pedestrians walking by. She put her glass down and reached for my hand.

"Om, I'm really sorry, I didn't mean to…"

"It's okay, it's not your fault," I interrupted.

She continued to hold my hand as we sat in silence. I gazed out of the window but focused on nothing.

"You miss her, don't you?" Rakhi broke the silence.

She snapped me out of my daze. I finally blinked and sighed as my eyes moved to the floor.

"The first time was on New Years Eve. I remember New York had been hit by a blizzard and everything had shutdown. Fortunately, at my insistence Preeti flew back from her vacation in California a couple of days earlier. I had bought tickets for us to spend the New Years Eve at Spa in Union Square. The only problem was neither of us knew where the club was.

"We exited the subway and walked up to the snow covered streets and began walking west hoping to find it along the way. There was a huge puddle at one of the junctions and in a poor attempt to be chivalrous, I wrapped my arms around Preeti and tried to lift her over the puddle. Instead, I ended up kicking her in the ankle by mistake. Fortunately it was only a scratch and we continued our search for the club. A few blocks later, we realised we hadn't a clue where we were going. Preeti started crying and eventually told me that she couldn't walk any more because her feet hurt. It was then I realised her pain. She was wearing open toed shoes and her feet were covered in snow. Add to that, the injury to her ankle, which had started to bleed, and the fact that we were lost, it was no surprise that she was upset.

"She sat on a short wall and as I knelt down, I brushed the snow off her feet. Her ankle was bruised and the tips of her feet were blue. I placed my gloves in my coat pockets and began to vigorously rub my hands together. She smiled through the tears as I placed my warm palms on her tiny feet, and apologised for ruining the night.

"We eventually discovered we were heading in the wrong direction and only arrived at the club thirty minutes before the New Year. Our evening immediately took a turn for the better as soon as we stepped into the venue. We grabbed a couple of drinks, and hit the dance floor. Only a few minutes of the year remained when I pulled her to the bar and ordered some champagne. The DJ counted down the final seconds and at that moment I leaned over and whispered in her ear, 'I love you.'

"I pulled my smiling face back and read her lips. 'I love you too.' The expression on her face was almost painful. It was as if a lifetime of yearning had finally come to an end and she had unloaded an emotion that was too heavy for her. 'Really?' I smiled.

"She nodded and looked as though as she was about to cry. I embraced her tightly."

Leaning back I looked away, as the night replayed in my mind. Rakhi sat patiently and watched as I floated away into my own world. Minutes must have gone by before I snapped out of daze and turned to her. After a heavy sigh, I leaned forward and looked at the menu.

"I'm sorry, Om, I didn't mean to drudge up old memories."

"No worries. So what are you going to have?"

"You really did love her, didn't you?"

I raised my head towards the window once again and stayed silent.

"More than she'll ever know," I sighed after a few seconds.

I turned my head back and looked down at the menu.

"I think I'll get the grilled chicken salad, what about you?"

❖❖❖

# Chapter 22

*Dear Om,*

*I am writing this letter to you while in the air. Hon, I am so scared and I can't sleep. I was so desperate to talk to someone that I contemplated calling you from the air phone but instead, I took your advice and just decided to write. I figured I ought to write to you since you're the one I always talk to about all this.*

*Firstly, I'm sorry for keeping this from you but please understand. I was scared of jinxing things and putting 'nazar'. You know how my love life has been so far and I just didn't want to take any chances. Also I couldn't bring myself to share my joy when I saw how sad you've been, it would've been in such bad taste. I hope you understand.*

*Anyway, I informed Sunil that you now know everything and he was relieved. Isn't that funny? It's as if he felt worse that I kept the truth from you. I tell you, Om, he's such a sweetheart. I always fight with him but he just lets me get away with it. He is so understanding and giving. I really want you to meet him. Wait, what am I saying, I haven't even met him myself!*

*I have butterflies in my stomach or as mum used to say, "Kuwa Paet Mei." My Sindhi isn't that good, I'm trying to say 'mice in the stomach', did your mother ever say that? Anyway, I'm excited and scared. Even while writing this letter, my hands are clammy. I hope the ink doesn't smudge. You know what you said about emails and text messages increasing the value of a handwritten letter, well you were on the money. That's why I decided to write this out because I know you'll appreciate it. Problem is my hand is already killing me! I'll tell you something else the 'spell check' option has ruined my spelling too!*

*I didn't tell you this earlier, but I also feel bad leaving you knowing what you're going through. I'll call you from Hong Kong though and I promise to keep an eye out for some hot 'kudis' for you. No Om, they're not ALL gold diggers in Hong Kong… just most of them. But seriously, I'll do some major PR for the most eligible bachelor in the market today… and maybe a little bit for you too. Just kidding, love.*

*I picked up the new issue of your magazine at the newsstand and saw the piece you wrote about 'Break Ups'. I think it's a fantastic piece and I'm very proud of you. I'm glad that you wrote this not only because it shows me that you're on your way to recovering but also others can benefit from your experience and advice.*

*I'll show it to Sunil too, I'm sure he'll be impressed. Have I told you that I love the way you write? Can't wait for your book, I just hope it's not about the 'Indian Porn' that you keep going on about.*

*I laughed so hard just now, I woke up the guy next to me. Even when you aren't here, you make me laugh. Anyway, I'll call you when I get to my aunt's.*

*Miss you!*

*Love,*

*Princess Mona*

## Chapter 23

Arun managed to raise his arm in time, shielding himself from the swinging wooden door.

"What's your problem, damn it?" Arun pushed the door open.

"You're an idiot, Arun!" howled Rakhi, "You said the movie had something for everyone. Where was the romance? The 'chick flick' part of it?"

Chuckling, Arun locked the door behind him.

"Babe, c'mon, you're upset about the movie?"

"Damn it, yes! You know how I am in movies like that. I'm going to have nightmares now," whined Rakhi.

"What about at the end when the two guys were lying on the floor and crying. Saying how they wouldn't lie to each other?"

"Arun, you idiot!" Rakhi turned around and clenched her fists by her side in frustration, "They were surrounded by blood and one guy had his fucking foot sawed off!"

Arun started to laugh which only irritated Rakhi further. He reached forward to embrace her only to be pushed away.

"No! You're an asshole, Arun!" Rakhi sat on the couch, "Why can't you be more like Om?"

Arun stood by the coat stand, stunned.

"Om? Where the hell did he come from?"

"Do you know how he treated Preeti, how much he loved her, the things he used to do for her?"

"What are you on about, woman?" Arun pulled the chair from under the dining table and turned it to face the sofa.

"He told me about how he felt for Preeti at lunch and..."

"Wait, wait, hold on," Arun interrupted, "When did you meet him for lunch?"

"I met him a couple of days ago. He was in the area and gave me a call."

"Why didn't you tell me?"

"Didn't know I had to. Arun, he's your best friend!" Rakhi stood up and walked into the kitchen.

"So what did Om say?" Arun raised his voice towards the kitchen.

Rakhi returned with a glass of water.

"Never mind," Rakhi leaned over and picked up the TV remote.

"No, tell me, I'm intrigued what my best friend and girl friend were talking about at a lunch I knew nothing about."

"Shut up Arun, I don't appreciate what you're insinuating," Rakhi sat back on the sofa, "He was just telling me about when he was with Preeti, about the things he did for her and how much he loved her."

"Trust me babe, you don't want me taking a page out of Om's book," Arun stood up and returned the chair to its original position.

"Why? It'd be a step up in my opinion," jabbed Rakhi.

"Damn it, you really want to know about Om," Arun slammed the chair on to the tiled floor, "I'll tell you! Sure he loved Preeti, and yes there was a lot of romance and mushy stuff; but believe me, there were tons of tears and most of it were Preeti's!"

"There is crying in any and every relationship, Arun, it's not unusual."

"Not like this, Om isn't an easy person to be with. He's very sensitive and possessive, and top it off with his conservative, old school mentality and you have a very dangerous cocktail."

Rakhi sat silently as she processed all the information Arun threw at her. Realising this, Arun took advantage of the situation.

"Om is needy and clingy too," he continued. "It's not like he's a stalker who follows women or anything, but he isn't the type to give a girl her space. Don't be fooled by his romantic side."

Arun walked towards the couch and sat next to Rakhi.

"Babe, the grass may look greener on the other side, but you don't know Om like I do."

Rakhi turned towards Arun astonished, "He's your best friend Arun, how can you say all those things about him?"

"Babe, don't get me wrong. I love Om like a brother, but that doesn't mean he's flawless. He's human like all of us."

"Did Preeti tell you all this? I wouldn't believe anything she had to say," Rakhi crossed her arms in disgust.

"No she didn't, she never spoke to me about their relationship."

"Then how do you know all this?"

"I saw it when they were together. I saw how Om used to behave. Trust me Rakhi, you and me, we have it good," he smiled.

❖❖❖

## Chapter 24

Jim sat outside sipping on his coffee as he flipped through his short story. New Yorkers consumed with thoughts or conversations, pounded the pavement back and forth unaware of Jim at the corner café.

"Om! You dirty Indian!" he raised his 6'4" broad frame and gave me a big hug.

"How have you been, you horny Canuck?"

Jim and I used to work together during the days of the dot.com boom. He was my first real friend when I moved to New York and even though our professional lives took us our separate ways, we managed to keep in touch and maintain a good friendship. He was one of the few people who could make me laugh so hard that I'd be left in tears. It was always a pleasure to meet him, especially when he regaled me with torrid tales of his life that were so absurd, they had to be true.

"Great, loving life, and you really look like shit! But first, tell me, what do you want to have for breakfast? They make a fabulous bacon and ham omelette here, perfect for a pork fan like yourself. Actually, it doesn't matter what you want since I've already ordered it."

"Right, well I guess the pig omelette it is. What have you got there?" I gestured at the papers in his hand.

"It's a short story I've been working on. Actually, I wanted you to take a look at it," he handed it to me.

Once upon a time, between dating an FBI agent he met on a flight and a waitress, Jim dated an African American writer who achieved notoriety by writing 'Black Erotica'. I still recall my reaction as I repeated 'Black Erotica' a few times and finally asked, "How do they do it different?" Jim only smiled smugly and said, "You got to have soul to understand." Sandra, the erotic writer, had commended Jim on his fictional writing and since then he was hooked and enrolled in numerous writing courses.

"Sure, what is it about?" I asked.

"It's about Virginia Woolf and her sexual experiences."

"Excuse me?" I spluttered.

"The basic premise is that while in England, she is constantly depressed, lethargic and just all around ill. A friend tells her about the spas in New York and their effects. She jumps on a steam ship across the Atlantic on an adventure. When entering the spas, she is submerged into a world of sexual pleasures and experiments."

We sat quietly and looked at each other, while he waited for my response.

"Well?" he asked anxiously, "What do you think?"

"Jim, did you just ask me to look through lesbian porn?"

"Don't be an idiot! Seriously, tell me what you think, Om?"

"Well, it's an original idea, but I'll tell you what I think once I'm done reading it."

"Fair enough. Anyway, tell me, how is life treating you?"

"It's the same. Sometimes I can't help but feel that I'm just killing time," I sighed.

"Lord, how morbid! You're not still pining over that bitch that cheated on you, are you?"

"It hasn't been easy, Jim."

"Oh for fuck's sake, you silly Indian, she was a bitch! You're better off without her. What the hell is the point?"

"Jim, you don't understand, we were going to get married, we were together for…"

"Oh, shut up," he interrupted, "It's time you got over it, Om. The cow cheated on you, she was unfaithful. Dude, she wasn't who you thought she was. Let me give you a piece of advice, stop talking about her, it'll help you get over her."

"First off, you're an insensitive prick, secondly, you brought her up!" I snapped.

"Fair enough," he responded with his hands up in surrender.

We sat in silence and watched the New Yorkers amble by. Jim assessed the women passing by, undoubtedly grading them in his mind. I, on the other hand, looked out into nothingness and let my mind churn through the memories.

"You don't get it. I can't help but fade into thoughts of her. The other night I was lying in bed, and like I had on so many other occasions, I naturally floated into thoughts of us. I had found her so adorable. Whenever we used to talk, I randomly used to raise my finger in the air and she always had to look at it. Even after I pointed out that no matter where her attention is, she looks at it like a little child as soon as it pops up. In spite of being conscious of it, she still couldn't stop. It used to make me laugh so much. I pictured that moment and as I lay there, I smiled. That angered me, Jim. It frustrated and angered me. In so many ways I think I've recovered, and then shit like this just brings me back."

"Om, I understand it's not easy, but you need to focus on the future and moving forward."

"For fuck's sake Jim, what do you think I'm doing? Do you think I enjoy dwelling in the past and reminding myself just so that I can feel like shit afterwards?"

"No, I was just…"

"It's like torture having to relive the events months after it happened. Shit, I know I wasn't perfect. I know I took her for granted at times. I know that I was possessive and jealous. Sure, we fought about unreasonable things, but how does that differentiate us from other couples? What about the good I did? What about the right I did? I was loyal, I was honest, I never lied, nor did I cheat. You think I didn't have the chance? I could've gone out there and got laid every night. For Christ's sake, I live in New York! So what sense does it make? Why do I deserve this? What made it okay? Fuck!" I slammed my hand on the table as I ranted.

"That's it, decaf for you!"

The waitress brought our meal and placed the omeletts in front of us. Jim rubbed his hands in excitement. She smiled at him. Somehow, he always managed to charm the women around him. There were moments I thought they were looking at me but soon after we would discover that wasn't the case. I could never figure out how he did it.

"You know what, it is fucked up, and no, you didn't do anything wrong and you didn't deserve it. It's unfair and well, that's all there is to say. Simply put, shit happens."

"Great, I'm feeling so much better," I responded sarcastically.

"Didn't you visit Mona after all this happened? Wasn't that supposed to be a healing trip of sorts. By the way, how is she doing?" he chomped away on the whole-wheat toast.

"It did help, but then when I came back, so did everything I was trying to get away from. I felt like I was sinking all over again and…"

"Om," he interrupted, "You're really killing the mood here."

"You know what, you're right. I'm sorry."

"Om, I really think you should consider Mona. She's a swell broad and seems to have so much of what you want in a woman. You two really have a special bond, I've seen it."

"Jim, we've had this conversation too many times," I responded rolling my eyes, "Just let it be."

Jim always could make me forget about life's burdens and just enjoy the moment. It was one of the many reasons why I had decided to meet him.

"Either way, Om, it's time you enjoyed your freedom and fooled around," he shared as he gobbled on. "You see, when it comes to women, I'm the kind of guy that doesn't know where his next meal is coming from or what cuisine it's going to be. You, on the other hand are the type of guy who likes to know exactly what he's getting on which day. On Monday it's pot roast, on Tuesday it's fish and chips, on Wednesday it's some Indian curry. Where is the excitement and spontaneity in that? Heed my advice young man, take advantage of your freedom and enjoy yourself. Consider this new found single-dom a blessing from one of your Hindu Gods."

"One of my Hindu Gods?" I raised my eyebrows.

"Jesus, you have so many, just pick one, right?"

"Prick!"

"Anyway, I really don't want to hear about your depressing, melancholic life." Jim shovelled the omelet into his mouth. "Tell me about this Bollywood movie running at the AMC in Times Square, do you know about it?"

"Oh yeah, it's supposed to be the most expensive Indian movie ever made. I didn't know you were interested in Bollywood."

"I've always been interested in foreign films," Jim looked almost wounded.

"Well, I may be checking it out this weekend with a few friends. You're welcome to join us if you like," I offered.

"I may just do that. Let's see what all this Bollywood hoopla is about. There will be subtitles right?"

"I'm sure there will be, otherwise I have a friend who can translate the dialogue for you. She probably knows the language better than any of us," I responded reassuringly.

"Will this girl have to press her mouth close to my earlobe in order for me to get every nuance of the language?" he grinned.

"Jesus, you're incorrigible," I couldn't help but laugh along side him.

"Oh that reminds me, there's a story I wanted to tell you. On this last trip of mine, I met a colleague. You see..."

"Wait," I interrupted him, "Do I really want to hear this story?"

He ignored me.

"I had met her before on a couple of trips and I knew she was interested in me," he continued, "But I wasn't interested in her because, well you know, she was white."

"I still don't understand how the whitest of white Canadians could have such an intense fetish for only, and I do mean only, black women?"

"Anyway," he ignored me once again, "I finally gave in on this last trip and we fooled around in my room. After Joy left, I had a shower and when I came back to the bed I noticed some marks on the sheet."

"Marks? Dude, I don't think I want to know anymore."

"Seriously, I was confused, so I straightened out the sheet and looked closely."

"Oh God! Please stop!" I pleaded.

"They were shit stains, Om! Can you believe that? Shit stains, damn it!"

"I think I'm going to vomit," I said pushing my plate away.

"Yeah, tell me about it. Thing is, she's going to be at the next event in Paris and she's going to expect an encore performance!"

"I suggest getting some plastic sheets," I smiled.

"I have to find a way to avoid it."

"I think that's the most disgusting story of yours I've heard to date, Jim. It's worse than the one about the 'swimming goggles' and the 'room by the hour' story combined!"

"Om," he paused and put his cutlery down, "I had to live it!"

We both burst out laughing. Other patrons at the restaurant turned around startled. That was the first time in a long while that I laughed as hard as I did. As expected, I ended up in tears as the amusement continued.

## Chapter 25

Jim first met her during the early stages of our relationship. We snuck out of work for a quick coffee at Bed, Bath & Beyond on 6th avenue where Preeti was waiting. It had only been a few days since I had been dating this beautiful girl, and that too in my first month in New York, a city where I knew no one. To say I was chuffed would be an understatement.

When I first joined the company, I assumed Jim was my senior and that I had to answer him. It took almost a week before I discovered we shared the same job profile. From there a great friendship spawned. As we got to know each other, I discovered that he had a great sense of humour and, in spite of being in such a quiet and demure environment, we always enjoyed ourselves. Jim often regaled me with his weekly escapades over breakfast. His wild tales of picking up a hot waitress at a café to an FBI agent on a flight read like the script of a spy movie. During the day, he forwarded me emails he had received from his harem for analysis, after which we would convene in the conference room to devise an apt response.

We walked through the revolving doors shrugging off the November cold. Preeti was beaming as we approached. Her enormous, warm and welcoming smile was the first thing everyone noticed when they met Preeti.

"Hey, sorry to keep you waiting," I apologised.

"Oh don't worry, I haven't been waiting long," she said giving me a hug.

"This is Jim. Jim, this is the girl I've been telling you about."

"I've heard a great deal about you, Preeti," he shook her hand.

"Likewise," she beamed once again.

Jim and Preeti got along and I saw that she was able to handle herself well with others as she discussed her travels to foreign lands, while also providing insight into the political state of the country. The only subject she seemed to not have a clue about was popular sitcoms and dramas. Later I would learn that Preeti only watched documentaries and PBS.

"My brother is an O.B.G.Y.N," Preeti responded to Jim's query about her siblings.

"What? Obi-Wan Kenobi? Like from Star Wars," I chuckled.

Both Preeti and Jim looked at me for a moment before continuing with their conversation. In spite of feeling like the third wheel, I was pleased that my two friends were developing a rapport.

Dropping off Preeti at the subway was never fun. She gave me a hug and snuggled her head into my chest for a few moments after which she pulled away and smiled warmly. I never got tired of her smile.

"I'll come into town this weekend and we'll spend it together, so don't make any plans," she wagged her finger.

"Okay, I won't. Are you going to stay with your friend in Midtown?"

"No silly, I'll be staying with you. Okay, I have to run baby, I don't want to miss my train," and with a quick peck, her petite frame was lost in the descending crowd.

I arrived at my desk in awe of our weekend plans, specifically about her decision on where she'd spend the night. We had just begun seeing each other and I wasn't aware of the 'custom' especially with the local *Desis*. Do we share the same bed? Do I sleep on the sofa?

"Om," Jim broke me out of my questioning mind as he wheeled over to my desk.

"So, what did you think?" I asked as I sat.

"She's cute and seems quite nice. You guys make a good pair."

"Really? You think so? I actually don't know her that well," I expressed to Jim.

"I'll tell you what was apparent to me." He leaned closer, "She's really into you."

"Why do you say that?"

"It's obvious, Om."

"Well honestly, I've just moved here and I'm not looking to get into anything serious. I would rather just go with the flow, you know. I mean shit, I'm in New York! It's time to have fun, right?" I grinned like a kid in a candy store.

## Chapter 26

The ring tone buzzed over and over. Normally I'd have hung up by now, but in my current state, I'd have just kept redialling the number until someone picked up or I passed out.

"Hello!" she gasped. "Oh shit! It's all wet. Sorry, hello?"

Silence passed between us and we only heard each other breathing.

"Hello?" she repeated in a more gentle tone.

"Hi, it's me," I slurred.

"I know hon, something told me it was you."

"What you doing? Am I disturbing you?" I asked.

"No, not at all. I was just in the shower and had to run out to answer the phone. There's this trail of water from the bathroom to the bed." Her breathing had now calmed. "Tell me, how are you?"

"I'm fucked up! How are you?" the sarcasm in my tone was more than apparent.

"What's wrong?" the concern in her voice was clear.

"It's the same old shit. But tell me what's happening with your cyber love?"

"I don't want to talk about that, Om. Tell me what's going on with you, what happened?"

"No!" I raised my voice. "Tell me about him!" I insisted.

Mona exhaled and humoured me.

"Well, things have been going well. We've been spending a lot of time together and he's a darling. I'm going to meet his mother this evening."

"That's fucking brilliant, I tell you," I barked resentfully "Just fucking brilliant!".

"He's been taking me around Hong Kong and we've had a couple of romantic dinners, it's been good." She ignored my negativity and continued, "I think he may be the one."

"Praise the Lord! Alright, that's enough, I don't want to know anymore or I'll hurl!"

"Now that you know everything on my end, tell me what's going on with you, Om? What time is it there?"

"I don't know. It's late," I said between gulps of water.

"Why are you up?"

"I Just got back home."

"Back from where, Om?"

"A bar! Where do you think?"

"Did you go with Arun?"

"Nope, by myself," I stumbled to the fridge and reached for another bottle of water.

"Om, what happened to you? You were doing so well when you came out to LA. What changed?"

She was right, I had regressed. I had spiralled out of control and it all seemed to start after my confrontation with Ravi. It brought everything back. I had slipped back into the dark well from which I had been crawling out of, inch-by-inch.

"I don't know, I feel so lost, Mona. I feel so alone. I don't know what to do, where to turn," I pleaded. "I feel like I'm begging for help from every corner but nothing helps," tears began to streak my cheeks.

"I know Om, I know. God, I wish I was there right now." Her voice cracked.

"I just don't know what to do anymore, I'm just so lost."
"Om…"

"I had dreams Mona, a future planned with her and it's all vacant, it's all gone! There's nothing but a huge void filled with shattered memories. You've never experienced what I have. Giving all you have and coming so close to having it all and losing it all in an instant."

I could hear her sniffing, and with her voice barely audible I realised she too was crying. We stayed quiet and I was aware of her breathing which started to slow down.

"Om, you loved her, there is no doubt of that, but let me ask you this: If she came back to you now and begged for you to take her back, would you?"

More moments passed in silence.

"No," I whispered.

"Would you want to make those dreams a reality if she was at your doorstep right now?"
I didn't answer.

"If she came back to you right now begging for your forgiveness and promising she'd be the woman you want her to be, and will always be by your side, Om, would you take her back?"
"No," I whispered once again.

"Then let it go, Om. You gave her your best and if I know you well, that's more than most men. She'll realise what she's lost and mark my words, when she does, it'll tear her soul apart."

Her words shed light on the obvious. She had said it before and she knew all I needed was reassurance. Every time I heard it was her loss and that she would regret, it calmed something within me. I was assured justice would be served. As she continued, the sun began to rise.

"Take this as God's will, Om. Consider yourself saved, who knows how long she'd been cheating on you. At least you found out! Imagine if it continued and you never knew. Om, you were saved! You should be thanking God." The tone in Mona's voice grew more assertive. "You always believed that if you give your best, you should be able to rest easy at night, knowing that there wasn't anything more you could've done. Om, she just wasn't right for you, she wasn't the one. She neither appreciated nor respected you. Om? Hello? You there?"

Picking up the water bottle, I walked to the window overlooking the Hudson River. Sunlight began to illuminate the New York sky. A sense of contentment warmed within me.

"You know, I may have not always been perfect, but I was devoted to her and our relationship. I was open and honest, never unfaithful and always tried to think of her first. I may not have always succeeded and there was room for improvement, but I am human! It's not like she didn't make mistakes," the slurring had been cured.

With every second, the Sun began its ascent to the heavens and discarded the blanket of night.

"Om, I know that. I know what you have to offer and I know how much you loved her. You used to tell me about her all the time..."

"You're right, and you know what?" I interrupted, "The worst feeling is that I failed. That my best wasn't good enough. That after all I did, it didn't work."

"I can understand that, Om, but it's not your fault, you know that, right? You didn't fail hon, *she did!*"

"I do Mona, I realise that now and I guarantee you this, I will be the benchmark she will compare every other man to, and in time, she will discover that she will never find better. As time goes on and she learns more about the man she's with, she'll wonder about how it would've been with me, with us and it'll haunt her forever! FOREVER!"

A sense of elation surrounded me. It felt as though a burden had been lifted off my chest and I was afloat within.

"I am that benchmark! I AM! She thinks she'll get better? She gave it all up for sex? She's going to be haunted by thoughts of me! By what she did! By what she gave up!"

"Om, what I believe, what I know, is that you two were brought together for a reason, it was fate. What the two of you did with it was your choice and she made hers. Mark my words, from the day she realises till the end of eternity, she'll know she has lost out and there isn't anything in the world that's going to change that," she said with conviction.

Our silence and contemplation was interrupted by the alarm in the bedroom.

"I have to get ready for work," I said softly.

"Are you going to be okay?"

"I will, and thank you, Mona."

"Om, listen to me, time heals. Just remember that."

"Okay."

"Call me tonight after work, please."

"I will, I will," I mumbled as I put the phone back on the receiver.

Mona was right, even with the mistakes I made, I did the best I could. I *was* aware of my errors and faults and I had hoped to fix them, but this wasn't my doing. Her betrayal wasn't because of a fault of mine, but rather an illustration of her true character. I *was* saved. The memories that stalk me are of my love for her; my love, which I gave whole-heartedly and was in turn treaded upon without remorse. My mind has accepted the reality that I'm better off, it's the rest of me that was struggling to catch up.

Looking at the clear morning sky, it dawned upon me, that she didn't love me, she never had.

# Chapter 27

Arun threw the remote control against the wall, sending plastic fragments ricocheting throughout the living room.

"For God's sake Arun, just calm down!" Rakhi shrieked.

"Calm down? How the hell can you tell me to calm down? Do you realise *what* your family has said about me?" he yelled.

"I knew I shouldn't have told you! I knew you'd overreact!"

"Overreact? How the fuck can you call this over reacting?"

"Don't you DARE swear at me!" Rakhi stood and raised her finger.

His eyes swelled wide as he started to breath heavier. Moments passed with them staring at each other, both enraged. Rakhi's eyes began to tear, but she didn't budge.

"Fuck!" Arun screamed and walked into the kitchen.

Rakhi collapsed on the sofa and began sobbing into her hands while Arun released his rage on the kitchen cupboards. He paused and rested his hands on the kitchen counter as his chest heaved, and in a sudden, blinding rage he punched the door with a yell. Rakhi bawled louder. Arun stepped back, pulling his knuckles out of the dented wood and examined his throbbing fist. He slid down to the floor, mentally and physically exhausted.

An hour had passed before Arun finally got up off the floor and made his way to the sofa. Rakhi had cried herself to sleep. Sitting on the floor beside her, he placed his hand on the tear-stained pillow and watched her sleep. Seconds later she opened her eyes and smiled to see Arun in front of her.

"Hey you," she croaked in a husky voice.

"Here, drink some water. You must be thirsty," Arun handed her the glass as she sat up.

"Thanks."

Once again they sat in silence.

"Baby, your hand!" she reached for his bruised knuckles.

"Let it be, it's nothing," he retracted his hand.

"What are you thinking?"

She waited patiently for him to respond. Not wanting to set him off again, she stroked his arm with her hand.

"Rakhi," he began, "What do you want me to say?"

"Tell me what you're thinking baby, please!"

"Honestly, I feel like shit! Your parents just said I wasn't good enough for you."

"No they didn't, they..." Rakhi placed her hand on his stubbled face.

"Please! There is no need to sugar coat. Telling me that because I'm not in medicine or law, I won't make as much money as you and you'll be the primary breadwinner. Questioning if I'll be able to support you!"

"They're the parents and I'm their daughter, Arun. They're only concerned about me."

"They've known about us and they bring it up now? What kind of shit is that?" Arun's tone began to turn aggressive once again, "I'm a man, Rakhi, and it's questioning my manhood," his fist tightened, "I never knew someone whose profession is market research would be beneath you and your royal family."

"Arun, please calm down, it's nothing like that," she pleaded.

"I've given you my best, Rakhi. I've treated you with respect and given you the best I could. I've not only been patient with your med-school but supportive too. I never made it difficult for you and I've been by your side always. After all we've been through, for your parents to question my worth is an insult!"

"Arun, they didn't mean it like that, please," she reached out and grabbed his hand tight, "Try to understand baby, they just want to make sure I'm going to be secure and happy."

Arun turned and looked up at her as she sat on the sofa with a half empty glass in her hand. Arun asked slowly;

"What do you think about what they said?" Arun questioned.

"Baby, why are you asking me this?" she began to tear.

"Tell me, what are your thoughts about this?" Arun pulled his hand away, "I want to know. This isn't a small thing!"

Rakhi placed the glass on the coffee table and sat back as she wiped her eyes dry.

"Arun, I love you, and you know that. I can't and won't deny that I come from a privileged background and it's not something I'm going to apologise for…"

"I never asked you to apologise for it, damn it!" Arun interrupted.

"Please Arun, let me finish. My father has worked hard for the life he's provided for us and like any parent, he wanted to give us more than he had. It's true I've developed a taste for luxurious living, I'm not going to lie to you. I enjoy buying my handbags, shoes and jewelry, and if you want to know if it crossed my mind whether I was going to able to maintain that lifestyle with you, yes Arun, it did."

Her voice began to crack. She raised her eyes to meet his and knew that those words would've cut him deep.

"Go on," he whispered through gritted teeth.

"But I didn't want to think about that. I'm happy with you. I love you and those things can be figured out later. I wanted to focus on the *now*. But according to my parents, I'm getting older and need to think about marriage. That's how all this came up."

"And now that marriage has come up and you're faced with this reality, how do you feel?" Arun continued to probe.

"Arun, I still don't know. I mean, once I start earning money, you know, I mean, I could…" she began to stutter.

"You can buy yourself the luxuries that I can't?"

"I didn't say that!"

"You didn't need to," Arun stood up and picked up his jacket off the sofa, "I need some air."

"Arun please," she reached out trying to grab him but missed. "Arun, please don't leave," her eyes began to well up, "Please, please don't go, please!"

"I don't want you here when I get back…" he said coldly with his back to her, "Leave the key on the dresser."

Rakhi buried her face into the pillow, howling.

❖❖❖

## *Chapter 28*

The loud crack of thunder jolted me off the sofa. The lightning illuminated the Hudson River under an eerie glow and signalled the impending crash that was to follow. Picking up the Corona, I gulped the last sip of warm beer mixed with backwash and made my way to grab another, when the phone rang. It was four in the morning.

"Mona, what are you doing calling me at this hour?" I picked up assuming it could only be her.

"Om, it's me, Arun. Dude, I need to talk to you."

"Arun, what the hell are you doing calling at this time?" I asked as I reached for a beer.

I could hear the rain and thunder through the phone and realised he was outdoors.

"Om, I fucked up. I fucked up big time. I need to talk to you," the desperation and panic in his voice began to concern me.

"What happened? What did you do?" I asked as I sat at the kitchen counter. "Hello? Arun? Hello?" I could only hear the pouring rain in the background.

"Dude, talk to me!"

"Om…" his voice cracked, "I need your help."

"Alright, I'm coming, where are you? Hello? Arun, where are you?"

"Downstairs," he choked.

"Come up now!" I commanded before replacing the phone on the receiver.

The next couple of minutes seemed like hours as I anxiously paced back and forth, waiting for Arun to knock at my door. I couldn't remember the last time he had cried; in fact, I had never known him to cry. I impatiently opened the door and saw him outside, sitting on the floor of the long, narrow hallway, crying into his sleeve.

"Dude! Get up and get inside," I barked, "Arun, come on, I have neighbours!"

The yellow carpet beneath him soaked up the dripping water. Eventually, I grabbed him by the arm and pushed him into the apartment.

"What the fuck is wrong with you? What's going on?" I asked as I brought him a towel.

"Om, I'm screwed man, I'm so screwed," he whimpered through the tears.

"Can you tell me what happened? You're freaking me out," I was irritated, "If you don't tell me what happened, how do you expect me to help?"

"Rakhi and I had a huge fight about her parents and what they said," he began.

Over the next twenty minutes Arun informed me about what transpired earlier in the day and how insulted and emasculated he felt, how he couldn't shake his anger and had been out from one bar to the next. He ended up at Sliver completely drunk.

"Dude, I don't get it. You got angry, went out, got hammered. What's the big deal?"

At that moment he turned to me and for the first time in the years of our friendship, I saw both pain and fear in his bloodshot eyes. My mind began to scramble and fear started creeping in.

"What did you do, Arun?" I asked slowly and sternly.

He turned and looked back at the floor once again. He continued, unable to look me in the face.

"Rakhi kept calling and every time I saw her number, I got infuriated and drank more. I turned off the phone. Maria was there and she was getting off her shift. I told her to join me and we kept drinking. Afterwards…" he stopped

"Afterwards what, Arun?"

Tears began to trace down his cheeks as he said softly with shame.

"We went back to her place and…" the words weren't able to escape him.

"But, but… Maria knows you're in a relationship!" I couldn't control the confusion swirling in my head.

We stayed silent as I watched him. Maria would never in good conscience be the other woman or a home wrecker.

"I told Maria it was over," he whispered.

"You what?" I stood up in shock. "What the hell? Why did you do that?"

"I was drunk, I was angry, I was confused," he offered weakly.

"Oh fuck, Arun, what did you do? How could you do that?" I grabbed the beer and downed it, unsure of what to think or say.

"I know Om, I know! What do I do now?" he begged, "How do I tell Rakhi?"

"Right now you don't do anything. Right now, just get dry and get some rest. Get something from my closet and take the bed, I'll sleep out here tonight." My mind was engulfed in a whirlwind of confusion as I tried to process what I had just heard.

"Om, please I need…"

"Arun, there's nothing we can do right now, give me your phone and I'll send her a text. Meantime, just get some rest. We need clear heads to figure this out."

He sighed and as he walked towards the bedroom, he turned and asked as a child would, "Om, everything is going to be okay, right?"

I nodded.

❖❖❖

## Chapter 29

The flickering light from the television sporadically illuminated the room. They were selling another grill that was guaranteed to burn off 90% of the fat from all meats or your money back. The images reflected off her spectacle lenses, but Rakhi wasn't paying attention. Unable to sleep, she did whatever she could to keep busy. After taking a bath, oiling her hair, painting her nails and cleaning up the house, she had nothing left to do. She kept calling Arun in spite of knowing she'd only get his voice mail, and yet with every recurring call, she hoped and prayed that it would at least ring. If it rang, there was a chance that he may pick up and she could hear his voice and talk to him.

"You have reached the voicemail of..." the mechanical voice echoed.

A tear caressed her cheek as she slowly replaced the phone and turned towards the television.

"*Beta*, why are you still up?" her mum whispered as she came down the stairs.

Draped in a blue and grey kaftan, she tied her hair in a ponytail and sat beside Rakhi on the brown, plush sofa.

"I can't sleep, mum," Rakhi said transfixed to the television.

"Why? What are you watching?"

"Just can't sleep."

Pushpa placed her hand on her daughter's shoulder.

"Go to bed, try and sleep," she appealed softly.

"I tried, I can't," her response was cold.

"He'll call you, keep your phone next to you."

They sat accompanied only by the low volume of the infomercial.

"If I lose him because of this," Rakhi began without shifting her glare, "I won't forgive you or dad."

Pushpa turned towards her daughter in shock, not knowing how to respond. Minutes went by while she digested what Rakhi had said.

"*Beta*, we didn't mean for this to happen, we just want what's best for you," Pushpa held Rakhi's limp hand, "It's our duty as parents to look out for your best interest."

She waited patiently for her, response but there was none. Pushpa knew her daughter and understood it was best to give her the space she needed.

"I'm going back before your father wakes up. Try and get some sleep, *beta*," she kissed her forehead and made her way upstairs.

The tears began to flow once again but Rakhi stayed silent, not wanting to alarm her mother. Biting her quivering lower lip, she held back, waiting until she heard the bedroom door closing before she released. Sobbing into the cream silk cushion, Rakhi muffled her moans so as not to wake her parents.

Several moments passed before she regained her composure and decided to take up her mother's advice. Replacing the cushion on the sofa, she switched the television off and made her way up the carpeted steps to her room. The melody of her cellular phone immediately grabbed her attention. Her eyes widened and she ran back down the stairs to the coffee table and in one swift motion, grabbed and flipped it open to find a text message from Arun.

*"I can't talk right now, sorry. I'll call you in the morning."*

Instinctively, Rakhi dialed his number. When she heard it ring, her grip tightened and she sat down whispering, "Pick up, pick up, Arun, please pick up!"

As the uninterrupted ringing continued, Rakhi's eyes began to moisten.

## Chapter 30

It was nearly six in the morning, and I had polished off another Corona. Rakhi had called Arun's mobile four times since the text message, and I had been on the verge of picking up. She eventually gave up and sent him a response that read, "Please call me, I really need to speak with you. Please call as soon as you get this message. Love you."

Turning the ringer off, I lay down on the futon.

"Bastard," I whispered.

At that very moment, I loathed Arun. He was no different than Preeti. My heart went out to Rakhi and what she was about to go through, when she learned about Arun's transgression. I knew she would, the truth always has a way of coming out sooner or later, and she would suffer the same torment I had. I hated Arun because he was causing me to relive my agony. To feel the pain, anger and the humiliation all over again! I kept being dragged back into this hell! My anger continued to fuel itself and I wanted to wake Arun only to physically release my rage on him.

Regaining my composure, I made my way to the bathroom and splashed some cold water on my face. As hard as it was, I forced myself to try and be objective. Arun is my best friend, almost like a younger brother, and he had turned to me in his hour of need. Yet, a part of me yearned to pick up the phone and tell Rakhi. I was disgusted and was losing respect for him. I hated having him in my home. I despised being forced into such a conflicted circumstance. He didn't deserve to be forgiven. He didn't deserve to be with Rakhi, and she deserved to know the truth.

Torn apart from within, I looked at myself in the mirror. My grip tightened on the sink. An all too familiar feeling ran through me. I had felt this anger, hate and confusion and it was worse this time. I wanted justice for myself. Rakhi, too, deserved justice.

I rapidly made my way to the table and picked up the phone, and for a few seconds, all I could do was stare at the digits. Twisting open the bottle cap, I gulped down the beer and started to dial Rakhi's number.

❖❖❖

## Chapter 31

Deepak punched the accelerator on his new 1995 Honda Civic as the lights turned amber.

"Deep, take it easy!" I screamed like a girl.

"Om, can you feel that kick? This car is awesome!"

"Yes, yes I can feel the kick, now just slow down!" I yelled.

"Slow? Dude, this wasn't made to be driven slow," and with that, my 17-year-old cousin floored it down the streets of Charlotte.

Why is it that the young ones are obsessed with speed? Was I like this at his age? Then again, I was his age three years ago.

"His flight lands in five minutes, and I want to get there before he exits the plane, otherwise this sign is a waste," he hollered over the music as he snaked through the traffic.

Deepak and Arun had grown up together, and he'd been away for the summer visiting his grandparents in India. My cousin's excitement had deprived him of sleep the night before. He couldn't wait to show Arun his most recent acquisition, fully loaded with tinted windows, spoiler and alloy wheels.

"I'm telling you, cuz, you're really going to gel with Arun," he stated as he sped towards the off-ramp, "He loves movies, video games, and is a big basketball fan, like you, but I can kick his ass on the court."

"Great, I'm really proud of you," I expressed, unable to hide the trepidation in my voice.

"Chill," Deepak laughed, "I drive like this all the time; we're good."

Somehow, his reassurance did anything but reassure me. In fact, it worried me even more. There are only so many times you can tempt fate by driving like a maniac. At that moment, we drove by a bumper sticker that read, "Speed Kills!"

"Deep, slow down!" I screamed at him, "For God's sake, just slow down!"

"Damn, you're worse than my grandparents."

I didn't mind the dig since it finally did slow him down, although not for long.

We waited outside the gate as he held up a sign that read 'Doughnut Poker'. In spite of Deepak being blood, I refused to acknowledge him, and sat a few feet away from the gate.

Arun finally stepped through the gate and they hugged like long lost lovers reunited. I would later share that with them, only to have them turn all their jokes on me. Kids can be so cruel sometimes.

"Arun, this is my cousin, Om, he's visiting from London. Cuz, this is my old buddy, Arun."

"How you doing, Om? Deeps has been telling me about his 'cool cuz' from England for a while now."

"Ahh, well, what can I say Arun, Deepak's told me same old stories about you, too."

For some reason I expected him to be bigger, but he was the same size as my cousin, just chubbier. He stood about 5'7" and those three inches between them and me only made me see them more as kids.

"Really, what stories has this punk been telling you?" Arun raised an eyebrow.

"Guys, can we walk and talk?" Deepak commanded as he led the way, "Arun, I have got something to show you, it's going to blow your mind!"

"Well, he keeps telling me about how you guys would play outdoors as kids, and about the time you sat down to have your lunch, and you sat on a bunch of red ants."

"Oh shit! You told him that?" he turned to Deepak, who was already laughing.

"You began to itch, not sure what was going on, and after you saw the ants biting away at you, you threw your sandwich in the air, shrieked and ran home. When Deepak came over to see how you were doing, he saw you hiding behind your mum, naked and covered in Vaseline."

Deepak and I burst out laughing but Arun just stopped and shook his head.

"I'm never going to live that one down, am I?"

"Cuz, I got worse stories about him and his escapades with Vaseline! I'll tell you later," Deepak sniggered.

"I'm surprised you haven't already," Arun said giving Deepak a friendly shove.

❖❖❖

# *Chapter 32*

Gently turning the brass doorknob, Pushpa peered into Rakhi's bedroom.

"Rakhi, why are you still in bed? Are you okay?"

In spite of being a medical student who studied an absurd number of hours, Rakhi kept her room spotless. The pink comforter matched both the shade on the walls and the curtain. Stuffed animals were scattered on the floor by the foot of the bed.

"I'm fine *Ma*, just tired."

"Aren't you going to the clinic today?" Pushpa sat by her side with concern.

"No," her response was soft.

They sat in silence as Pushpa brushed her head tenderly. She heard Rakhi snivel and understood all she needed to do was let her daughter know she was there for her, and would always be there for her.

"Has he called?" Pushpa inquired.

"No, he hasn't," she wiped her face, "And his answering machine is still on."

"Have faith *beta*, he'll call. Just give him some space."

"*Ma*, I don't want to talk about it, please."

Pushpa leaned forward and placed a kiss on Rakhi's forehead before she made her way to the door.

"Breakfast is ready whenever you want to eat," and with that, Pushpa left the room.

Rakhi wept louder after she heard the door click shut. In spite of her daughter's attempt to muffle her sorrow, Pushpa heard everything through the door. A child's pain is worse for a parent, and Pushpa shared that sentiment. Witnessing what her daughter was going through was tearing her apart within. She too had cried herself to sleep the night before, however, she could never let Rakhi know. Climbing down the stairs, she felt a pang of regret for having stood by her husband as he questioned Rakhi about Arun's ability to support her. But she was only thinking about what was best for her child. How could that ever be wrong?

"Pushpa, where are you? I'm getting late for work!" bellowed Gope from the kitchen.

Hearing her husband yell, Pushpa scurried down the stairs and made her way in to the kitchen. Over the last 24 hours, Pushpa and Gope had exchanged no more than a few words. They were still dealing with the lingering after-effects of the incident that had left them both riddled with guilt, but also comforted in the belief that they did their duty as parents.

"Where is she?" he mumbled as he read the paper.

A stubby man with a pot belly, Gope insisted on rubbing coconut oil into his balding scalp, which not only made it glisten, but gave him a very distinct odour.

"In bed," Pushpa's words were soft and lifeless.

"Doesn't she have to go to the hospital?"

"Let her be today, she's been through a lot."

Neither Gope nor Pushpa looked at each other as she placed his plate on the table and sat beside him. Gope put the newspaper in his briefcase and began eating.

"This is life, Pushpa. We didn't do anything wrong," Gope broke the silence, "We have to do what's best for our daughter and she needs to realise that!" He looked up at Pushpa with blood shot eyes.

Gope had been working long hours at the motel since his General Manager had been hospitalized, and after this incident with Rakhi, he hadn't been able to sleep.

"What time will you be back tonight?" she asked.

"I don't know, I have a lot of work to do."

Pushpa's experience had taught her not to question her husband and risk agitating him further. She picked up his plate once he had finished and made her way to the kitchen sink.

"This too shall pass," she whispered with her eyes closed.

## *Chapter 33*

Arun breathed heavily at the edge of the bed. The alarm clock was surrounded with shards of white plastic on the floor.

"I'll pay for it, I'll get you a new one," he didn't move his gaze.

"Don't worry about it. I didn't know you were up," I said as I handed him a strong cup of black coffee.

Walking to the bedroom window, I gazed out at the Chrysler building and its iconic crown.

"Did you know," I broke the silence, "the Chrysler building was the tallest in the world for 11 months until the Empire State building surpassed it?"

Sitting with his back to me, Arun maintained his silence.

"Then there's Jersey over there," I gestured past the Hudson towards the neighbouring state, "which is considered the armpit of America in spite of being known as The Garden State. Tragic!" I continued, "Just tragic."

He turned towards me, squinting as the sunlight hit his face.

"Are you talking about last night or Jersey?" croaked Arun.

I was dreading this moment, but we couldn't ignore the elephant in the room any longer. My anger and hatred for him persisted, and was clawing its way out.

"Both," I looked down at the swirling coffee in my mug.

Silence ensued and neither of us moved. My disdain for him wouldn't allow me to look him in the eye.

"It just feels like a nightmare. It feels like it happened to someone else, but I know it didn't," he began, "I just want to erase it."

"I'm sure," I stated, as I took another sip.

"I don't know what came over me, I was just so angry and didn't stop drinking and then…" Arun leaned forward, placing his head in his hands. "My head," he mumbled.

I had some Tylenol in my hand, but I couldn't bring myself to give it to him. I wanted him to be hurt. I wanted him to pay for what he had done to Rakhi, for what Preeti had done to me.

"Om, what am I going to do?" he finally asked.

I struggled with the same question during the hours I'd been awake. My loyalties as a friend lay with Arun, but at the same time, I cared dearly for Rakhi.

"Om, help me," his voice cracked, "Please help me, I don't know what to do."

Listening to him break down and reach out for my help weakened the rage that had filled me within.

"I don't know who else to turn to, please Om, I'm begging you."

I handed him the pills and sat down silently as he continued to weep.

"Last night, while you were sleeping, I almost called Rakhi." I confessed.

Arun stopped crying and turned towards me in horror.

"Why? Why would you do that?"

"I didn't call her. I said I almost did," I replied.

"But why would you even think of calling her?"

"Because you're no different from Preeti," the words escaped without hesitation and released a heavy weight within.

Stunned, Arun was dumbfounded.

"Tell her the truth and hope she forgives you," I continued, "That's the only reason I didn't call her. She needs to hear it from you."

"Om, I can't. I'd lose her."

"That's true, she'll probably leave you, but this way you would do the right thing," I made my way towards the door.

"I can't do that. It's just not an option," his voice more coarse now.

At those words I stopped and turned towards Arun.

"Arun, the truth always comes out. Eventually, one way or another, she will find out." With that, I shut the door behind me.

❖❖❖

## *Chapter 34*

The Tir Na Nog pub at 5 Penn Plaza was my salvation for the night. I couldn't go back to Sliver, it was temporarily disowned. Instead of trendy furniture, hottest music and the iconic aquarium, I'd make do with the wood laden tables, chairs, benches and the stench of beer.

Placing the sheets of paper on the slab, I slipped off my grey jacket and sat down on the barstool.

"Om, my son, haven't seen you in a long time, mate," Paul snapped from the corner of the bar.

"How's it going, mate? It certainly has been a long time."

Paul was a tall, gruff man with an iron handshake and a hearty laugh. He had been pulling pints behind the wooden bar since anyone could remember.

"Caffrey's, is it?" Paul knew the preferred poison of each of his regulars, even those who had been away.

"Please. I see you've got some new glasses, Paul?" I asked pointing at the thin, silver-framed instrument that sat on his disfigured nose.

"Aye," he placed the frothy glass in front of me, "My eyes ya know and the missus, she's been busting me nads. Says, I eye up all the totty in the pub and when I told her I'm flipping blind, she got me these buggers," he laughed. "Only problem is, now I can see all the totty and I'm loving it!" He laughed louder this time, "Oye, you think the talent will think I'm more distinguished with these on?" He stood up straight and posed by placing his hands on his hips.

"Oh definitely, you're a regular Brad Pitt."

"Aw bollocks, that Pitt lad is a pussy!" he continued making his way to one of the regulars at the end of the bar, "Enjoy your pint."

"Cheers," I raised the glass.

Picking up the papers, I started to read the last article from the backup stash, hoping it would keep my mind occupied. Monica's deadline was around the corner and I hadn't found a permanent cure for the crippling writer's block I suffered. As I read through the old words about an Indian man's turn-offs, my mind wandered in to thoughts of betrayal. Halfway through the pint, I dialled Mona's number only to be diverted to her voicemail. I was struggling to keep it together and needed to talk to someone. Arun's stupidity threw me into an emotional and mental whirlwind and I could once again sense myself slipping.

"You in a rush?" Paul returned as I downed the rest of the pint.

"Just thirsty Paul, just thirsty."

"Yeah, I've seen that kind of thirst. What *his* name?" he winked.

"I still like women, Paul."

"Ahh well, you've been away for a while, son, you never know," he chuckled.

"Don't you have a sheep to shag or something?"

"That's the Welsh, you twat. I'm Scottish!"

"Well, you're all sheep shaggers to me," I responded quickly.

"Don't get touchy, I'm just taking the piss, mate!"

"I know, so was I."

"She fucked you up pretty bad, ey?" he asked pulling another Caffrey's.

"It's a little more complicated than that."

"Aye, isn't it always?" he handed me the glass, "I may be an old tosser who doesn't know much, but one thing I do know is you won't find yer answers in there, son."

He nodded at me flipping his towel over his shoulder.

"Cheers to that, Paul," I raised the glass before downing the whole pint and ordering another.

"What you got there?" he gestured towards the papers in front of me. "I didn't know you could read."

"It's my next article."

"Right, right," Paul nodded, "It's for that Paki magazine of yours. Let's have a butchers."

## The Desi Guy's Kryptonite

*Since the beginning of time, men have been plagued with one weakness or another, some of which have been the cause of their downfall. For instance, Adam had Eve, the great Achilles had his Achilles, and Bill Clinton had Monica Lewinsky (and a propensity for Cuban cigars)! Then you have Superman's weakness which, contrary to popular belief, isn't a penchant for tights (or a compulsion to wear his chaddi on the outside) but rather, Kryptonite. When exposed to the glowing green substance, Kal-el, of the planet Krypton, loses the ability to use his powers and immediately falls gravely ill. With this premise in mind, I started to ponder about the desi guy's kryptonite with regard to the opposite sex. In lay-woman's terms… what turns a desi guy off when it comes to the opposite sex.*

### *Ram Ram HAIR-e-ram*

*To many, this is an obvious turn off. However, its importance cannot be stressed enough. A girl may have a sexy walk, sultry voice, stunning figure, sensual lips, seductive eyes, but any hint of a muchi and you can forget it! Unfortunately to prevent such a scenario, women have to suffer through electrolysis, waxing treatments, sugaring, plucking and bristly hair caused by repeated shaving. So I'd like to take this opportunity to say, cheers, we appreciate you staying 'clean'.*

*What makes it worse is the wayward mentality of a few individuals out there. For instance, when I was a young'un I was told that women are beautiful, hairless creatures, and being an innocent child, I believed them. You can imagine the damage done to my psyche when I discovered women had hair all over, and not just in the obvious places! If you think that's bad, I know kids who believed women had penises, and fortunately for them, some do! For more details, check out the Tenderloin district in downtown San Fransisco.*

*The 'hair' issue works both ways. Women find men with hairy backs repulsive and in the same way, men are turned off by hair in unexpected locations such as legs, arms, back, chin, top lip, butt… ugh! So ladies… let the men sport the goatees, while you don the Prada bag. For those that are wondering, 'Unibrows' and Ashanti style 'Side Burners' just won't do and nor will bleaching. You aren't fooling anyone!*

### *Stankonia*

*I was sitting in a car with a female friend when suddenly an odour whisked by my nostrils causing discomfort to my sinuses. At first I couldn't place the scent, but as seconds passed, the stench grew more pungent and I realised it was one of my biggest fears, BODY ODOUR! My mental DVD player immediately rewound to the start of the day and replayed the events. I let out a sigh of relief as I confirmed that I had used my deodorant. Still, the source of the pong remained a mystery until I realised it originated from the female I was with! Sadly, this wasn't a one off situation, as a couple of meetings after that incident confirmed that she had a bit of a B.O. problem (and a friend concurred that he too could sniff the ghastly smell). As a good friend, I felt I should inform her about her predicament; however, other females suggested otherwise.*

*Ladies, you need to understand that men visualise you as sweet and pretty creatures. You stimulate all our senses, from our eyes with your beauty, our ears with your voice, our touch with your skin and our sense of smell with your scent. In our mind you're a human flower that's in constant bloom, so please stay that way. I understand a rose by any other name is still a rose; but if it smelt like a fart, you certainly wouldn't want them by the dozen! We understand you can't be perfect all the time, and Lord knows you need to get your sweat on, but don't be stingy with the deodorant, body spray and perfume. On that note ladies, let's keep it fresh!*

### Klingon

*Men are human beings and we too enjoy attention and affection, but there is always a limit. Receiving 14 missed calls when you're playing basketball with your friends is beyond that limit. Asking 'why?' repeatedly like a kindergarten child isn't attention, and questioning our whereabouts and people we were with isn't affection. There is a well-known phrase; "Absence makes the heart grow fonder", so do yourself a favour and allow us the opportunity to miss you, to appreciate you and to think about you. Eventually we'll run with our arms wide spread, through a field of daffodils screaming your name and that too with only two outfit changes.*

### Digger

*Hong Kong, London, Spain, Philippines… they're everywhere! They aren't always easy to spot since they can transform into the sadhori sati savitri. Once they dig their claws in, all you can pray for is that you earn faster than they can spend. If a guy hears a girl is a Gold Digger, she is deleted from his mental rolodex immediately. All we can hope for with these women is that they realise there is a scarcity of quality men and learn to appreciate more than the almighty "Bling!"*

## Gamer

*Men always have to battle the stigma of being a 'player', however, I must protest that women are no different. A majority of women follow their own personal 'good book', otherwise known as "The Rules: Time-Tested Secrets for Capturing the Heart of Mr. Right" by Sherrie Shamoon & Ellen Fein. Now ladies, before you run off and order you own personal copy, please finish reading the rest and remember, this is a piece about 'Turn Offs'.*

*This book guides the reader on how to trap a man and maintain his interest. Some of the suggestions are along the lines of:*

- *No conversation should last over four minutes. Time the conversation and end it once the four minutes is up. – What I want to know is: does the time spent on call waiting count too?*
- *Never return a call until he has left three messages. – So three messages is good, four messages is stalking?*
- *Never agree for a Saturday date if called after Wednesday night. – So instead sit at home with tears in your eyes, fatty ice cream in your hand and Pretty Woman on the box? Good plan!*

*For the curious, other suggestions include; never meeting him halfway, training him to call early in the week and if you're sitting watching television on a Friday night, keep the answering machine on in order to make men think you have a life.*

*A friend of mine tested out the methods, and I admit she not only got her man but by feeding him enough for him to know he was hungry, also kept him on his toes for a while; unfortunately, after dating for a long period of time, she eventually got played herself. Point is ladies; the only kind of guy a book like this will get you is one that responds to games. The review itself reads, "The idea is to return to pre-feminist mind games, exploiting the male." Even if you agree to play the game for eternity, just remember, everyone loses eventually.*

*Just ask Lesley Cronin of Santa Monica who writes; I tried the tricks in this book, and wound up messing up what could have been a really good thing. If you want to learn everything NOT to do – then read this book. It's filled with all the games the guys see through, and it DOESN'T WORK!*

*My suggestion is if you want to play games, invest in a Nintendo. Want a quality guy? Be open, honest and straight forward.*

*I'm sure the men out there would like to list some other qualities that turn them off, and women that would like to know about them, but sadly, there is only so much allotted space. So to summarise, don't suffocate, there is more to life than the mighty $$$, in playing games you'll end up being the loser and like Outkast said, be sure to stay, "So fresh and so clean-clean!"*

*Now who wants to wax my back?*

*The Mind of Om*

❖❖❖

## Chapter 35

Mona extended her clammy hand as Sunil's mum approached. A petite woman dressed in a simple yellow *salvar khamise*, Radha carried the joy of the world in her childlike smile. Brushing Mona's hand aside, she spread her arms and embraced her as tight as she could. Mona knew that Sunil's mother was relatively old, but she never realised the effects of time until she saw her for the first time. The crow's feet, wrinkled upper lip and neck made her aware of how wicked time could be. Leaning back up, Mona was surprised how deceptively strong this aged lady was. Radha squeezed Mona's cheeks with her right hand as parents do with little children.

"So pretty, no?" said more as a statement, even though it came across as a question.

Those were the first words Mona ever heard from her potential mother-in-law, and she couldn't have been more pleased. We all seek acceptance and more so from those who matter most to our loved ones.

"Thank you Aunty, that's sweet of you to say," Mona blushed.

"My *beta* has done so well to get such a pretty girl. So fair!" Radha seemed sincerely surprised, which only fuelled Mona's confidence. Displaying her bleached white teeth as she smiled, Mona felt thankful to her Aunty Maya for insisting Mona purchase a large stock of a particular ayurvedic fairness cream.

"Aunty, you're too kind. Sunil has been telling me so much about you. I've been very anxious to meet you."

"Yes yes, okay okay, sit sit," Radha gestured towards the chair.

The Mandarin Oriental coffee shop was anything but a coffee shop. With numerous servers in white standing by as many stations, serving an array of dimsum, sushi, pastries and everything in between. The cream walls housed a variety of colourful fruits and oils amongst other things in symmetrical squares that had been cut in to the walls. The polished marble floors reflected the ceiling spotlights which created a runway along the floor.

Mona turned toward Sunil as she sat and noticed a smug and proud grin across his stubbly face.

Sunil was a tall, broad man and complimented Mona perfectly in physique. Being a workaholic left very little time for personal grooming or extracurricular activities, which lead to his typical Indian potbelly. He had been athletic in his youth, but all his aspirations of maintaining his fitness vanished once he drowned into the rigours of his work schedule.

"And, may I ask, what you look so chuffed about, Sunil?" Mona questioned with a smirk across her face, too.

"Can't I be happy that the two ladies of my life are meeting?" his smile broadened.

"Well, I'm just happy your third lady isn't here," Mona stated as she placed the napkin on her lap.

"Third lady? Who?" Sunil was genuinely perplexed.

"Your work!" with that, all three of them laughed.

"Yes, I tell him he is working too much. Many years I have been telling him to find a wife," Radha began, "But you know these boys of today, money, money, all the time only money!"

"Yes mum, but someone has to work and it's not easy you know, with the economy the way it is and…"

"Yes I know inflation, oil price," she interrupted her son, "You sing the same song all the time. But what about your mama, soon I will have to join your papa and I want to see you settled, na?" her head bobbed as she spoke.

"Mum, please, can we not talk about such morbid things? You have a long time ahead," Sunil shook his head in disapproval.

"Always talking long time and one day, time gone," she turned to Mona, "But it's okay, today you brought me this beautiful girl and my heart is happy."

Mona blushed and squeezed Sunil's hand under the table.

"You already feel like family, *beta,*" Radha held Mona's hand on the table.

Sunil almost choked on his water while Mona's bottom jaw dropped.

"Mum, please!" Sunil exclaimed once he stopped coughing.

"Don't mind me, *beta*, I'm just an old woman ranting, you don't mind, no?"

"No, of course not, Aunty," Mona replied quickly, unsure how else to respond.

Turning to Sunil, Radha reached out and took his hand in her own. With both their hands in hers, she exhaled a deep sigh before lowering her head. Mona and Sunil looked at one another confused, waiting politely for Radha. A few moments later, she raised her head and smiled warmly.

Radha looked back and forth between them and squeezing their hands, her gaze settled on Sunil, "I approve *beta*, she's perfect!"

❖❖❖

## Chapter 36

Mona's shrill voice almost ruptured my eardrum. She was overjoyed and did nothing to hide it.

"Om, and then his mother grabbed my hand and said I was PERFECT! Can you believe that? Om, I was sweating so badly, so profusely, sorry, not sweating, I was perspiring. But oh my God! I can't even begin to tell you how anxious I was! Oh My God! Oh My God!" like a child she kept ranting.

"I'm happy for you dear, very happy," I blurted as she took a breath.

"Om, I have to tell you, I think he's the one. I mean everything has just been so seamless, I don't know what to say. It's just," she paused momentarily, "Bizarre!"

"Well sometimes it just works out that way," my tone was bland.

"Anyway, so that's why I didn't pick up the phone and I'm telling you Om, as soon as Sunil's mum left, I just couldn't wait to call you and tell you all this. Isn't it exciting?"

Mona's sunny disposition was beginning to get on my nerves. I wanted to be happy for her, but I couldn't help but feel envious.

"Yes, very."

"Om, what's wrong with you? How can you be so blasé about such fabulous news? Why can't you just be happy for me?"

"Mona, I am happy, I've just had a rough couple of days."

"You know, I've been there for you when ever you've needed me," her frustration grew by the second, "And from all the people, I wanted to call you and share this news with you, and you just can't get out of yourself and be happy for me?"

"Mona, listen to me, I am happy, really happy!"

"You don't seem to be," Mona fumed.

Moments passed and all we heard was each other breathing.

"What happened?" she asked softly.

"Mona, it's okay."

"No, it's not, and you might as well tell me. I need you to be truly happy about all this and unless we sort out your worries, it's not going to happen. You know at the end of the day it'll come out and you'll tell me, so might as well save us both the time and trouble. Tell me now."

I so desperately wanted to share what had transpired, but felt I'd be compromising my loyalty to Arun and our friendship. Yet every part of me desired to reveal.

"Arun, he..." I choked.

"Arun what?"

"Arun came over the other night, late at night. He, well…"

"He what, Om?"

"He cheated on Rakhi."

"WHAT!"

I continued and filled in the blanks for Mona and once I started I couldn't stop. The more I opened up the lighter I felt. The more I shared the less I carried. She understood how it took me back to my own experience, how my loyalty was to Arun, and yet my heart went out to the victim. How I felt conflicted and believed it was my duty to save Rakhi, and for Arun to be punished.

"I'm lost for words, Om" she gasped, "Did he tell Rakhi?"

"I don't know, I haven't spoken to either of them."

"Well, I think you should wait. Arun is a decent person and he'll probably tell Rakhi when he's ready. Either way, this is their burden to wield."

"It's just taking me back to…"

"Om," she interrupted, "It's been long enough. You can't wallow in self-pity any longer. You are going to come across numerous situations like this and you can't let it affect you," her tone was almost harsh, "I don't mean to sound inconsiderate or insensitive but I'm your best friend and enough is enough. You have to stop doing this to yourself."

Her words pierced deeply, but she was right. Perhaps I had found comfort in the darkness and pain of the past. It's where I wanted to stay.

"Please don't be angry with me, but Om, you need to get out there and start meeting new people. It's time."

She waited patiently, waiting for her words to sink in. I tried to focus beyond the wounding words and take in the message they delivered.

"I don't know what to say," my voice was barely audible.

"Om, if each time you come across a cheat and fall in to this hole, how do you expect to recover? How do you ever expect to move on? Are you going to let that slut keep you in this hole for the rest of your life? Om, life's a bitch and you got dealt a bad hand but are you going to hold on to that or start playing the next hand and win?"

For a few moments again silence filled the space.

"Full of metaphors today, aren't you?" I smiled.

Mona burst out laughing, sensing my mood had lightened.

"I was thinking exactly the same thing."

"I know you're right, and I'll tell you what, it's fucking annoying to feel this way all the time."

"That's the spirit," she cheered.

## Chapter 37

Rakhi switched her cell phone to silent and placed it in her Gucci bag, which hung on the chair. Arun had finally called and insisted on discussing their situation in person. Desperate to resolve the differences, Rakhi called in sick for a second time that week. She nervously spun the silver fork as she stared at the wooden revolving door, anxiously waiting for Arun to enter.

"Hey there," a chirpy blonde waitress blindsided Rakhi. "Welcome to the Olive Garden. Can I get you a drink?"

Her gleeful demeanour wouldn't normally have irritated Rakhi, but considering how high strung she had been over the last few days, she wanted to stab her with the fork.

"Thank you, I'm actually waiting for someone."

"Would you like to hear our specials?" the blonde leaned over smiling.

"No thank you, I'd rather wait."

"How about a drink?"

"Some water please."

"Sure, I'll be right back," the waitress skipped away.

"Cow!" Rakhi whispered.

Her gaze once again settled at the front door. The waiting was starting to take a toll on her. She began to regret arriving earlier than planned, but she knew she'd be going through the same agony at home. Before she left, Rakhi kept looking at the clock. Eventually, frustration got the better of her and she figured that by commuting to the restaurant, at least she would be doing something!

"Here's your water dear," the waitress placed the glass on the table once again catching Rakhi off guard. "Would you like to hear the specials now?" She leaned over again allowing Rakhi to peer right down her dress.

Rakhi's eyes widened. She knew it was common for staff to flaunt their assets to maximise their tips but this was a family restaurant, and it was only lunchtime!

"Err… no, no thank you. Not right now. Perhaps later," with that Rakhi turned away.

Time continued to drift as patrons walked in and out of the swinging doors, but there was still no sign of Arun. As each moment passed, Rakhi began to fear that he wasn't going to show. Gripping the fork tight as she could, she bowed her head and began praying under her breath.

"God, please don't take him away from me. I beg of you not to punish me for my sins in this manner. I love him and pray that you help me and bring him back to me." Tears began to roll down her cheeks. "Please God hear my prayer, please forgive me and help, please God, I beg you, please God."

"Rakhi, are you okay?"

His voice broke her out of her trance. She looked up with her tear stained face as he towered above her. Their eyes were transfixed on one another for the next few moments until Arun broke the silence.

"What?"

Immediately Rakhi dropped the fork that had left its impressions deep in her palm, and embraced him tight. Her force knocked Arun back a step. Nearby diners gave them a momentary glance before returning to their meal.

"I'm so sorry, I'm so sorry. I love you. I'm sorry," she blubbered in between kissing him on the cheek, "None of that matters, I'm sorry."

"It's okay, it's okay, sit down," Arun steadied her and returned her back to her seat.

"I was so scared you changed your mind and weren't going to come, I was waiting and waiting," Rakhi spoke a mile a minute.

"But… I'm on time" Arun looked confused.

"No, I mean, yes. I was here earlier. I just couldn't wait at home anymore and so I decided to come early."

"Oh okay. I get it, I think," Arun sat down across from her.

"Why are you sitting so far away? Come sit beside me."

As Arun switched seats, Rakhi's chipper friend returned.

"Oh! I see your friend has arrived. Would you guys like to hear our specials?"

"Jesus Christ! What's with you and the specials? Can we get a few minutes please?" Rakhi snapped uncontrollably.

Both the waitress and Arun stared at Rakhi in absolute shock.

"I'm sorry, I've just had a rough day. Would you mind giving us a few minutes? We'll let you know when we're ready," Rakhi continued.

The waitress simply nodded and walked away.

"What the hell was that? What happened?"

"I'm sorry Arun, it's just been stressful for me. I haven't slept in the last few days and it's taken a real toll," she reached for his hand.

"I know, it's been hard on me, too, I've been doing a lot of thinking."

"So have I. I was so scared I was going to lose you and you weren't picking up your phone or returning my messages," Rakhi's tears started to appear once again.

"I was really angry and…"

"I know, Arun," she interrupted, "And I understand and am so sorry for that. I've been thinking about it all and I don't care about those materialistic things. It doesn't matter to me, you're what matters."

Arun sat silent and stared down towards the glass of water in front of Rakhi.

"Arun, say something."

"I don't know what to say."

"This isn't such a big thing, people go through so much worse. The important thing is we realised what matters, right? Right?"

"Rakhi, I was so angry that I did some crazy things."

"What do you mean?"

"After our fight I just went on a bender. I was hopping from bar to bar and kept on drinking."

"Is that why you didn't pick up your phone or call?" she asked.

"I was just so angry and then I ended up at Sliver."

"With Om?"

"No I was on my own and…"

The waitress once again interrupted their conversation, this time smiling as she placed a glass of water in front of Arun.

"What were you saying? You were at Sliver and?"

Arun took a few sips of water before he turned to Rakhi.

"After everything that happened I realised that I didn't want to lose you," Arun confessed.

"I don't want to lose you either," she gripped his hand tighter, "Arun I love you and..."

Arun placed his fingers on Rakhi's lips and asked, "Rakhi, will you marry me?"

# Chapter 38

Pushpa gently shut the bedroom door once she realised Rakhi had entered the house. Turning to Gope, she gestured for him to relax, which only enraged him further.

"You want me to stay calm?" he said with no attempt to conceal his anger, "Our daughter wants to marry that pathetic loser with no future, and you want me to stay calm?"

"We need to handle this with a cool head. We have to think things through, Gope."

"Don't you care about your daughter's life?" he questioned.

"Of course I do," Pushpa responded sternly at the accusation, but managed to keep her voice low, hoping Rakhi wouldn't hear. "She's my daughter, too! I carried her for nine months! It was I who gave birth to her!"

"Oh, for God's sake Pushpa, please stop giving me the birth story."

"My point is, I do care about my daughter. She is a part of me. But she's not a child anymore, Gope. She's a grown woman and we have to deal with this in the right way."

"How can you even contemplate letting her marry that lowlife? What future do you think he'll give her?"

"Gope, it's not that…"

"Not what?" he interrupted, "I worked hard to give my daughter the better things in life and keep her happy. She's accustomed to a particular way of living! He can't give her that, she'll be miserable! She deserves better Pushpa, he's not of our standard!"

"Gope! Please, Rakhi is home, keep your voice down," Pushpa knew Gope had been spread thin recently but she was beginning to lose her patience.

"I don't fucking care! It's my home, don't tell me what to do."

Gope stood up from the four-post bed and stomped aggressively towards his petite wife.

"Don't you dare curse at me, Gope! I'm not your employee," Pushpa raised a finger to her husband as a warning.

"Move that finger from my face, woman," Gope took an intimidating step towards his wife.

"Enough Gope, I've had enough!" Pushpa didn't budge, "What will you do to me? Hit me?" She yelled.

"Pushpa!" Gope screamed as he gripped her arm tightly causing her to grimace and yelp in pain.

The wooden door flew open and bounced off the inside wall as Rakhi burst through.

"What the hell is going on here?" screamed Rakhi.

Startled, they both turned towards their daughter who had tears streaming down her face.

"Nothing, *beta,*" Pushpa attempted to reassure her, but her tears said enough.

"You're not marrying that boy!" Gope commanded as he walked out of the room and home.

"Mum, what happened?"

"Nothing, darling, nothing at all," Pushpa sat at the edge of the bed wiping away her tears, "How was your day at work?"

"Mum please, tell me what happened."

"Nothing *beta*, your dad has just been stressed at work, that's all."

"I know it's about Arun. What happened, what did he say?"

Pushpa raised her hand and brushed her daughter's head, "What is it that you want me to say, Rakhi, that won't upset you?"

They wept in each other's embrace, each for a different reason.

❖❖❖

## Chapter 39

Sunil drew the blinds open and stretched his arms as he took in the view from the Langham Place Hotel in Mongkok. Turning his back to the window, he watched Mona relaxing in the bath through the windowed partition.

"Now that's what I call a view," he murmured under his breath.

Mona turned her head towards him and smiled. Smiling back, Sunil wondered if she had heard him. Surely not, it was barely a whisper.

He walked over to the DVD player and inserted his 'Sex-CD' as he liked to call it. Maxwell piped into the bathroom once he pressed 'Play', and Mona immediately knew what it meant. She looked through the glass and saw Sunil pulling off his Giordano T-shirt as he made his way towards her. Without a word, he slipped into the bath opposite her and smiled.

"What would your mother think if she knew you weren't in China and were corrupting me instead?" asked Mona as she blew the foam in the palm of her hand towards him.

"I think she knows I'm the one being corrupted," he sniggered.

"Funny!" she couldn't help but laugh.

A moment of silence passed between the lovers as the water sloshed around them. The marbled bathroom with heated flooring had taken Mona's breath away at first, but as she lay in the soapy water, all she could focus on was the man she shared it with.

"So, mum really liked you. She couldn't stop praising you."

"That's sweet," Mona was unsure how to respond.

"She loved how fair you were and I couldn't stop telling her about your eyes," Sunil could see the impact of his words from the goosebumps on Mona's wet skin.

"I like her too, she's a sweet lady," she almost whispered.

"This is moving quite fast, isn't it?" he asked.

"Yes," Mona said softly as she nodded, unsure of where to look.

"Does it scare you?"

"Yes, but…" she hesitated.

"But what?"

"But it feels right. It feels…" she paused, "Natural!"

"I was going to say the same thing. It just feels right!"

Sunil reached across from the tub and grabbed his toothbrush.

"You're not going to brush your teeth in the bath, are you? Not with me in it!" Mona sat upright in alarm.

"Yeah I am, why? What's the big deal? You don't want me to kiss you with morning breath, right?" Sunil began to brush away.

"That's disgusting, Sunil!"

Pulling out the brush, Sunil gave her a foamy smile.

"Well if we continue on this path, you may just have to get used to it," he winked.

Mona blushed and sank in the tub. ❖❖❖

## *Chapter 40*

Mona's rhythmic pounding on the whirring treadmill echoed throughout the desolate gym. Lost in thought, she paid no attention to the panoramic city view from the 41st floor of the Langham Hotel. She hoped a 3am jog would give her some clarity and tackle her insomnia. She had been in Hong Kong for over three weeks now and besides racking up a notorious hotel bill, she was stressed about where her relationship with Sunil was heading.

The relationship had developed smoothly and quicker than she had expected. A shiver travelled through Mona's spine each time she thought about how soon she had slept with him. She convinced herself that it wouldn't be relevant if they were to get married eventually, and with that she was able to come to terms with her actions.

In a few hours, Mona would have to pick up her mother's call and answer the identical barrage of questions she had been asked for the past few weeks, "What have you decided? Should we fly down? Should I call his mother? How long are you going to stay there for? You know you're not young any more and it's not as though the proposals are flooding in. What are you doing with your life?"

Her neck would tense at the sound of her mother's voice. She longed for companionship, and watching her friends getting married wasn't easy, especially with the battery of questions she endured with a smile at each wedding. The pressure society put on her, compounded with her mother's guilt trips left her sleepless.

Increasing the volume on her iPod, Mona tried to drown out her mother's voice which reverberated in her head. Increasing the speed on the apparatus, she ran harder, hoping to escape from herself.

With Sunil, she didn't have to run. Everything was forgotten and she had slipped into the dream that it felt like. Maybe it was a dream? People usually say when it's too good to be true, it is. But what do the sceptics know? They don't believe in *kismet,* destiny and soul mates. What if she had to wait to find the right person? What if this is exactly how it was meant to be and she should continue to flow? Why question it? She remembered reading something to the effect of the universe and destiny bringing our soul mate to us in every life, and what we did after that fell into the realm of free will. Our decision dictates whether we lead a life of love and joy, or one of loneliness and misery. How could she risk that? Maybe it *is* supposed to flow this easily? And why not? She's waited and been patient.

Thumping the giant red switch, Mona brought the treadmill to a halt. Panting, she stepped off and stared at her tanned reflection. Her skin glistened with beads of sweat that snaked down her skin and dripped on to the carpet.

"I deserve it!" she whispered.

## Chapter 41

Jaymee flirtatiously placed her hand on my arm as she laughed. Tall and slender with a smooth, olive complexion, Jaymee was truly beautiful. She was in New York for a modelling assignment, and would only be in the city for three more days.

"You're so funny!" she commented, as she put her other hand on my shoulder.

Jim, who was surrounded by his harem, shot me a smile from across the room, acknowledging my progress.

The vibration interrupted my conversation in mid sentence. Pulling my phone out of my pocket, I asked Jaymee to excuse me. Whenever the phone rang, a small part of me still hoped it was Preeti. Instead of getting frustrated, I accepted that this too would fade.

"Hello?"

"Om, it's Mona. How are you?"

"Wait I can't hear you, hold on."

Making my way through the crowd I stepped out on to the street.

"Hello?"

"Om, it's Mona. It's so loud, where are you?"

"Fatty! Where the hell are you?"

"I'm still in Hong Kong."

"What? What are you still doing there? You've been gone a month!" I stated.

"It's a long story. Where are you? Are you busy?"

"I'm at Madam X with Jim. You remember that sexy, red bar downtown, on Houston?"

"Yes, how could I forget?" Mona giggled. "Arun said I'd feel horny as soon as I walked in."

"Yes, that's the one," I laughed, "Jim insisted I come out with him. He assured me he'd get me laid and I must admit it's very entertaining."

"Oh! Okay, why don't we speak later then?"

"No, no, shoot. What's up? How are things with you and your cyber lover?" I asked as I sat down on the curb.

"Well, that's what I wanted to talk to you about. Things are going really well, I mean, we've gelled so smoothly, Om, it's freaky!"

"Well that's great news hon, I'm happy for you," I said with a genuine smile.

"Yes it is. I met his mother and we got along great! Not only that, but the mother said to him that she approves of me."

"Why wouldn't she? You're a catch and a half, Mona."

"Thanks, sweetheart."

"The fact that you are cool with the family is a huge advantage and it just makes things easier for the two of you."

"You're right," Mona whispered.

"So, what's bothering you then?"

"How did you know I was bothered?" she sounded perplexed.

"Why else would you call me at this hour?" I smiled.

"Om, I think I'm," she paused, "I'm going to move ahead with this."

"Move ahead?"

"I'm going to ask my family to come meet his so that we can take things forward and maybe get engaged."

"WHAT?" I yelled.

Startled pedestrians turned in my direction.

"Om, I'm not getting any younger and I just feel that this is right. We get along and I'm happy," she almost pleaded.

"Mona, you hardly know the guy!"

"I've been in touch with him for a few months and have spent almost a month here. I have been thinking about this and it makes sense."

"That still doesn't mean you know him. All you've witnessed is him putting his best foot forward! This may not be the real him, Mona! You still need to spend more time with him. If it's right today, it'll still be right tomorrow!"

"I understand what you're saying Om and I appreciate that you're only looking out for me. But I have other things to think about. My mother is the only parent left, and it scares me that she may not see me settle down…"

"But that's not…" I interrupted.

"Wait! I wouldn't get married for her sake but it *is* something I have to consider. I also want kids Om, and I'm nearly 35. Look, I've pondered over this a lot and I'm going to go ahead with it. I just would like you to be happy for me and be there."

The New York nightlife in the background echoed through the phone as I kept silent. Standing up from the curb, I brushed my jeans and sighed, "If this is what you want, I'm happy for you and wish you the best. I'm there for you."

"Thank you Om, that mean's a lot to me. You're the only one that knows so please don't tell anyone. I'm going to call mum and speak to her. She's going to be thrilled!"

"I'm sure. She's been waiting for this."

"Anyway enough about me, how are things with you?" Mona asked.

"Things are good, thanks. Don't waste your money, I'm going to head back and get a drink to celebrate."

"Okay, sorry to take you away, and thank you. Please tell Jim I said 'hi'."

"Don't be silly, we'll talk later."

"Okay, and Om, if you do get laid, please use protection."

"Sure Mona," I laughed, "Bye."

Returning the phone to my pocket, I tried to digest what I had heard. I was scared of losing Mona and letting her move away even further. But what had me alarmed was the pace she was moving at with Sunil. Did she know about Hong Kong men and their reputation? Was she aware of the superficial and pretentious society? Should I have suppressed my urge to tell her?

My phone vibrated once more, "Hello?"

"Where the fuck are you?" Jim screamed.

"I'm outside, I had to get a call."

"Okay, well, can you come inside? You're going to lose the Filipino chick, and trust me, she's a sure thing!"

"I'll be right in."

"Om…"

"Yeah?"

"I promise you, '*she love you long time*'," he laughed before hanging up.

Walking back in, I was engulfed by the red velvet that was draped all over the lounge. With the matching sofas and staff donned in red, unsuspecting first timers usually suffer a sensory overload when walking through the doors.

I hoped to come to terms with Mona's situation. She was a smart woman and only she knew what was best for her. I wanted to be happy that she had found someone. She deserved to be happy.

Making my way to the bar, I slipped my hand around Jaymee's slim waist and whispered in her ear, "Miss me?"

She turned and smiled, "I thought you forgot about me." She pouted.

"Forget you? Never!" I turned to the bar tender, "Let's get a bottle of champagne, my friend's getting engaged!"

❖❖❖

## Chapter 42

Icy bullets ricocheted off my body, wrenching me out of my sedated state. Instinctively jumping upright, I gasped for air and screamed, "FUCK!"

Disoriented, I grabbed onto the plastic and attempted to pull myself up only to have an inexplicable force push me back into the cold, white coffin.

"Stay there and take a moment, Om," said a familiar voice.

The shock of the cold water had transformed the colour of my skin to a burning shade of red. Releasing the plastic, I squeezed the edges of the freezing tub as my chest heaved back and forth rapidly.

"How you feeling?" the baritone, male voice was faint in the back of my mind as I focused on processing my surroundings.

White tiles, which matched both the tub and floor surrounded me. A rail of blurry spotlights shone down on me from the heavens as I stared at the generic chrome faucet which conspired to drown me in an icy tundra.

"Om," a hand reached out and touched me on the shoulder, "Are you okay?"

Snapping my drenched head around, I noticed the silhouette sitting on the commode. My bottom lip quivered as my eyes focused on the figure.

"Jim?" I shivered.

"You had me worried there for a while." Reaching forward, Jim turned the tap and halted the flow of water.

"What the…"

"Here dry up," he handed me a towel. "Get changed, I'll make you some coffee."

Pulling myself out of the tub, I reached for the towel rail only to stumble and bounce off the wall. My head spun like a carousel off its axis as I toppled back and forth trying to gain my balance. Holding on to the rail I closed my eyes and took a deep breath hoping to gain my composure, only to be overwhelmed by an intense wave of nausea.

"What the fuck?" I slurred, as saliva dribbled off from my blue bottom lip on to the wet floor.

"Easy there, big guy," Jim lunged forward and grabbed me.

Putting my hand over his shoulder, he helped me into the living room and sat me up right on the futon.

"You really did it this time, didn't you?" he handed me a mug, "Have some of that, it should wake you up."

Time trickled on as we sat in the living room in silence. Eventually, the spinning slowed down and with it faded the desire to vomit.

"What happened?" the question escaped from my lips softly.

"What happened?" You got smashed! That's what happened!" Jim responded with a condescending smile.

As much as my mind's eye attempted to penetrate the thick fog saturated with intoxicating fumes, I couldn't recollect the evening.

"You kept going on and on about Mona's engagement and didn't stop ordering shots and bottles of champagne. I think you bought everyone in the bar a drink."

A grunt was all I could offer as I brought my hand up and rested my face on the clammy palm.

"You started slurring and falling all over the place until you finally collapsed and couldn't get up. If you hadn't kept slurring and apologising, I would have taken you to the hospital."

Unable to offer a response, I shamefully shook my head.

"You kept talking about Preeti, how she had failed you even after your devotion," Jim continued, "After that, you moaned about Mona and how you feel like you're losing her now that she's going to get married and you're going to be alone."

"I'm sorry Jim," I murmured.

"Sorry?" he chortled, "You've got that right, you are a sorry sight."

"I'm sure."

"Look Om, I consider myself a good friend of yours and you know I'm not the type to pull any punches, but you are really in a pathetic state."

"I'll be alright tomorrow," I responded as I finished off the last of the coffee.

"That's not what I mean, Om. I think you may have a problem."

Raising my head, I looked at him with an expression of confusion across my face.

"I should've said something earlier, but I was hoping it would sort it self out."

"What problem? Said something about what?"

"Om," Jim leaned forward, "I think, you have a drinking problem."

Engulfed in silence, we stared at each other.

"I'm not saying you're a full blown alcoholic, Om, and I should know, I've seen plenty in my time. But you're on your way there and you need help. Trust me, I know the signs."

Jim sat back and waited for me to speak, probably expecting me to acknowledge and agree with his bold accusation.

"Jim, thanks for taking care of me, but I think I'm going to get some sleep now."

"I understand, it isn't an easy thing to hear," he persisted as he stood up and reached for his jacket, "But as a friend who cares about your welfare, it's my duty to tell you the truth. This isn't who you are, Om. I know it's been hard on you but if you continue like this, you are only allowing Preeti's actions to affect you still, to control you and drive you to this. It's time to let go."

"I'll call you tomorrow."

"You can't ignore this, Om, it's a beast that will eat you up unless you take care of it now."

"Goodnight Jim," I snarled.

"Night, Om," Jim shut the door behind him as he exited the flat.

"Fucking asshole!" I opened the fridge and reached for a beer.

The state of intoxication dissipated and gave way to anger. Enraged by Jim's accusation, I slammed the refrigerator door and heard the contents fall over each other.

Sliding open the windows of the living room, I leaned out and felt the cool, gentle breeze caress my face as I brought the bottle to my lips and took a sip. As the beverage wet my pallet and slipped down my throat, the wave of nausea returned. Dropping the frothy bottle on the living room floor, I raced to the bathroom and violently purged myself of the poison that had corroded my insides. As I sat on the floor teary eyed and with my head over the toilet bowl, Jim's words began to echo in my mind. A part of me knew the truth, it had always known. Each day, I knew I was slipping further but I convinced myself tomorrow would be different. Instead I justified it to myself and tomorrow never came. Initially it was supposed to be an aid. It was a tool to help me escape from the toxic memories of Preeti. But that tool had developed into a crutch that I started to lean on whenever life became the slightest bit uncomfortable. I used one source of poison to escape from another and had lost myself. I convinced myself that if I didn't admit it to myself, it wasn't a problem. Turns out the only person I was kidding was myself and worse yet, I knew it all along.

Grabbing the sink, I pulled myself up and stared at my pale face in the mirror. I hardly recognised myself. A sarcastic smile crept across my face as I shook my head. Never would I have imagined falling this far in life.

Splashing cold water on myself, I looked up at the stranger's reflection and whispered under my breath, "It's tomorrow."

Reaching into my pocket, I pulled out the mobile and called Jim.

"Hello? Om, are you okay?"

"Yeah, I'm fine. I'm sorry for being rude, Jim."

"It's alright, I apologise if I crossed the line, but..."

"No," I interrupted, "You were right, Jim, I needed to hear that. You were right."

❖❖❖

## Chapter 43

The bright lights of Lan Kwai Fong left Mona wide eyed. Walking downhill, she peeped into the bars on either side in awe.

"So this is like the Time's Square of Hong Kong?" she squeezed Sunil's hand.

"I guess so, I've never been to the States," he laughed.

Mona snapped her head around in amazement as she slowed her stride.

"What do you mean you've *never* been to the States?"

"I never needed to, nor did I have the time. I did apply for a visa once but I got rejected," Sunil shrugged.

"I never knew that. What passport do you have?"

"Indian of course, I'm a patriot!" he announced proudly.

"Patriot? How often do you go to India, Mister Ramchandani?" she smiled.

"Err… once every five years!" he laughed, "Okay we better rush, we're late and everyone will be waiting."

"I'm so excited, I love sushi!"

"Oh, you'll love the tuna tartar, I could have three orders on my own!" Sunil rubbed his belly.

The other three couples welcomed Mona and Sunil with kind words and warm hugs as they entered.

"So, we finally get to meet you!" expressed Navin as he hugged Mona. "Sunil has been going on and on about you but he never brings you out!" he said as he introduced Mona to his wife, Rachna.

Hiding her anxiety, Mona met the group and hoped she'd remember all the names. She had been nervous the entire day since it was her first time meeting Sunil's friends, and the public appearance made their relationship official.

"Mona, sit next to me, I want to know all about you," Rachna held Mona's hand and guided her to a chair.

As the evening progressed, Mona warmed to the group. Dishes of sushi were ravaged and copious amounts of Saki consumed. Laughter echoed through the dimly lit Japanese restaurant, irritating other patrons, but the Indians didn't care. Mona began to envision her future with Sunil and being a part of the group as his wife. She smiled to herself at the thought.

"So Sunil, does this," Navin nodded towards Mona, "mean you won't be going to Mong Kok any more for your massages?" He chuckled.

Sunil's smiling face turned sour in an instant. Mona noticed the change but was puzzled.

"Mona," Navin turned toward her, "Did you know that you're with a local celebrity? They were going to change the name of Mong Kok to 'Sunil's Kok'," he joked, sending the rest of the table roaring.

Sunil stood up forcefully, sending his chair across the floor.

"You motherfucker!!!" he screamed, "You think that shit is funny? Humiliating me in front of her?" he pointed at Mona.

The faces on the table spelt horror. Navin gulped and attempted to calm Sunil down, "Dude, I was just kidding. Why don't you calm down and take a seat?" Navin held up his hands in surrender.

"Don't tell me what to do!" Sunil reached across the table and grabbed Navin by the collar.

Rachna held Sunil's wrist and pleaded, "Sunil, we're in a restaurant, please, calm down!"

Taking a moment, Sunil looked around, having been made aware of his environment. He turned back to Navin, refusing to loosen his grip.

"Let's take this outside, you bastard!" he screamed. Globs of saliva flew across on to Navin's face.

The manager and waiters surrounded Sunil and insisted he vacate the restaurant.

"Let's go Mona," he commanded as he threw dollar bills on to the table.

Mona, petrified, was unsure of what to do. Turning to Rachna, she apologised and picked up her bag before following Sunil out onto the bustling street.

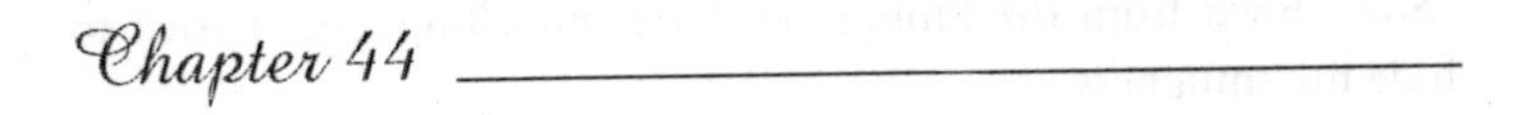

# Chapter 44

Standing in front of the mirror, I debated for over ten minutes whether to tuck my shirt in or not.

"Fuck!" I was exasperated.

I hadn't been on a date in years and wasn't sure how to go about it. First dates were intimidating enough, but with a model, it magnified ten fold. Jaymee must have been wined and dined by the elite of society, how could I measure up? Then again, I was fortunate that she wanted to see me after my embarrassing deed at Madam X, and since it was her last night and I probably wouldn't see her again, I had nothing to lose.

The intercom buzzed, indicating that Arun was on his way up. During a brief conversation the previous night, Arun had politely requested to meet in person. The truth was I had nothing to say to him. His decision of proposing to Rakhi rather than telling her the truth disgusted me. The fact that he would get away with his transgression angered me. Justice wasn't served, and as for *karma*, it was a lounge on the East Side of Manhattan, nothing more.

"Hey, how's it going?" he asked walking in.

Our usual customary hug had been substituted by a formal handshake.

"What are you all dressed up for?"

"I have a date in an hour. Want something to drink?" I inquired.

"A date? With whom? When did this happen?"

"A few days ago. I met someone when I was out with Jim."

"With Jim?" asked Arun puzzled, "Who is she?"

"She's down from the Philippines for a modelling gig," I tried to hide my smugness.

"Wait, you're going on a date with a model?"

"Yep, she's staying at the Marriot Marquis," I informed him as I handed him a Corona.

"Where's yours?" he asked as he grabbed his beer.

"I'm good. So what's going on with you?" I asked, sitting across from him.

Arun stared at the beer as he slowly coiled it around in his hands. Drops of condensation slid down the bottle and moistened his fingers while the froth ascended to the neck of the clear bottle. The temptation grew stronger and I wanted to join him. A voice within me tried to justify just having one beer. Perspiration gathered on my forehead as my palms moistened.

"I'm going to cut to the chase," taking a giant swig, he leaned forward, "Rakhi and I are getting married and it's important for me to have your support. You're one of my best friends and I want you to be a part of every step," he raised his eyes to meet mine.

"Does she know about Maria?"

"No, and she doesn't need to."

"Do you think that's fair to her, Arun?"

"It's not about fair, Om! I made a mistake and I realise that. There is no reason for us to throw away our future because of it."

"Don't you think she also has a right to make that choice?"

"What the fuck is wrong with you?" Arun yelled, slamming the bottle on the coffee table, "You're supposed to be my best friend, why are you being such a fucking dick?"

"You cheated on her, Arun! You betrayed her trust! What gives *you* the right to do that and get away with it?" I responded with equal aggression.

"What gives *you* the right to judge *me*?"

"I'm not judging, I'm just…"

"Of course you are!" he interrupted, "I am aware of what I did and I have to deal with it. I don't expect my friends to keep throwing it in my face and crucifying me for it."

"Arun, I'm…"

"I know Preeti fucked you up, but why are you projecting your anger and bitterness onto me? Ask yourself, if you weren't cheated on, would you still be acting this way? Would you still be trying to punish me? I was there for you when you needed me," he stood up and made his way to the door, "You cried to me over Preeti and I stood by your side. I helped you through it, and now you have the balls to look down at me from your pedestal?"

I noticed Arun's eyes welling up before he turned his back to me and opened the door.

"I came here to speak to my friend and when you're done being a self-righteous bastard, you know where to find me."

He slammed the door, sending vibrations through the flat. I couldn't move fearing that he may have been right.

❖❖❖

## Chapter 45

The keys gently slid across the cherry brown console table. Grabbing a six-pack of beer, I slumped on the couch and replayed the day in my head.

Jaymee turned heads throughout the Marquis lobby as she walked towards me. Her spiked brown hair drew attention to her slender neck that lips would beg to kiss. The fitted white dress, embroidered with a green and pink floral pattern, highlighted her slim and sexy figure. She was stunning. As she leaned in and kissed my cheek, I noticed the entire hotel lobby of people staring at us. I felt a lucky man.

Her demeanour was as flirtatious as it had been at Madam X. She was anticipating a wild night of fun on her last evening in the city, but I wasn't myself. Having to wrestle with Arun's accusations less than an hour prior and the urge for alcohol had overwhelmed me. Instead of laughter, our dinner was peppered with awkward silences. Her flirting eventually came to an end and our conversation deviated to mundane topics like the weather and gas prices.

Breaking off a beer from the pack, I stood up and made my way toward the window. Leaning against the waist high air conditioner, I stared out into the night, pondering. His question echoed within me ever since it left his lips. If Preeti hadn't cheated on me, would I have behaved the way I did towards Arun? Was my desire for him to pay for his act a perverse and desperate attempt to seek justice for what happened to me?

The can cooled my hand and I started to pull the ring, only to let it snap back. It felt good having it in my hand, almost natural. It was during moments like these that I turned to such libations for numbing comfort.

Leaning back on the sofa with the unopened can still in my hand, I continued to ponder. Would Rakhi's knowledge of the truth and her possible decision to leave Arun help me in any way? Even if I did feel relief, it would only be temporary. I'd go through the same bitterness the next time someone I knew was guilty of infidelity.

Arun was right. I wanted him to pay for Preeti. Even though I didn't respect his actions, I could have been a better friend. He had always been there for me, especially through Preeti's betrayal. Although Rakhi was clearly the victim, she was only a friend because of Arun to begin with. How, then, did I owe her any more than I owed Arun? Yes, I wanted to do the right thing. But I also had to maintain my loyalty to my friend. I could only, therefore, urge him to be forthright with her. I didn't owe Rakhi any more than that.

Placing the can on the side table, I picked up the cordless phone and dialed his number. The realisation of my actions brought on a surge of guilt. When Arun turned to me in the middle of the night, in his hour of need, a curtain of bitterness had forced me to ignore his fear and remorse. My blinding rage for Preeti had kept me from seeing the plight of a friend. Instead, I added to his burden. I needed to speak with him, I needed to purge myself.

The call was transferred to his voice mail. It was 4am, he had to be asleep. Replacing the phone to its cradle, I sat back and flicked through the channels, hoping for a distraction. ESPN sportscenter repeated the same results while BET had on a 'Krump' marathon. I arrived at the biography channel, which was broadcasting a documentary on Walt Disney. Preeti would've enjoyed this. Letting out a deep sigh, I chose to keep on watching and confront the memory.

## *Chapter 46*

Staring out the window in amazement, Preeti squeezed my hand and pulled me closer to watch the city fly by underneath.

"This is so exciting!" she stated as she kissed my cheek, "You know, I've never done something like this before, going away on a holiday with my boyfriend."

"Nor have I, but I'm glad I'm sharing this with you."

Turning around to face me, Preeti placed her hand on my cheek and kissed me. Her hand slid higher and she ran her fingers through my hair, pulling me closer.

Months before receiving my tax refund, I had decided to surprise Preeti by taking her on a vacation. It had always been a dream of mine to visit Disney World with my girlfriend, and the extra influx of money provided me with that opportunity.

Loading the bags into the car, and after a quick word with the driver, I gestured Preeti to come closer.

"Why won't you tell me where we're going now?" she pouted.

"It's a surprise!" I smiled and hugged her.

Pressing her head into my chest, she wrapped her arms around my waist.

"I love you!" she whispered.

Exhausted, Preeti rested on my shoulder and dozed off on the drive to the hotel. Even though she had claimed to be a terrible liar who always managed to get caught, Preeti still managed to concoct and maintain a web of lies that made the trip a reality. Unfortunately all that spinning with her parents had taken a stressful toll on her.

"Preeti, wake up. We're almost there." I shrugged my shoulder.

Rubbing her eyes, she looked around for a clue to our location.

"Where are we, baby?" she kept searching.

"Just wait," I had been more excited about the surprise than her, but that was about to change.

Leaning forward she squinted as we drove closer to the entrance. In an instant, her eyes widened and with a snap of her head, she turned.

"No way!"

I smiled as she gripped my arm tightly.

"We're staying at the Disney Resort? Oh my God, oh my God!" she bounced in her seat, "I've always wanted to stay here, how did you know?" In her excitement, she leapt across, wrapping her arms around me and smothered my face with kisses.

The vacation played out delightfully. After enjoying the rides and entertainment at both Disney and Universal studios, we unwound and relaxed at the themed hotel. From sleeping in together and romantic nights in the jacuzzi, to the minor, uneventful mishaps, it was all perfectly scripted.

As we strolled back to our room with our arms wrapped around one another, Preeti expressed her appreciation, "Om, thank you for this, I've had so much fun. I can't begin to tell you how happy I've been this whole trip."

"You're welcome. You know, we should do this more often, go away together and spend some quality time away from work, family, obligations and all that other drama."

"Yes, we should, but next time, I'm paying," she smiled, "When we get back, you need to get in shape." Preeti tapped my stomach.

"I am in shape," I declared.

"Then what is this little tummy here?" she kept tapping away and smiling.

"This is just here so there is more for you to love."

"Om's got a tummy, Om's got a tummy." she teased.

"Okay, I'll prove it to you. You see that palm tree? I'm going to climb it. Watch!"

Kicking off my slippers, I walked briskly on the lush grass towards the trunk.

"Om, don't. I was kidding."

As the base approached, the walk accelerated into a jog. Gathering momentum, I leapt up and hugged the large trunk. Pushing off with my bare foot, I began my climb only to yelp seconds later. Preeti ran to the tree.

"What happened?"

"I'm in pain!" I squealed.

"Then come down. Why are you still holding onto the tree?"

"It'll hurt more when I move," I explained.

"What?"

Gingerly, I released my grip and winced as I stepped down from the tree.

"Babe, what happened?" Preeti asked again.

Extending my arms toward her, I turned my palms upwards.

"Oh my God!" she cried out, "So many splinters!"

"On my feet too," I grimaced.

On our last night, Preeti meticulously removed every splinter from my hands and feet.

"Om, you're so silly," she laughed as she removed the last splinter, "But it's okay, I still love you." She said, kissing my forehead.

## Chapter 47

He paced back and forth as Pushpa watched her husband from their king size bed.

"If you don't talk to me, Gope, how am I going to understand what's bothering you?"

Continuing to walk, he contemplated her words before finally coming to a stop,

"When did it get like this? How did it get like this, Pushpa?"

"What?"

"Our home! I can't communicate with my daughter, and as for us," he paused, "We're like strangers."

Pushpa struggled to hold back her tears. She was angry at him for torturing her with his temper. But as he stood there, appealing to her for help, her love for him softened the resentment.

"I'm losing my family, Pushpa," he turned to her as his eyes welled up.

Climbing off the bed, she walked to Gope and put her arms around him. Pushpa knew her husband wasn't the sort of man to express himself and she could count the number of times he had cried on one hand.

"You're not losing your family, we're right here with you," she brought him to the bed and sat him beside her.

"What am I going to do about her? She's throwing her life away with that boy."

"Gope, she's your daughter, but she's also a grown woman. We did the best we could raising her, and we have to trust her now. We have to believe that we raised her right."

"So what do you want me to do, Pushpa? Give her my blessing to ruin her life?"

"No, I'm not saying that. But listen to your daughter. Try to understand her. Talk *with* her instead of talking *to* her. She is hurting too, Gope, she wants her father by her side."

"She's my child and I just want her to be happy," tears began to stream down his face.

Wiping his tears with her bare hands, Pushpa began to cry.

"Don't cry, my dear, don't cry. It'll be okay. Just talk to her."

"She doesn't even want to talk to me."

"She will and when she does, just listen."

Rakhi's parents sat in silence, lost in thought and confusion. Gope turned to his wife and said, "Pushpa, I don't know what to do."

"Give him a chance," came a voice from the entrance.

Rakhi stood in the doorway weeping. She walked to her father and embraced him.

"Just give him a chance, papa, please, just give him a chance."

## Chapter 48

Arun scanned the room before giving Rakhi a quick hug as he entered the five-bedroom house.

"This should be fun. So, where are they?"

"In the kitchen," Rakhi responded. "Thank you for doing this, it means the world to me."

"Let's just get this over and done with, please."

Rakhi led Arun into the living room and gave him a quick peck before calling out to her parents. Sitting on the leather sofa, he admired the artifacts from the ivory tusks to the African masks placed around the room.

"Hello Arun, welcome to our home," Pushpa greeted him with a hug.

"Thank you, Aunty, thanks for having me over."

"Uncle will be coming in a moment, he's on the phone with the motel. Please sit, *beta*, sit."

"I must say you have a beautiful home, Aunty."

"Oh, you have to tell Rakhi, she really put a lot of work to make this ho,ne beautiful. What do you want to drink, *beta*? Would you like a beer?"

"I'm alright for now, thank you, Aunty. I'll have something later."

"At least have some water. Rakhi, get Arun some water please and tell your father to finish his work and come."

Pushpa and Arun exchanged an awkward silence while Rakhi had made her way to the kitchen. It was hard to be anything more than cordial, especially with all the drama that had transpired.

"How's your family, Arun?"

"They're fine. Thank you, Aunty."

"How's work? Are you very busy with your research?"

"It's pretty much the same."

Arun stood up as Gope entered the room.

"Sit, sit," he instructed as he shook Arun's hand, "Did you have any difficulty finding the house?"

"No Uncle, Rakhi's directions were easy to follow."

"Water? Don't you want to have a beer or something?"

"Maybe during lunch, thank you."

Rakhi broke the uncomfortable silence, "Papa, you remember Mona? Om's cousin, the one from LA? Well, she's getting engaged to this boy from Hong Kong!"

"Really?" Pushpa jumped in, "Who is the boy?"

Rakhi had skillfully provided a segue way for Arun to continue.

"His name is Sunil Ramchandani. He has an import/export company. They were introduced over the Internet through friends and got to know each other by chatting online. In fact, her family flew to Hong Kong a week ago to meet his family," Arun informed.

"I don't believe in this Internet nonsense. You can't *know* someone without spending time with them," Gope declared.

"I'd have to agree with you, Uncle. I've never been a big fan of Internet dating or setups."

Pushpa and Rakhi smiled at each other as they recognised their two men found a common ground.

"Yes, Gope, I agree also. I think it's important to spend time with someone and get to know them, right Rakhi?" Pushpa winked at her daughter.

Acknowledging what his wife was implying, Gope let out a soft growl.

"Arun, let me give you a tour of the house," Rakhi offered.

The two men headed towards the den after an uncomfortable lunch. Rakhi and Pushpa stayed back in the kitchen and cleaned up, giving the men an opportunity to talk privately.

"Do you want another beer?"

"No, I'm quite alright, Uncle."

"Arun, I'm not a man who beats around the bush, so I'm going to get to the point. You want to marry my daughter and she feels we should get to know you. Putting tradition aside, and the fact that you didn't ask me for her hand, what else should we know about you?"

"No disrespect, Uncle, but since we're being frank, you and I both know that you don't approve of this union. This meeting, as you so rightly stated, is at Rakhi's behest. Thus, being aware of your stand on our relationship, I knew what your answer would've been if I asked," Arun disguised his nerves by responding confidently. He had decided not to give an inch, "But let's not forget, we're both here for the same reason, for Rakhi's happiness and that's what is most important, I'm sure you agree?"

Gope nodded.

"I love your daughter and always have. I care about her and want to take care of her. I know I'm not your preferred choice, but you won't find someone who loves her more than I do."

"That's all very romantic, Arun, but let's come down to reality for a moment," Gope did very little to hide his condescending tone, "How much do you earn, thirty, forty thousand dollars before taxes?"

"Something like that, yes."

"How much of that do you save a year, two thousand? *Chalo*, let's even say it's five thousand."

Arun nodded at Rakhi's father in agreement. He had dreaded this part of the conversation, since he wasn't able to formulate an appropriate response. This only gave Gope ammunition to rain down on him.

"That apartment you stay in, I understand you don't own it. It is rented, no? So explain to me son, what life can you offer my daughter?"

Arun was unable to answer as Gope watched him patiently.

"As a father, it's my right to know, don't you think? It's all well and good that you love her, but love isn't going to put food on the table or take care of her needs."

Arun contained his anger. Rakhi's father had demeaned him, but he had to respect him nonetheless.

"You're right, my financial position isn't ideal right now, but now that I've taken this step, my priorities have changed. Besides that, it's only a matter of time before Rakhi is earning and at that point we…"

"I know you're a man of integrity, so obviously you don't expect my daughter to support you!" Gope interrupted.

"Of course not!" Arun snapped back resenting the implication, "But in this day and age, a dual-income family is common."

"So what plans do you have now that your priorities have changed?"

"I… I… I've been in touch with some people about an idea that…" Arun stammered vaguely, "I would rather not talk about it until it's cemented."

Gope watched Arun stew in his anger. He felt sorry for the young man, but as a father it was his duty to ensure his daughter's future.

"Relax Arun, I'm not trying to embarrass you. I just want to understand what future my daughter has in store for her if she marries you."

"Uncle, I'm not going to pretend to have any blueprints in place, but I can assure you that I intend to keep Rakhi happy."

"I'm sure that's what you intend to do, but the '*how*' is what I have to know."

A long, awkward silence followed as Arun sat back, unsure of what to say.

"As you rightly said, I want my daughter to be happy. She can be naïve, but she is smart and a good girl. She claims to love you and tells me you make her happy. My wife and I have been thinking about what we can do about this situation and I have a proposal for you to think about."

"A proposal?" Arun responded puzzled.

"Yes, a proposal. I'd like to offer you an opportunity to work with me, at the motel. I have a managerial position open and it will pay more than your current job."

He sat bewildered with the unexpected turn of events.

"Why don't you think about it and we can discuss it at another time?"

Gope walked out of the den, leaving Arun to contemplate the offer. He sat motionless, uncertain of how to react. In the instant that it was mentioned, he had been angered by the proposal, but it soon dawned upon him that this was an indirect acceptance of him and his relationship with Rakhi.

The Mission Impossible theme derailed Arun's train of thought. Reaching into his jeans, he pulled out his mobile and stared at the name flashing on the screen, Om.

❖❖❖

## *Chapter 49*

Sunil's giant arms enveloped Mona as he wrapped them around her.

"Isn't this view fantastic?" he asked as he looked at the Hong Kong skyline across from the Tsim Sha Tsui Promenade.

"It really is magnificent!"

"I've wanted to bring you here for the longest time. Come, I want to show you *my* favourite part of this pier!" grabbing her by the hand, Sunil briskly led Mona to the black statue.

"This? This is your favourite part of this whole pier? This is what you like the most?" she pointed at the figure.

"Yes! Isn't it so cool?" Sunil asked.

Mona simply shrugged in response.

"Do you even know who this is? It's Bruce Lee!" he almost pleaded.

"Okay, as long as you like it, I like it. Now let's go get some coffee, I'm feeling cold.

Placing her café latte on the table, Sunil noticed Mona was lost in thought as she stared out the window.

"Babe, what's wrong? You've been so distant these few days. I thought you'd be happy after our families met. Did they say anything that upset you?" Sunil reached across the wooden surface for Mona's hand.

"No, no, it's nothing like that. They really liked you and your family, they couldn't be happier."

"Then what is it, Mona? Is it going too fast? Aren't you happy?"

"Of course I'm happy," she smiled, "It's just…"

"Just what?"

"Sunil, we haven't talked about what happened at dinner with your friends. It… it was frightening."

"Frightening? Why?" Sunil pulled back confused.

"I haven't seen that side of you. I never knew you could get that angry."

"Babe, I'm sorry you feel that way, but I'd never hurt you. You know that, right?"

"No, I know, but I was scared, Sunil, and it made me think about what else I don't know about you."

The irritation began to appear on his face.

"Look, that night was Navin's fault. That annoying bastard likes to instigate trouble and push people's buttons. He was trying to humiliate me in front of you," he said raising his voice.

"Sunil, please calm down."

"He was talking about massages and shit, which was uncalled for. He's no saint, you know. He's down in Macau getting special massages and going on about how *happy* his ending was!"

"Sunil, I really don't want to…"

"Guy fucks hookers and bribes his clueless wife with handbags and diamonds and he has the balls to call me out?" he put his coffee mug down with a thud, splashing a few drops on to the table.

"Sunil, please! You're scaring me!"

Finally noticing the concern on Mona's face, Sunil stretched his hand out and apologised.

"Babe, I just get irritated at the thought of him, I'm sorry."

"Sunil, I just don't know. This has all happened so fast, I mean what else do I not know about you?"

"Well, ask me, I'll tell you whatever you want to know," he smiled.

"Here? Right now?"

"Yes, why not, go ahead."

Mona contemplated the offer as she looked around.

"Is this really about Navin, or do you have a temper?"

"Babe, I am temperamental, but its just Navin who gets my blood boiling. He's a snake who always has an agenda."

"Then why do you hang out with him?"

"He's part of the group, I can't exactly avoid him. Anyway, what else do you want to know?"

"What he said, about the massages in Mong Kok, was that true?" she asked in a softer tone.

Sunil looked down and stared into his coffee mug uncertain how to answer her probing question.

"See, this is exactly what Navin was trying to do. Motherfucker!" he muttered angrily under his breath.

"Please Sunil, this isn't about him. I just want to know the truth."

"Yes, it's true, I have been to the massage parlours and received the 'special', but that's common everywhere! Most guys do it," he stated defensively, "And it's not as if I've done it while I was in a relationship, unlike other men."

"Have you ever slept with a prostitute?"

"Of course not!" Sunil snapped, insulted.

"Please don't be angry, I had to ask."

"What about drugs?"

"I'm not going to deny, I have a past, but who doesn't? The point is how I am now. I'm sure you've got some skeletons in your closet, but you don't see me interrogating you!"

Sunil's face was flushed and Mona noticed him gritting his teeth.

"I accept you as you are. I don't ask you how many guys you've fucked, do I?"

Horrified, Mona's eyes widened as she covered her mouth with her hand.

"I'm sorry, I'm sorry. That came out wrong," he squeezed her hand, "I've just been stressed and then I was nervous about meeting your family and Navin's topic just got me all fired up. I'm sorry baby."

"Sunil, I… I've never been spoken to like that."

"Baby, it was a mistake, I'm sorry. Please, forgive me."

Unyielding, Mona began to pull her hand out of his. Sensing the motion, Sunil moved to the seat beside her.

"Mona, I love you…" he whispered to her for the first time.

## Chapter 50

Radha placed the rice on the table beside the *daal* before sitting across from her son.

"Eat before it gets cold," she instructed, "How was your day with Mona?"

"Yeah, it was good, mum," mumbled Sunil.

"Her family is very nice, don't you think so? And her sister, so pretty! If I had another son, I'd marry him off to her too. Did you see the jewellery on the mother, those giant diamond *yakos*?"

"I didn't really notice," Sunil grunted with his mouthful.

"Have you taken her to your office? Good, don't take her. No need to share too much now. The mother was asking me about your dad and the business. What does she need so much information for, I don't know? I felt like I was at a police station!"

"I'm sure she was just making conversation, mum."

"Nonsense, she was prying. You don't know how these aunties are. They show one side and then behave another way. Anyway, you don't need to think about the mother. Focus on Mona and be sure to not let this one go. You're 38 years old and it's high time you settled down."

"She's not going anywhere, she's the right one, mum."

Sunil couldn't help but feel confined in the modest two-bedroom apartment. Surrounded by furniture from the economical Giovani store, and subjected to the fan rather than the air conditioner, he found himself in a constant state of irritation at home.

"After you get married, you will get your green card so you have more options for the future," she blurted before scooping a glob of rice into her mouth with her fingers.

"Mum, I'm going to marry her for her, not a green card."

"I know, but I'm just saying it gives you options. How much longer is she going to be here for?"

"Another week or so."

"Wow! She's staying in that 5-star hotel for so long? They must be so rich to afford that."

"She got a discounted rate from her contacts."

"I don't want you bringing her home, she may complain about the size of our flat and cause problems. These Americans are used to big, fancy places."

"You already told me, mum, I won't bring her," he moaned.

"Anyway, we have to meet her family for lunch tomorrow, so don't be late. At least when they leave we'll be done paying for all these expensive meals!"

Sunil kept his head down and continued eating, letting his mum prattle on.

"Neither of you is young so you better think about children soon. I don't know how much longer I'll be around and I want to see some grandkids."

"For fuck's sake!" Sunil slammed his fork on the table, "Can you please stop pressuring me!" he roared as he stormed in to his bedroom.

❖❖❖

## Chapter 51

**S**tanding in line, I flicked through the sports section of the New York Post. The fact that Café Habana didn't take reservation irritated me at first but once I saw the crowd the tiny restaurant attracted, I figured I'd never get a reservation.

"What's going on, you been waiting long?" Arun joined me in the queue.

"No, about ten minutes. We should get a table in another ten."

"What? You're kidding! Why don't we just go somewhere else? This place looks like a hole anyway, not like your usual joints," Arun declared looking around, "Wait, are we in a fucking trailer?"

"It's worth the wait, trust me. When you try the corn and the garlic chicken, you'll complain that I didn't bring you here sooner."

"I hope so, I'm starving! What you reading?" he nodded towards the paper.

"Reading about how the Knicks still suck!"

Nudging me, Arun gestured with a smile towards a table occupied by four females. I scouted the table, baffled, until I realised what it was, a woman whose jeans had slipped down revealing her butt crack.

"Arun, that's just gross. That's the last thing I want to see when I'm about to eat."

"It's hilarious, Om! I don't know about you, but these days I'm seeing ass cleavage more and more. I think it's a new trend."

"I hope you're talking about women," I sniggered.

"Dude, I'm being serious, ass crack is the new thing."

"So this is what does it for you now? Ass crack?" I asked turning to him.

"I don't know man, I'm confused. It's too new for me to decide, but I guess I could grow to like it."

"Well, I'm fine with regular cleavage, thanks!" I turned my attention back to the news.

"Yeah, but check out her friend with the tattoo."

Raising my head, I noticed a Mauri tribal tattoo sprawled across the small of the blonde's back. I couldn't deny that body ink ignited a primitive inner desire in most men.

"Now that's hot, right?" Arun continued.

"Yeah, definitely!"

"I bet she's a wild one."

"Because she has a tattoo?" I asked.

"Yeah man, I remember reading something about how women who get tats are freaky, especially those who have them on their lower back."

Arun had a point, most men somehow felt there was some sort of correlation between tattoos and promiscuity.

"Man, just once I'd have liked to have had a shot with a blonde with a tat," he sighed.

Arriving at the table, Arun immediately ordered the chicken, corn and two beers. The voice once again justified having one and I pondered the prospect for a moment.

"I'll pass dude, I'm detoxing. I'll have a coke," my resolve shone through.

"So, how's work? What can we hope to read about next?"

"Well, Monica is still a pain, but as long as I keep submitting my articles, she stays off my back. Problem is, I'm struggling to find stuff to write about."

"Why don't you write about the allure of ass cleavage?" Arun sniggered.

"Very funny!"

"But seriously, I read your breakup piece, quite insightful I must say," he nodded with approval.

"What about you, what have you decided?"

"I don't know, Om, I'm confused. I mean at first I thought the father would just bitch me out, which he did, but this offer was a curveball. I'm torn!"

"Torn?"

"Working for your father-in-law is a little emasculating, don't you think?" Arun stared at me wide-eyed.

"I can understand where you're coming from, but you have to look at the bigger picture."

"I'm sure Rakhi will stick with me even if I decline his offer."

"If you take the offer, you have a higher income, a solid job, her parents' blessing and most importantly, Rakhi would be incredibly happy!"

"And I will owe her father and remain under his thumb forever!!"

"Perhaps," I mumbled with a mouthful of corn, "I wouldn't want to be in your shoes."

"Thanks, you're a true friend."

Arun wanted a clear, cut answer, but I knew better than deciding on his behalf, and later, be blamed for it. This was a dilemma he'd have to solve on his own, however, I was thankful for the opportunity to redeem myself and be there for him.

"So has Mona set her wedding date?"

"I don't think so. They just got engaged, so the dates aren't set, but they're thinking about having a church wedding in the Philippines in two months."

"Church wedding? Philippines? Two Months? Why?"

"He's got family there and according to Mona, there's no reason to wait. Also she's always dreamed of a church ceremony."

"It's all a bit too fast, don't you think?" asked Arun as he bit into the garlic chicken, "Oh shit, this is good!"

"Well, I can see it from her point of view. She's waited this long and Sunil is almost forty, so the sooner the better. In fact, she already called the hotel she works for in LA and said she isn't coming back."

"You mean, she's staying there in Hong Kong? What about her stuff?"

"Her family is flying it over."

"Wow, just like that, huh?"

"Yep, just like that!" I nodded.

"She's happy with Hong Kong, she feels she can live there?"

"Mona said it's going to take some adjusting. The Indians there are very different from what she's used to. According to her, people there are very 'status' conscious."

"What does that mean?" he gulped down his beer and ordered another.

"It means they're fake and pretentious. She mentioned many of them are heavily into branded goods and showing off. Mothers act and dress like teenagers, people gossip and pretend, and nothing is what it seems."

"Sounds like you have another article right there."

"It does, doesn't it?" I nodded.

"You should list all the types of aunties and describe them. Like there are those that are religious fanatics and go overboard, and those who pretend to be religious for the public and are anything but when they're out and about in society, you know the kind, right?" He asked.

"Yeah, and then you have those that are constantly looking for gossip and information so that they are always in the know, like a human search engine!"

Arun and I burst out in laughter as we continued to identify the traits of each and every Aunty we could think of.

"Wait, so she's still ready to settle down there?"

"Seemed like she was. I've never heard her so happy! She says Sunil treats her well and is everything she could've ever asked for."

"Wow! Maybe you should look into Internet dating too!" he sniggered, "Wait, that means you can meet that Filipino model friend of yours, Jaymee! You two still in touch?"

"Yup, she's in Hong Kong on a shoot right now." A smug smile crept across my face.

"So how's *that* going?" he asked with a cheeky grin.

"Surprisingly well! I didn't expect to hear from her when she left but she's been calling a lot. I'm telling you, Arun, I can't get enough of her accent. Not to mention she's smart, funny, down to earth..."

"And hot!" he interrupted.

"Yes, and hot!"

"Did you tell her you might be coming?"

"Yeah, she's looking forward to it," I grinned.

"ALRIGHT," he howled, "My boy is finally gonna get some!"

I tried to keep a straight face as I enjoyed the praise. Jaymee, without a doubt, was out of my league and not even in my wildest dreams did I ever think I'd have a shot with a woman like her.

"Honestly Om, you had me worried for a while there. I never thought you'd get over Preeti. But, here you are, bagging super models half way across the world. You *are* over her, aren't you?"

I thought about his question as I sipped the coke only to yearn that it had some form of alcohol in it. Placing the glass down on the table, I let out a deep sigh before answering his question.

"Yes and no. I still find myself reminiscing about her. If I denied our unique connection, I'd only be lying to myself. The truth is I think I'll always love her. The only difference is, I have accepted it and moved on."

"Wow, that's some crazy shit!"

"Amen to that."

"So I guess Mona is the only one flying high right now?"

"I guess so!" I said raising my glass, "Here's to Mona and flying high!"

"Cheers."

❖❖❖

## *Chapter 52*

Monica waved her hand signalling me to enter. Her office reeked of smoke and the stench only intensified the closer I got to her.

Covering the mouthpiece, she turned towards me.

"Don't be a moron and sit down!" she commanded before returning to her call.

Her mahogany table was littered with financial documents which were weighed down by a carton of cigarettes. Monica could put the 'Marlboro Man' to shame.

"Alright Om, I don't have much time. What can I do for you?"

"Err… you asked to see me."

"I did?" she asked confused, "Oh that's right."

Pushing the scraps of paper aside, she found the current issue.

"I wanted to talk to you about this piece you wrote."

Once again she threw the magazine towards me with an assassin's precision as it landed inches from the edge. I was convinced she practised this unique sport whenever she got the opportunity.

"Our readers have responded positively to your new article. So much so, that I decided to take a look at it. Now, you know I've never liked the drivel you write, but I have to give kudos where it's due. This piece was an entertaining one and perfect for the South Asian subscribers. The ironic thing is that readers from other communities, such as the Jewish, wrote in expressing that they can relate."

I couldn't help but smile. It was like receiving rave reviews from Simon Cowell after a performance on American Idol.

"Alright, wipe that bloody grin of your face. As far as I know, this could be a fluke or something from that 'stash' you were referring to."

"Actually, this is an original piece. I got the inspiration from a friend of mine in Hong Kong."

"I'm mystified," she responded sarcastically. "Anyway, your work seems to have improved," watching the smile creep across my face she continued, "From crap to piss! Now get out of my office and have your boyfriend stroke your ego."

As much as I hated having to answer to Monica, she had been able to turn the magazine around. What she lacked in tact and bedside manner, she more than made up for in business savvy. In her few months at the publication, Monica almost doubled subscriptions and increased advertising sales.

Sitting at my desk, I decided to revel in the moment before returning my calls. Picking up the magazine, I made a mental note to thank both Arun and Mona before I flipped through to my column.

**The Aunties**

*We know and interact with them almost on a daily basis. In most cases, we forget their names and are dumbfounded, and forced to pretend when they call and ask, 'Do you know who this is?' They're a constant, and sometimes an unwelcome feature of our lives. They aren't related to us, yet we refer to them as 'Aunty'.*

*Like most things in life, 'Aunties' fall into a variety of groups, owing to their specific traits. For instance, we have the* **L'Oreal Aunties**, *who refuse to go silently into the night and continue to cling on to their youth. These elderly women usually purchase make-up at wholesale and apply it with nothing smaller than a paintbrush.*

*There are some ladies who take their 'fashion' sense up a notch by adding a touch of the urban. These 'trendy' aunties are easy to spot with their giant puffy hair that puts any African to shame. We refer to them as the* **Afro Aunties**. *If you were to ask any of the aunties, 'Why the need to be so excessive?' their answer would be simple, 'Because I'm worth it… beta.'*

*Fashion isn't only restricted to the older group of ladies as our community is also blessed with the* **Status Aunties**. *This breed of women is all about designer wear and making sure you, me, and everyone knows about it. Besides kindly informing us what brand her blouse is, she'll also be sure to let you know its value while stating it was something she simply 'threw on'. If not, she'll mention that her thoughtful husband 'Gyan' bought it for her on their first class trip to the honeymoon where they sat next to Bollywood superstar, Shahrukh Khan. You'll find some tend to have a superiority complex because of the money they have, claim to have, or married into. This Aunty also strives to be part of the upper echelon of society, and is sure to be found at all the 'IT' parties, making sure she's surrounded by all the 'IT' people, dropping names, prices and other 'priceless' information. Often, she's the loudest one.*

*The fashion victim,* **'Yummy Mummy'** *Aunties encompass a large group of ladies from the young mothers to the fifty-plus who insist on dressing like a provocative sixteen-year-old cheerleader. Most men would argue that the younger women who stay in shape, remain well groomed, and highlight their hair to high heaven, do attain somewhat of an allure. However, they fail to understand that with age, that very allure fades and no matter how blonde your hair is, 'sexy' is not coming 'back'.*

*Then there is the group of women which also includes 'Status' and 'Yummy Mummy' Aunties, who get together to form the* **Kitty Party Aunties**, *otherwise known as 'Rummy Mummies'. Besides getting together in their glitziest gear to play some pato and mastering the art of using a chopstick to drag a card, they exchange all the 'juicy' information they've gathered since their last session. You can be sure that all your personal and private information is divulged within this network of rummy experts. At the end of the session, they'll know who wore what twice, whose daughter is seeing whom, whose son is snorting cocaine, whose husband is cheating, and which aunty uses tabs from old designer clothes on her new Marks & Spencer's wardrobe. Scandalous!*

*The information exchanged at the kitty parties is usually gathered by a particular breed known as the* **Owl Aunties**. *We've all come across this particular type, since they are the ones who constantly ask us, 'When are you getting married Putu? Why aren't you married yet beta? So handsome/pretty, why no boyfriend/girlfriend?' After they're done with you, you can expect your parents to suffer the same barrage of questions. They also tend to make a mental note of who's wearing what clothing and jewellery, and when intrigued enough, they not only inspect closely with their eyes and hands but throw etiquette to the wind and openly inquire of its quality and price. No wonder men head to the bar and stay there at social events! Antics of the 'Owl Aunties' are not only restricted to social events. When they grace your abode, they'll be sure to inspect everything from the paint and upholstery to your kitchen and the nationality of your maid. Beware, since these aunties move with great stealth and precision when needed. For example, while standing face to face, they'll reach behind their back and feel the texture of your tablecloth, simultaneously nodding away, leaving you clueless. Perhaps, they feel simply asking is impolite.*

*Sometimes, the curiosity of the 'Owl Aunties' gets the better of them. That's when they evolve into the* **Nosey Aunties**. *The 'Nosey' like to get into everyone's business, and often ask questions such as, 'Why did the divorce* *take place? Why are they closing down their business and moving? Why did the venue of the wedding change? Why did your sister get botox?' And so forth. Often enough, these very aunties put forth their own negative reasoning, which in turn become rumours that spread throughout our society. How can we not be proud of such problem-solving and upstanding citizens of our community?*

*The headliner at the Kitty Parties is none other than the* **Google Aunties***, otherwise known as the INN (Indian News Network). This human search engine is not only able to sniff the tiniest details, but does it at a speed that makes the Internet look like a slug. If ever you want to know about a particular boy/girl's family, she'd be the best source of information (although some of it might be skewed).*

*In contrast, there is a group who haven't been seduced by the glitz and glamour of the social scene and have taken a more spiritual and/or religious path. They're known as the* **Hari-Om Aunties***. At times mistaken as borderline fanatics, these aunties attend almost every satsang, fast at every opportunity, and have so many havans that the mahraj gives them a discount! The annoying thing about the Hari-Oms is that they'll be sure to let you know all the days in the year when you have to be vegetarian. Either way, you know they are on the guest list to heaven, so better to be on their good side.*

*It is important not to confuse the Hari-Oms with the pseudo Hari-Oms, otherwise known as the* **Contradictory Aunties***. These are the ladies that do almost everything that the Hari-Om's do, but still carry the traits of the other aunties. After singing their bhajans in 'bling', you'll find them donning their low-cut Versace top with a martini in one hand, bitching about how their neighbour is broke and her husband's niece is cheating. Bol Jhulelal Aunty, Bol Jhulelal!*

*Each Yin must have its Yang, and hence, an equilibrium. There is a selective group of ladies who no matter how wealthy, remain humble. No matter how small their home, their giant heart welcomes all. No matter how sick and twisted her neighbour may be, she still remains* *fair and just. Even though they attend social events and are dressed classy or chic, they don't get caught up in society and its ever changing demands. These women are more enlightened as human beings and are envied only because of the respect they attain. One can only admire the **Balanced Aunties**.*

*Regardless of their traits, Aunties, in whatever shape or form provide colour in our lives, sometimes, literally. Some are role models to be aspired to, while others consider themselves models. Some incessantly express faith, while others ooze of hate. There are those who are victims of fashion, status and society, and then there are those victimised by society and its fickle principles. Whatever they may be, I thank them for giving me enough to write about in this article.*

*Finally, the best kind of Aunty is the one with cute single daughters. You're my favourite kind. Care to invite me over for some Chai?*
*The Mind of Om*

## Chapter 53

Returning to the flat after distributing the remaining alcohol I owned between the doormen, I was alone with my craving. Needing a distraction, I collapsed on the futon and dialed the Hong Kong number. Mona picked up her mobile only to ask me to hold on.

"Sorry Om, it was Sunil. He's going to be here with his mother soon."

"Do you want me to let you go?" I asked.

"No, we can chat for a little bit. Have you booked your seat for Boracay?"

"Yep, I'm coming via Hong Kong."

"What about your room?"

"It's all booked, Mona. I'll be there, chill!"

"Okay fine. It's just been really stressful putting it all together."

"You sure that's all it is? You've been out of sorts of late, Mona."

"'Course', it's just that there is a ton of things we need to accomplish in a month! Oh, I've been meaning to ask you. Did you ask Jaymee to come? Would you like me to call her and invite her personally?"

"No!" I squealed, "Mona, I hardly know the girl!"

"I thought you two have been in touch."

"Yes, but I've only spent a few hours with her in person. I can't have her attend your wedding, Mona, it would just be odd."

"So? I got to know Sunil over the phone and Internet and look where we are," she stated defensively.

"Yes Mona, but I'm not looking to marry Jaymee. It's more like an…" I paused momentarily as I searched for the appropriate expression, "*Unexpected adventure*, that's all. Besides, imagine all those uncles and aunties gossiping about us if I brought her."

"I don't think you need to worry about that, they'll be talking about you after your last article!" she laughed, "Anyway, if you do change your mind, she's welcome."

"Well, I'm stopping in Manila for a few days before Borocay, so we'll just go with the flow."

"Sounds like a good idea. I saw her pictures on the web and she's beautiful, Om, just beautiful!"

"I know! Can you believe someone *that* hot is interested in me?"

"Yes, I can. You know if I was younger or if you were older, I'd have totally gone for you."

"Really?" I was stunned by Mona's confession.

"Of course, Om, you're an amazing guy, what woman wouldn't want you?"

"Preeti didn't."

"Om, I'm sorry, I didn't mean to…" the concern in her voice was evident.

"Relax, it's okay," I interrupted, "I'm not bothered. I'm in a good place, Mona, and it's perfectly fine."

"Okay good, she was a stupid cow anyway."

"No she wasn't," I laughed, "But yes, she did lose out." I smiled.

"Om, I'm so proud of you! Look at all this improvement," her voice cracked with a hint of lamentation.

"Mona, what's wrong. I can hear it in your voice. Are you sure about this wedding?"

"It's nothing."

"Tell me, what is it?" I insisted.

"I don't know, maybe its cold feet."

"Maybe?"

"I don't know. I just had this very uncomfortable conversation with Sunil and his mother the other day. I can't be sure but I think they were hinting at a dowry."

"Wow!" was all I could pathetically offer.

"Well, I can't be sure. They weren't direct about it but they were talking about Rolex watches for their relatives. You know what, it's probably my imagination. They're good people and they treat me well."

"I don't know what it is, but I sense you're apprehensive. Just be sure. Remember, it's better to part ways now rather than later."

The hotel phone rang unexpectedly.

"Hello? Hi Sunil, are you here already? No, no, I was talking to Om on my mobile. Yes okay, I'll be down. No. Sorry. I'm sorry. Yes I'm coming. No, I understand. I'm sorry. Yes, I'll be right down."

Returning to her mobile, she said, "Om, I've got to go, I'm sorry," she said frazzled.

"Mona, is everything okay?"

"Yes, I'm sorry I've got to go," she hung up.

❖❖❖

# Chapter 54

Stabbing his knife into the flesh, Sunil ripped the meat apart violently before biting down on the steak.

"Well, it's unexpected, but it's an opportunity I can't let pass by, Mona."

"But I don't understand how this affects our wedding?" Mona stressed.

"Babe, I just don't have enough money available right now. Most of it is tied up in this deal."

"So what do we do? We've sent the invitations out, paid the hotel deposit, I've ordered my outfits and our guests have booked their tickets and rooms…"

"Yes, I know everything," he interrupted, "I've been there every step of the way." Sunil munched away, indifferent to Mona's concern.

"So, what do we do about it all?"

"I guess, we just postpone."

"Postpone? Till when? Jesus, are you going to take this seriously or just stuff your face like this happens to you every day?"

"What the *fuck* do you want me to do?" Sunil hissed snapping forward.

Startled, Mona jumped back. Her eyes widened, and within seconds, they began to well up with fear.

"What is it that you want me to do? Turn down this deal so we can have enough money to go ahead with the wedding and be broke afterwards?"

"What do you mean 'be broke afterwards'?" Sunil's words stunned her, "Are you telling me this is all the money you have? Don't you have savings for the future, for our future? Didn't you consider the financial aspect before proposing to me?"

Realising the magnitude of what he had let slip, Sunil looked down at his plate and continued shredding his steak.

"Sunil, what did you mean?"

"Of course, I'm not broke. I have money tied up in investments and goods that are being delivered. Once those bills are paid, I'll be liquid again. I had money set aside for the wedding, but I had to use it for this lucrative business opportunity. Mona, this *is* for our future."

Pushing her plate away, Mona wiped away her tears.

"Fine, we'll do the needful and postpone," she muttered through her hands that covered her face.

Sunil finished his meal while his fiancée sobbed quietly into her napkin. Wiping his oily mouth, he broke the silence.

"There is another option so that everything can go as planned."

"What?" she sniffed.

Leaning in, Sunil pulled her hand from her face and, as he held it in his, stroking it gently with his fingers he said, "Your family could pay for the wedding and we could reimburse them."

❖❖❖

## Chapter 55

Placing the sinfully indulgent grande caramel frappuccino on the table, I stared at the blinking cursor on the screen. With a looming deadline that was set to expire in less than 24 hours, I had an inclining of what Jack Bauer must feel like when saving the world repeatedly. With my backup stash of articles exhausted, I arrived at my local Starbucks in desperate search for inspiration. My plan had borne little success and instead I clicked on the random pictures on Facebook. I never understood why women insisted on uploading glamour shots when all they did was set the stage for disappointment. If their objective was to garner attention and land a potential partner, it was a poor plan, for they'd never match up to that glamour shot in reality.

Letting out a deep sigh, I returned to the blank page and contemplated on how I could write two pages on 'Butt Cleavage'.

"Dude, she dated Kevin!" a deep voice barked beside me, "How could you?"

"How? Dude, she's hot!" was the response of his colleague. "How could I not?"

"I don't care how hot she is, if she hooked up with a punk like that, I wouldn't touch her with a barge pole."

Smiling at my newfound inspiration I started to type.

"You're only pissed 'cause you didn't get to hit that."

"Whatever, dude!" The bark had now calmed to a voice of disdain.

"Don't deny it! You're pissed 'cause she dick-teased you."

"Dude, bitches like that just want attention." He snapped forward and returned to the barking tone. "They ain't gonna give it up, all they wanna know is if they could have you and when they do, dude, it's over! They go around telling all their *bitch* friends how the guy was all into her and she wasn't interested. She forgets to mention how she flirted, teased and led the brother on."

"I don't know about you, but this brother *tapped that ass*!" the colleague laughed as he covered his face. "I'm sorry man, but it's alright, plenty of other honey out there, man."

It was at moments like these I wish I had a digital recorder.

"Tell you what, I'll set you up with a sure thing?" the colleague boldly announced, hoping to appease his distraught friend.

"Really, who?" curiosity had transformed the bark into a purr.

"Anne, that chick you brought to the club last week. Dude, she'd be all over you!"

Staring at his colleague, the friend began to speak through gritted teeth.

"You are offering to hook me up and you suggest *my* friend, to me? You are suggesting the person *I* introduced *you* to, to me? Are you serious?"

"Yeah, so?" the colleague shrugged.

"Do you realise how fucking retarded that is? She's my friend. I already know her. Do you think because you suggest it that somehow an invisible veil will be lifted from my eyes and I'll magically go for her? Who the fuck do you think you are, Harry Potter? David Copperfield? Or maybe you think you're David mother-fucking Blaine?"

I let out an uncontrollable chuckle as I continued to type as briskly as I could. Both turned and looked in my direction probably wondering if I was eavesdropping, but I couldn't stop, this was gold!

"Dude, take it easy," the colleague ignored me and continued, "You shouldn't let her aggravate you like this. So what if she teased you, it was probably for the best. You know they say everything happens for a reason and things happen for the best."

"They? Who the *fuck* is they? Who is this 'they' you're quoting?" the bark had now become more vicious.

"Dude, you've lost it," the colleague stood up, "Let's bounce."

With that, my muses had departed as suddenly as they had arrived and even though I was sad to see them leave, I was certain they had given me enough content for my next article.

My fingers rapidly danced on the keyboards as I licked my lips in excitement. The sweet rhythm of the irregular clicking had me hypnotised as my journalistic magic began to flow from within me once again. The article was finished in what seemed like an instant and all that remained was an appropriate title. Raising my head I scanned the crowd in the coffee shop only to observe another woman whose shorts had fallen low, revealing her butt cleavage. Smiling I whispered, "Observations."

As I typed the title, a subtle vibration coursed through the wooden table. The caller ID read 'Rakhi'.

"Hello?"

"Hey, Om, are you busy?"

"Actually I just finished work. What's up?"

“Can we meet?” she asked in an almost frenzied tone.

“Sure, I’m headed to the court right now. Do you want to meet me there?”

“Perfect, I’ll see you there in an hour, bye,” she hung up abruptly.

Momentarily baffled by the peculiar call, I turned my attention to my Pièce de résistance and smiled smugly. Clicking on the save icon, I started to read the article.

## Observations

*Throughout life there are multiple observations that we make on a daily basis, and these numerous thoughts that cross our minds are stored way at the back. After much pondering, I felt it was time to put pen to paper and bring some of these long lost thoughts to the forefront.*

### *Glam Shots*

*Facebook, Friendster, My Space and every other social website is littered with vanity shots on crack. Some have them up for fun, while others utilise them as a tool to garner attention and interest from the opposite sex (or maybe the same sex). The issue is that ‘Glam Shots’ are simply no more than false advertising. The individual never looks as good as the picture, and he/she is only creating high expectations in turn, setting the audience (and themselves) up for disappointment. So boys and girls, next time you drool over a glam pic of a supposed hottie on Facebook, just keep in mind, ‘Glam’s a scam!’ and demand a Polaroid!*

### *Reflections and Ratings*

*As the saying goes ‘the friends you keep reflect who you are,’ and as one matures, we learn that there is a certain level of merit to that statement. Mingling with the likes of the serial party crasher or the pseudo spiritual who, in reality, is a slave to society, can (and does) alter the public perception of you. The thinking is, ‘if his/her circle of friends is damaged, then by association, he/she must be too'! Of course, this isn't always the case; every rule has its exception. But more often than not, the theory holds. Hence, we are victims of perception by association - this is no truer than when it comes to the dating scene. The fact is that we are often rated by our past transgressions or conquests which can work both for or against us. To illustrate this notion, I'll share a dialogue that occurs ever so often:*

*A: Dude, what about Amy, she's cute?*

*B: She is, but she dated Jay and he's an absolute wan*er.*

*Such ideology is a two-way street, which is to say when an individual is involved with someone out of their league, it only raises their stock value in the eyes of the public. Many will argue that such thinking is superficial. Unfortunately, such is the society we live in.*

### *Another Notch*

*We're all aware of individuals who womanise and 'manise' and etch another notch on their bedpost with every conquest. However, there is another method of 'notch accumulation'. There are people who lead others on and keep stringing them along for the constant slew of attention they receive. They never take it further; knowing that they could have them at the drop of a dime is just as good as actually having them. In turn, they continue to feel better about themselves while once again increasing their appeal. If actress Karisma Kapoor was the girl next door as opposed to the Bollywood diva she is, she would hardly be as coveted as she is. That 'appeal' and the desire to conquer is as much of an aphrodisiac as anything else on the market.*

### *Haters*

*We've all grown up with them and know exactly who they are. These malcontents, who stew with envy stemming from some void in their life, find constant pleasure in insulting and putting down others.*

*Like politicians, they smile in front of you and wish you well in your endeavours, while hoping and praying for your failure within. Enveloped by their negative aura, they infiltrate our life in sheep's clothing and turn it toxic. That cancerous insecurity grows until they project their bitterness at every conceivable opportunity and mock at you behind your back. Instead of encouraging you and rising to your achievements, they belittle you and find more pleasure in watching you fall to their level. Unenlightened, these unsatisfied dark souls traverse the Earth and lead a life by feeding on the misery of those they feel more fortunate, completely unaware that what they hate most is themselves.*

## *Crack*

*Often we've been dining at a public restraint, enjoying the wine and company, only to be blindsided by the woman in our peripheral vision. With her back to me, she seats herself at the table in front of me, and POW… 'Ass-Crack'. Arguably, this new means of seduction has gained some support with woman-kind as more and more are starting to reveal their 'Butt-Cleavage', perhaps expecting it to have the same allure as the original cleavage. However, the reaction by the male species has been anything but positive. Ladies, your ass-crack doesn't have the magnetism to draw us to you, but it does give us a reason to point and laugh.*

## *The Stupid Cupid*

*How many times have we been with a friend or acquaintance and they decide to take up the challenge and state, that they'll find us someone, only to start listing our friends to us? It's as if they believe when they make their suggestion, the magic in their voice will lift the proverbial veil, revealing the sparkling reality and we think, EUREKA! Just to set the record straight, for those wannabe cupids, there is no veil, nor is there magic in your voice. Suggesting people to us that are our friends is redundant and borderline retarded! Almost all reasonable human beings have considered those they met at one point or another; it's only natural for it to cross our minds. You're just going into our fridge and trying to sell our own meat to us.*

## *Body Ink*

*They are eye catching and sexy. When a woman with a visible tattoo crosses the path of a heterosexual man, more often than not it will grab his attention. The ink adds a mystery, a certain je ne sais quoi. While the tattoo does conjure up some fantasies, the flip side is that many of those very men (and even some women) correlate such permanent body art with promiscuity, which is what feeds that 'naughty girl' fantasy. Can this be considered narrow minded and ignorant? Yes. But that certainly doesn't change our thinking pattern.*

## *They?*

*Who is this 'They' that we constantly refer to in everyday life?*

*'They say it's the thought that counts.'*

*'They say the journey is the destination.'*

*'They say it's the darkest before the dawn.'*

*Armed with an abundance of phrases, we always quote them to others and attempt to find solace in their advice, but who are 'they'? Is it an individual or a collective? How did he/she/they come by such knowledge, wisdom and insight? Do they have any qualifications or do they just jabber on while high on ganja and we, like sheep, follow it as gospel? Are we ever to know? Or can we just be expected to listen, nod and adhere with a Borg-like mentality? Is the truth really out there?*

*Certainly there are numerous other universal observations that can be discussed; however, there are only so many allotted pages. Till next time, keep observing and 'Just say No to Ass-Crack!'*

*The Mind of Om*

# Chapter 56

Slipping through the gym doors, Rakhi sat on the bleachers and waited for the game to finish. With Arun working late, she had grabbed the opportunity to talk to me.

"Hey, you're early."

"Yeah, I figured I'd come and wait till you were done," Rakhi smiled, "I was hoping you and I could go for a coffee afterwards."

"A coffee?"

"Unless you're busy, it's no big deal," she retracted.

"Oh no, it's okay. Let me just grab a quick shower, okay?"

"Sure."

Returning from the shower, I watched Rakhi flip aimlessly through her medical journal before jamming it into her bag.

"Hey Rakhi, you ready?"

Seeing her face buried in her hands. I ran up the bleachers and put my arm around her.

"Rakhi, what's wrong?"

"It's Arun," she buried her head in my chest and wept, "He's not the same."

"Take a deep breath, it's okay, just breathe."

A few minutes and a cup of water later, Rakhi began to disclose all that had been weighing her down for the past few weeks.

"I don't know what it is. After our fight, he's just been so withdrawn. It feels like something's broken."

"Rakhi, I'm sure it's nothing. He's probably preoccupied with your dad's offer and is deciding if he should take it or not."

"No, Om, it's not that! He was distant before that. When we're together, it's not the same anymore. He isn't as affectionate anymore and rejects my advances. He seems constantly inattentive and distant. There have been so many times when I've been talking to him and he's staring out the window in another world, paying no attention to what I'm saying. The worst thing is that he's become so much more irritable! The smallest thing sets him off."

"Have you talked to him about this?"

"No," she whispered.

"Well, don't you think you should?"

"Om," lifting her head, she looked at me with her tear-stained face, "You're his best friend, he tells you everything. Is there something you think I need to know about Arun?"

I could feel my face getting flushed, as parts of me desperately wanted Rakhi to know the truth. I wanted to reveal the reality of her situation and save her, but it wasn't my place.

"Rakhi, you should talk to him about this. If there is something, you should hear it from him."

"But I'm asking you, Om."

"Rakhi, Arun loves you dearly and the fact that he proposed to you and is even considering taking your dad up on his offer illustrates that he would do anything to be with you."

"I guess, you're right," she exhaled.

"I can tell you this: he would go through great extremes not to lose you."

"I know, but you would tell me if there was something I needed to know, right? You know, you're like a brother to me."

Her words began to tear through me. I hated being in this situation and going against my instinct, but I had to maintain my loyalty.

"Of course," I lied hugging her.

## Chapter 57

Arun chuckled from across the table as I skimmed through the Chevy's menu. Leaning in, he asked, "Why are you looking at the menu? We come here all the time and you always order the same bloody thing!"

"Well, you never know. Maybe they've added something new," I shrugged.

"Just shut the fuck up and order your chicken salad," he laughed.

"So, are we going to see you managing a Jersey motel anytime soon?"

"Honestly, I don't think so. I know Rakhi would like me to and if I did, it'll make everyone happy," he sunk in his seat. It was apparent the decision was taking a toll on him. With bags under his eyes and sudden weight loss, he looked truly haggard.

"Everyone?" I interjected.

"Everyone, but me. If I did accept the old man's offer, I don't think I could respect myself as a man. Rakhi would still be with me if I don't. After some time, the parents would come around and accept us. I mean she is their only daughter, after all."

"I wish I could help you, Arun, but you're the only one who can figure out what's best for you and your future with Rakhi."

"Yeah, no worries, I'll figure it out."

"How much longer is Rakhi going to be?" I asked as I looked at my watch.

"She should be here soon. You know how she is when it comes to Chevy's. She's probably jogging down 42nd street as we speak!" he laughed.

"Arun, I wanted to talk to you about something before she gets here."

"Let me guess, your friend Jaymee is into threesomes and you want me to join you. Normally, I'd say no because it involves another male, but seeing what a fine piece of ass she is, count me in!" he smiled taking a swig of his beer.

"Yeah, you wish! No, but seriously, I wanted to talk to you about Rakhi."

"About Rakhi? What about her?" Arun asked taking a more serious tone.

"She turned up at the gym to have a chat with me."

"At the gym? You mean the night when I was working?"

"Yes, she wanted to talk to me about you."

"About me?" Anxious, Arun knocked over his beer but managed to grab the bottle before it spilled. "What about me? What did you tell her?"

"Arun, bro, calm down. I didn't say anything. She was concerned about you."

"Concerned, how?" he growled.

"Dude, just relax. She said that you haven't been the same since the fight. Since," I paused, "Since the night you came to my flat."

Looking down, Arun rubbed his hand over his face.

"Did you tell her anything?"

"No, of course not."

"Good, keep it that way," he snapped.

"Arun, Rakhi knows something's off. She said you haven't been the same since and asked me what was wrong. She asked if I knew of anything that she needed to know."

"Well, as long as you didn't say anything, Om, it'll be alright."

"I haven't, but I'm giving you advice as a friend. The truth always comes out and eventually, she will find out Arun. You two are getting married and to keep this buried isn't a good idea. I can see the guilt tearing you apart from within and honestly, as your best friend, your older brother, I suggest you come clean now."

"You keep your *fucking* mouth shut, alright?" he roared through his teeth, "You're not God. It's not your place to get involved, got it?"

"Arun…"

"YOU GOT IT?" his finger hovered inches away from my face, "I'm not Preeti and she *will not* find out!"

Swiftly turning his head towards the entrance, Arun retracted his hand as he saw Rakhi walk in. Turning back to me he whispered, "Not a word!"

Standing up he spread his arms wide, "Baby! You took so long! I was missing you! Come sit and let's get you your favourite."

With that Arun placed a kiss on Rakhi's cheek.

# Chapter 58

Unable to sleep, Arun left Manhattan early taking the Path train into New Jersey. Rubbing his clammy palms together, he waited anxiously in the bare foyer for Gope. Noticing Arun's nervous behaviour, the night manager shuffled closer to the alarm. Oblivious of the manager, Arun continued glancing at his watch as his knee bounced unconsciously.

Arun, surrounded by pale yellow walls and a six-foot counter where guests checked in, drowned out the Bollywood music blaring from the 17-inch television that hung from the wall.

"He will be here shortly, sir. Perhaps you'd prefer to get a coffee from the diner across the road while you wait?" the manager proposed in a thick Indian accent.

Normally Arun would've mocked him, instead he simply responded, "No, it's alright. I'll wait here."

Arun had tossed and turned the previous night as Om's prophecy haunted him. What if he was right, what if the truth came out? She was already suspicious and went digging for the truth behind his back. Rakhi could never find out, he couldn't afford to lose her.

"Arun? *Beta*, what are you doing here at this time?" the bell chimed as Gope strolled in through the door.

The manger relieved, let out a sigh.

"Morning, Uncle."

"Is everything okay?" Gope noted Arun's jittery behaviour immediately.

"Yes, yes, I just wanted to have a word with you."

"Sure, just give me a moment with my staff," he said before heading back into the office with his manager.

A wave of nausea passed through him as he sat down. Reaching into his backpack, Arun pulled out a bottle of water. Beads of sweat dripped down his brow before his head started to spin. Arun began to breathe deeply, trying to combat the sickening sensation. Closing his eyes, he tried to visualise his future with Rakhi. In the past, dreaming of their life together was second nature, but since his lapse in judgement, everything seemed to be a struggle. He now passed through a labyrinth of thorns before arriving at that very image of their blissful future.

"Sir will see you now in his office," the manager stated.

Wiping his face on his sleeve, Arun took a deep breath to settle his stomach.

"Come Arun, have a seat. Do you want some coffee or tea? We have some *masala* tea if you like."

"No thanks, Uncle."

"Have you had breakfast? How about something to eat? My staff can run across to the diner and get you some pancakes or a sandwich if you like?" Gope offered with concern.

"No, that's quite alright, thanks."

"Is everything okay, you look worn out, *beta*."

Arun was surprised by Gope's hospitality. It was hard to be confrontational when your opponent was warm and welcoming.

"Y… Yes it is," stammered Arun.

"What did you want to talk to me about?"

The nausea returned. A proud man, Arun tried to portray strength but he knew the mental and emotional fatigue that plagued him was now physically visible.

"Uncle, I…" Arun lifted his hand over his face and hid his eyes that began to well up, "I…."

Perceiving Arun's vulnerability, Gope walked behind him and shut the door. Grabbing the opportunity, the young man quickly wiped away the tears with his sleeve. Standing behind him, Gope patted Arun on the shoulder,

"Take your time, *beta*."

As hard as he tried to hide his angst, Arun's bloodshot eyes revealed the truth.

"Uncle, I accept your offer," his eyes welled up again, "But on one condition."

Gope felt a mix of contradictory sentiments. He was pleased the arrangement played out in his favour. He could now keep a close and controlling eye on his daughter's future. Satisfied to have subjugated the younger and prouder man, he couldn't help but regret as he watched him break in front of his eyes.

"What's the condition?" Gope asked sternly, contesting the temptation to lower his guard and dominance.

"That Rakhi and I get married next month."

Gope's eyes widened with surprise. Uncertain of the reason and fearing the worst, Gope himself began to perspire.

"Why the rush? Is my daughter pregnant?"

"Of course not," Arun managed a chuckle at the absurdity, "The truth is that I want to start building for a better future for Rakhi and myself, and I rather start now."

"Well, you can start working here now and get married later if that's your reasoning," Gope countered.

"Uncle, I'm not marrying your daughter so I can work for you. I'm working for you so I *can* marry your daughter!" he voiced boldly, "I want to start my life with her as my wife and if being able to do that means joining you, I accept. But, I have no desire to wait."

Gope observed his future son-in-law and he knew he should've been content, but for some reason, he couldn't help but feel a nagging reservation.

## *Chapter 59*

**P**lugging the phone into charge, I walked out of the bedroom to grab my dinner from the kitchen when it started to ring.

"Hello?"

"Hey, it's Mona."

"HEY YOU!!!!" I hollered with excitement. "How are you?"

"I'm good, are you busy?"

"No, of course not. I just got off the phone with Jaymee. She's so thrilled about me coming."

"I'm glad to hear that."

"I'm telling you, Mona, I get excited every time I speak to her!"

"That's wonderful, Om, I'm happy for you."

"And oh my God, she is kinky! She could really teach me a thing or two. If I'm being honest, I'm sort of intimidated," I laughed, "Listen, I may take you up on your offer and bring her to the wedding, but nothing's confirmed yet. I'm still going to see how things go in Manila."

"Om…" she whispered.

"But we're going to have to get her another room if she comes, one next to me if you know what I mean," I chortled.

"Om!" Mona roared.

"What?" I yelled back.

"It's off."

"What?"

"It's off, Om, the wedding, it's off."

"WHAT! What do you mean the wedding is off?"

"We called it off."

"Why? What happened? Are you okay?"

"Yes, yes, I'm fine. Nothing happened, we just found out that both of us are thalassemic minor."

"You're thala-what?"

"Thalassemic minor! It's a blood disorder where the red blood cells have a shortened life span."

"Red blood cell life span? Sorry Mona, but I'm lost."

"Basically if two people are thalassemic minor, the chances of them having a healthy pregnancy are slim. It just means that Sunil and I wouldn't be able to have a child, and if we did, they'd need to have blood transfusions for life."

"Wow! I don't know what to say!"

"It's okay, Om, it's no one's fault. Better we found out now than later. You know I've always wanted kids and I'd want to have them soon after marriage. If I discovered this after, I'd be devastated. No, it happened for the best."

"Yeah, you're right. I'm so sorry, Mona."

"Thanks, Om."

"How is Sunil taking it?"

"Well he's dealing with it the best he can."

Sitting down on the futon as the shock refused to dissipate, I asked Mona the glaring question,

"What are you going to do now?"

"I'm moving back to LA in a few weeks. I'll drop off my stuff, get settled and then I'll be there for Arun's wedding."

"You're going to come to New York?"

"Of course, I am. I wouldn't miss it for the world! I was planning to come after my wedding anyway."

"What about the hotel and the guests and everything?"

"It's all been taken care of. We're informing everyone and refunding payments wherever we can. The only thing we can't do anything about is the tickets."

"Shit, I don't think mine's refundable!"

"Well, I'm sure you can change the date. They may charge you a penalty, which I'll pay for."

"Please, don't be silly, Mona!"

"Anyway, Om, I have to make a bunch of calls, so I better go," Mona's voice was thick with sadness.

"I'm really sorry and you know I'm there for you if you ever need to talk."

"Yes, I know, thanks," she sniffed.

"Chin up, it's like you always said, each person we go through brings us closer to the right person."

"Right…" she murmured.

"It wasn't meant to be, Mona, and like you said, better now than later."

As much as I tried to comfort her, my words fell on deaf ears.

"Thanks, I better go. Bye," she said as her voice cracked.

Mona hung up before I could say anything. I lay on the bed and tried to process the information. Mona had been waiting for this moment for most of her adult life and when it finally came, she had immersed herself completely into the relationship. She had to be devastated.

Opening the fridge door, my eyes scanned for the beer as a force of habit. My palette craved a sip of the amber nectar, but I had remained unwavering and witnessed the cravings subside. But at times like these, the beast surfaced violently. Cracking open a bottle of water I took a sip and hoped in vain it would quench my *real* thirst.

❖❖❖

# Chapter 60

Paul wiped each of the pint glasses before placing them on the shelf under the wooden bar slab.

"Paul, you fat bastard, how are you?" I yelled walking into the empty pub.

The aroma of the ale that flowed through the pub freely was like an aphrodisiac for me. I wanted to be enveloped by the scent and soak it in through my pores.

"Om, you dirty Paki! What are you doing here? Don't you have a job?" he asked in a strong Scottish accent.

"What can I say? I missed your beautiful mug!"

"Aye," he laughed, "Caffrey's, is it?" He began pouring the pint before I even answered.

"No, I'll have a Redbull. I need to wake up!"

"I didn't know a pussy had walked in through the doors," Paul continued to pour the Irish ale.

"I'm driving, mate," I jingled my keys, "Where's the crowd?"

"It's not even lunch, you silly drunk! It'll fill up in an hour."

Paul poured a pint with perfection. Tilting the glass, he brought it upright with smooth precision. It was poetry in motion.

"You look like shit, mate."

"Yeah, I know, I was at a friend's bachelor's last night and it just ended a few hours ago and I'm bloody knackered!"

"Here, I've poured it now," he placed the pint in front of me, "It's on the house."

Paul made his way into the back to set up for the lunch rush leaving me alone with the war that ensued between temptation and my resolve. Reaching forward, I wrapped my naked fingers around the curvaceous cold glass and licked my lips unconsciously. A sip couldn't hurt. I hadn't had a drink in over a month and had controlled the beast within. Maybe I could just wet my lips with the froth.

"You really know how to pick a place. Where are all the people?" Jim slipped into Tir Na Nog unnoticed, "If you wanted to have a quiet, romantic drink with me Om, you could've picked a more romantic venue!" he smiled as he slapped me on my back. "Are you drinking?" Jim stopped suddenly.

Turning to him, I handed the glass to him.

"It's for you," I smiled.

"I can't fucking believe you're drinking, Om, and that too at this hour," he roared unconvinced.

"Jim, I'm not an alcoholic and besides, I knew you'd be hung-over and would need it. *Hair of the dog* and all that."

"What? What do you want me to drink? Dog hair?" Jim shook his head in utter confusion.

"*Hair of the dog* is an English expression used in reference to the drinking of alcohol as treatment for a hangover."

Jim observed me as the definition sunk in and once it did, he smiled.

"Well, I'm more familiar with doggy style but I think right now I'll settle for one of those 'Hairy Dogs'."

"Jesus, you're incorrigible!"

"Last night was madness, I'm sure Arun dreamt of all those naked titties he had in his face all night!" he laughed.

Redbull spluttered across the bar as I almost choked at Jim's comment.

"Fucking Pakis can't handle their pussy drinks! I hope you're going to clean that up, you tosser?" Paul threw a rag at me as he walked by.

"Piss off!" was my only response.

"I don't suppose we're going to meet Arun today?" Jim asked as he took his first sip and sighed in approval.

"No, I'm sure he's recovering. Besides, I have to pick up Mona from the airport later."

"How's she doing? Terrible, what happened to her," he shook his head.

"Yeah, but I guess, it's fate, you know."

"How are you doing? Can't be easy for you either."

"Yeah, I'm alright. I mean it's not easy, but it's best that it happened now."

"Good of her to come for Arun's ‚ lough, especially after what she's been through," Jim was halfway through his pint.

"Yeah definitely. I was surprised, but she's a tough one."

"You know, if she needs some comforting, you can guide her to me," he winked.

"You keep your filthy mitts off her! She doesn't need to be comforted by a man whore!"

"Om, if I had feelings, that would hurt."

"Yeah, *if!*" I laughed.

"What are you going to do about Jaymee? She was really disappointed to hear you were no longer coming."

"Yeah I know, but with Mona's wedding called off, I couldn't really go," I expressed with genuine disappointment.

"I think you should make a trip out there nonetheless."

"Naah, it's too much of an effort. I mean, it would've been fun, but it's not like there's a future in it, you know?"

Jim put the pint glass down and turned toward me baffled.

"No actually, I don't know. How can you say there's no future there without even trying, Om?"

"Well, because she isn't Indian."

"And?"

"And I want to settle down with an Indian. My family expects me to settle down with someone of the same race, Jim."

"That's a bit racist, don't you think?"

"No, it's just how it is. By being with an Indian, there is a common understanding of the intricacies that are relevant to the culture and race. It's not something that can be learned, but it's more to do with the influence of your upbringing. For instance..."

"Blah blah blah!" he interrupted. "Did any of your family own slaves?"

"You wouldn't understand."

"What I don't understand is when two people have a lot in common, enjoy each other's company, share an understanding and are attracted to one another, and I *know* you are attracted to her because you're one giant erection when she's around, then why isn't there a future? Because she's not Indian? Because she doesn't worship a trillion Gods? Because she doesn't have a tiny red target on her forehead?"

"It's more complicated than that, Jim."

"You know, it surprises me. You see how difficult it is especially after what Mona has been through, after what you've experienced with Preeti and yet you discount someone just because they weren't born in a particular race? It's pathetic, Om."

"Since when the *fuck* did you get so deep and philosophical?"

"Since I learned about hairy dogs!" Jim broke into a cocky smile.

"Anyway, I can't see myself having a future with someone like that."

"Someone like what? A Filipino? Now *that* is definitely racist, Om."

"No! You referred to her as a 'sure thing', remember? I just can't have a future with someone who has been around and is easy."

It was Jim's turn to almost choke on his pint. His laughter echoed through the empty pub.

"What? What's so funny?" I asked.

"Om, you silly fool. I just said that to build your confidence!" he continued laughing.

"What?"

"Yeah, you were in such a shitty place that I figured you needed a confidence booster. I figured by telling you Jaymee was a sure thing, you'd believe you couldn't miss and wouldn't be so conscious of your game. Instead of trying hard, you'd be yourself when you gave it a shot."

"So, she's not easy?"

"Om, I hardly know the girl!"

Jim almost fell off the stool laughing. I fast-forwarded through every incident and conversation with Jaymee in my mind. Her flirtatious behaviour, reciprocating my gestures, initiating physical contact on our date was all the result of a genuine chemistry.

"You fucking dick-head! What if it backfired and she rejected me?"

Jim regained his composure and placed his hand on my shoulder.

"Om, one thing I know about is *women*. I knew, if you'd just be yourself, you'd bag that girl and, bugger me, *did you bag her*!"

Ignoring Jim's laughter, I neared the bottom of my drink as I attempted to make sense of everything.

"Om, you should make a trip out there, she seems like a wonderful girl. Remember, the only way to rid yourself of temptation, is to yield to it," he winked.

As Jim's words echoed in my mind, I wondered if that would apply to my desire for alcohol. If I gave into the temptation perhaps I wouldn't desire the forbidden libation as much and be better equipped to control the desire?

"Arun needs me here for the wedding. He has a lot to deal with and I need to be there to help him," I responded before I could consider Jim's suggestion.

"Yeah, he looked fucked up yesterday!"

"Well, he probably drank a whole bottle of Vodka! What do you expect?"

"No, Om, the guy has lost weight and looks as though he's aged! He almost looks sick!"

Jim was right; I had also noticed the drastic change in Arun. He looked pale and worn out. I could only attribute it to the guilt festering within him.

"It's eating him up inside," I murmured under my breath.

"It's what?"

"I said it's probably the stress from the wedding. That's why it's important for me to be here!"

"If that's wedding stress, I'm never getting married."

"Jim, you could never get married, it would mean knowing what meal you're having every night."

"Right you are," he raised his glass, "To never getting married!"

# Chapter 61

Crowds of people walked in and out of Kennedy airport as I waited for Mona. Flicking through the New York Post, I looked up at regular intervals in case she didn't spot me at our meeting point. Several months had passed since I had last seen Mona and so much had transpired within that period. She had met someone, practically moved to another country, got engaged and weeks before her wedding, she called it off.

"Can a cousin get a hug?" she smiled taking off her sunglasses.

"Mona!" I squeezed her tight.

"I can't tell you how badly I've needed this hug."

Slowly, Mona pushed me away and asked.

"Why do you reek of smoke?" she asked, "You haven't started, have you?"

"No, I was at the pub with Jim earlier."

"Oh, how is he?"

"The same, horny as ever!"

She covered her mouth and laughed in acknowledgement.

"Mona, what happened? You've lost so much weight! Haven't you been eating?"

"Silly boy, I was getting in shape for the wedding, remember?"

"I'm sorry, I just…"

"It's okay Om, you don't have to walk on egg shells with me."

Mona had changed drastically. Besides the weight loss, her skin had broken out and she had humongous bags under her eyes. I put it down to stress and the six-hour cross-country flight.

"How was the flight?"

"Exhausting! How's the wedding preparations coming along?"

"As expected, stressful!"

"Don't I know it!"

Mona remained quiet as she stared out the window on the way to the city. I couldn't even begin to comprehend what she had endured and the fact that she was attending a friend's wedding right after calling off her own must've compounded the anguish she suffered.

"Mona, are you okay? Mona?" I squeezed her hand.

"Sorry, I was lost in my own world, hon."

"I was just asking if you were alright?"

"Yes, I'm fine, dear. I'm just tired after the flight. I think, I need to take a nap once I get to the hotel."

"I still don't understand why you're staying at a hotel when you can crash at my place."

"Om, with the rates I get at the hotel, you should get rid of your flat and move in with me," she smiled.

"Good point! So, what do you want to do tonight?"

"Honestly Om, I just want to catch up on my sleep tonight and be fresh for the wedding tomorrow. Do you mind?"

"Sure hon, we can catch up after the wedding. I have to meet Arun for a drink tonight anyway. I think he wants to have a man-to-man talk before he bites the bullet, you know?"

"Yeah, I think he probably needs one. It must be a nerve-wracking time for him."

"Jesus, it'd be nerve-wracking for anyone, don't you think?"

"Yeah, it is," she whispered.

"Shit, I'm sorry! It's so insensitive of me going on about the wedding and everything, I'm sorry. This can't be easy for you."

Mona reached out and placed her hand on mine.

"Om, that's sweet, but don't worry, I've come prepared. Of course, you're going to talk about the wedding, your best friend is getting married, after all! Please, just be yourself, and don't treat me like I'm handicapped." She smiled warmly before turning to look out the window again, with a vacant stare.

# Chapter 62

Arun held the large mug of black coffee with both hands as he gingerly sipped away.

"You're really in bad shape, aren't you?"

"Om, I couldn't even take the subway to get here. My head's pounding so badly that I had to take a cab."

"You know a beer or two will fix that hangover right up?"

"Stop! You're going to make me puke," he said, covering his mouth with his hand.

"Is this really how you want to spend your last night of freedom, with a coffee in Starbucks?"

"Yes. After last night, this is *exactly* how I want to spend my last night."

"Jim wanted to know if you dreamt of titties last night," I smiled.

The sudden roar of Arun's laughter caused patrons to turn and stare at us.

"So, are you ready, young man?" I reached across the table and patted him on the shoulder.

"As ready as I can be."

"Okay, well, I guess that's good enough."

"Seriously though, thanks Om."

"Thanks for?" I asked.

"For being here. After everything that happened, I wasn't sure if you were going to be beside me through all of this."

"It's your wedding, dude, of course I'm going to be here."

The mobile phone vibrated against my thigh. Mona had sent a text informing she was calling it a night. As I texted back, Arun expressed his fear, "I'm scared."

"Scared of?"

"That I'm doing all this for the wrong reason," Arun wheezed.

"That's just cold feet, I'm sure. It happens to the best of us, Arun, you can't put too much stock into it."

"No, I don't think it's that," he shook his head, "Om, I haven't had a comfortable night's sleep since being with Maria. I can't stop thinking about what I did. I constantly feel guilty and whenever I'm around Rakhi, I'm just angry and I take it out on her."

"Arun… "

"Let me finish," he interrupted, "I accepted the job at the motel out of guilt and a fear of losing her. When I did, I felt something break inside me. What's worse is I've started resenting her for it. I'm angry that she's elated while I'm so miserable."

"Arun, it's not too late."

"Not too late for what?"

"To tell Rakhi the truth, to tell her about Maria. Arun, it's killing you inside and you need to purge. The guilt is going to destroy you. Look at you, you look like you've aged several years in these past few months."

"I know, I do look like shit, don't I? Well, I feel even worse."

"Arun, it's not too late."

"I can't, Om, I can't lose her."

"But what do you have with her now? You're not happy and this isn't the relationship you two shared. You've become distant from her and from the person you used to be. Arun, you're a good person and I know this lie is the reason for your breakdown."

"Om, if I told her, she'd call it off and leave me."

"Maybe. Maybe not! At least you would've been true to her, to yourself and to your relationship. At least you'd rid yourself of this burden you've been carrying all this time."

"I can tell her after we're married."

"And if she leaves you then? Arun, that's a divorce for you and her. It's not fair for you to do that to another person."

"But that's why I *would* tell her afterwards, she wouldn't leave me."

"Arun, you aren't thinking straight. That's just being plain manipulative. Can you understand you're doing that to the woman you love and are about to marry? Don't you find that perverse?"

"She'd forgive me after a while, and this way I wouldn't lose her," he justified.

"So you'd allow this marriage to take place under false pretences?"

Arun remained silent.

"Let's say she doesn't divorce you after you tell her. What kind of marriage would that be? She'd be miserable, a part of her would be broken, Rakhi would never trust you and it would never be the same again. At least now you have the opportunity to tell her before she takes that step. She can see how much you love her, cause you are getting married to her and took a job with her family. It's possible she'll forgive you and move forward. It may take her some time to heal and the worst she may do is postpone the wedding." Leaning in, I stressed, "Arun, it's not too late to tell her the truth."

"Maybe you're right," he whispered. ❖❖❖

## *Chapter 63*

Mona kicked off her shoes and let out a deep sigh as she lay down on the couch.

"Tired, aren't you? Do you want some coffee or tea?"

"Got anything stronger? Some whisky maybe?" she requested.

"Sorry, I'm out of booze," I responded proudly.

"Alright, whatever you're having then. By the way, I love what you've done with your place, Om, I'm quite impressed."

"What can I say, I got in touch with my feminine side," I smiled.

"Well, don't touch her too much, young man, especially not in public."

"What?" I laughed, as I tried to make sense of Mona's jab.

Placing the tea on the table, I sat beside her. I always felt happy to see Mona in New York. It was where our friendship began, and we always had a grand time whenever she visited.

"That was a beautiful reception. I like that it was classy and yet, not gaudy. You know how some Indians tend to go over the top and make their weddings more of a spectacle for the public."

"You must've seen a lot of that in Hong Kong?"

"Yes, some," she whispered.

Dropping my head in frustration, I apologised. Since Mona had arrived, I had consistently made unintentional comments that forced her to regress. I kept reminding her of the anguish she must be trying to escape.

"Mona, I'm sorry. I don't mean to say such insensitive things," I expressed as I reached out and held her hand.

"It's okay, Om, it's part of life. The daily reminders pale in comparison to people asking me directly just to get the latest gossip," she began to tear.

Reaching forward, I embraced and attempted to console her.

"Mona, it's not your fault. There is nothing to feel ashamed about. There are some things we don't have control over. You'll meet someone else and now that you're aware of this condition, it'll be something to look out for."

Pushing me away, Mona sobbed into her hands.

"Mona, it's okay, you'll get through this," I said, softly rubbing her back.

"It's a lie, Om." She whimpered.

"What's a lie?"

"The reason. It's a lie. There was no blood disorder, it was just an excuse."

"What?" My jaw dropped.

Mona fell to the floor weeping. Shocked, I watched her curl up into a foetal position as she broke down in front of my eyes. Instinctively, I dropped to the floor beside her and rubbed her arm, feebly attempting to calm her down. Once her tears subsided, I helped her up on to the sofa and brought her some water. Taking a sip, she lay quietly until she dozed off.

❖❖❖

## Chapter 64

Pretending to read, I turned the pages aimlessly. Mona was the rock I always turned to, my beacon of positivity and strength. The image of her collapsing on to the floor and falling apart would forever be etched into my psyche.

"Hey," she knocked on the ajar bedroom door, "How about that tea?" she asked wrapped in a blanket.

We sat silently on the couch cradling our cups. Mona would open up to me in her own time.

"It was wonderful to start with, just like a fairy tale. I was so happy. I had everything I could ask for. He took care of me, made me laugh, his mum was adorable and treated me like her daughter. I believed what I finally received was what I had I always deserved, wanted and prayed for." She managed a smile, "But as time went by, I began to see their true colours. He had a frightening temper that intensified each time it erupted. I convinced myself it was a minor flaw, after all no one's perfect. The mother started to pry more and more about my family and our finances but I put that down to the fact that she was old and most aunties are just nosey. Close to the wedding, he told me he sunk all his money into a profitable deal. Playing on my feelings for him and desperation to settle down, he manipulated me to ask my family to pay for the wedding. Ashamed to ask them, I decided to cash in all my savings and gave it to him. He later told me he invested part of those savings into another venture and forced me into compromising for a smaller wedding. Spitting out my anger, I accepted it. I told myself it was for the best and focused on the bright side that once we got married we would have more money to raise a family. But, it didn't stop there. One night after we had been out drinking with his friends, we went into a convenience store for some ice cream and in front of them he..." tears from her face descended to the floor, "He stuck his hands down the front of my pants."

I reached out to embrace her but she moved away.

"Please Om. I'm sorry, but please, don't touch me."

Embarrassed and uncertain of how to help her, I leaned further away from her to give her the space she seemed to need.

"When he did that, I was shocked and scared. He just laughed. Some of his friends sniggered along and others stared. He had violated and humiliated me. I justified that it was the result of the alcohol."

Mona continued to drink her tea quietly as she regained her composure and the tears stopped.

"A few days before I called you, the two of us shared a romantic dinner after which we had a few drinks. He then took me to his flat for the first time. It was a tiny two-bedroom flat that he shared with his mother. She was fast asleep in her room when we quietly snuck in. After a brief tour he proudly asked me what I thought of my home to be."

She turned towards me, "You know me, Om, I am not superficial and I didn't really care about the size of the flat. But I did have one question. I asked him how we would raise our kids in that flat."

Her eyes began to moisten and her bottom lip quivered. I wanted to hug her but was scared to upset her further.

"He bruised my arms by grabbing them tightly. He said I was a snob and his mother was right, that I'd complain and have problems with their home. Inches from my face, he screamed that I was a bitch. The mother woke up and saw us. He threw me against the wall and told his mother to kick me out and that he's done with me." Bent double, Mona began to sob uncontrollably. All I could do was sit next to her and watch.

Later, Mona would tell me that Sunil tried to reconcile but she could never return to him. Instead, she packed whatever she could and escaped to her home.

❖❖❖

# Chapter 65

My stomach grumbled as I flipped through the channels on the television desperately trying to find something to take my mind off my hunger when the phone rang.

"Hello?"

"Hey, it's Rakhi, are you busy?"

"Hey! No, not at all, I'm just waiting for a pizza. How's the honeymoon?"

"It's good, thanks. How are you? I'm sorry we didn't get a chance to call when we left, it was really chaotic."

"That's alright, we were all recovering from the reception anyway," I responded.

"I hope you guys had fun."

"Oh, we had a blast. Jim and I just dropped Mona to the airport and she was telling us how happy she was that she came."

"Oh, please tell her that Arun and I were really touched that she made it."

"Definitely. Hey, is Arun there, can I speak to him?"

"He's still in the room. Actually that's what I wanted to talk to you about."

"About what?"

"Arun. Om, you need to tell me what is going on."

"Sorry, but I'm sort of lost here, Rakhi."

"You're like his brother and if *anyone* is going to know what's going on, it's sure to be you."

"Rakhi, what happened?"

"All he does is sleep and stay in the room all the time," the frustration in Rakhi's voice grew stronger.

"I'm sure he's just tired, hon."

"Om, he hasn't *fucking* touched me on our honeymoon!" she snapped, "Does that sound normal to you?"

I had guessed Arun kept his secret alive. The fact that he couldn't look me in the eye, while Rakhi was radiating at the wedding was a good enough indication that nothing had changed.

"Rakhi, you two are married. If there is something wrong, you need to speak to *him* about it."

"I did and he told me the same crap that you did, that he's just tired".

The bell rang and I hoped it would be my saving grace. Walking to the door with cash in hand, I tried to circumvent Rakhi and her inquisition.

"I have to get the door."

"Om, you *know* what the problem is and you're keeping it from me."

"Rakhi, I can't get involved, this is between a married couple and you two need to figure it out for yourselves."

"Om, you let me get married knowing something was…"

Reaching for the doorknob, I almost dropped the phone.

"Rakhi, I didn't *let* you do anything. You're a grown woman and…"

"Hello? Om?"

"Rakhi," I whispered, "I'm going to have to call you back."

"Om this is *important*!"

"Preeti's here."

I hung up before she could respond.

## *Chapter 66*

Her smiling face beamed as tears trickled down her cheeks. Preeti's shiny, shoulder length hair was now streaked with hazel highlights. Tight fitted jeans hugged her toned legs. Standing at my doorstep, she looked as beautiful as ever!

"Hi! May I come in?"

Unable to respond, I stepped aside letting Preeti walk into the flat.

"Thanks," she placed her hand on my shoulder and kissed my cheek.

"Do... do you want something to drink?" I stuttered.

"A glass of water, please."

Even as she wiped away her tears, she continued to smile nervously.

"Are you surprised?" she asked, sitting on the couch.

"That's an understatement!"

"Well, you always liked it when I showed up unannounced, right?"

"And obviously you didn't," would have been my response if I hadn't held my tongue at the last second.

"Right. You look well."

"So do you, are you still playing basketball?"

"Every week." I was surprised she broached the topic of basketball since that's where I, and probably she, had met Ravi.

"You don't have that 'tummy' anymore."

"No, that was a long time ago."

"We had fun that time at Disney though didn't we?" she shuffled closer to me.

"Yeah, it was fun," I answered coldly.

"That was the best vacation of my life. I was looking through the photographs from that trip just last week."

Non-responsive, I drank from my glass and wondered one thing, what the *fuck* was she doing in my home?

"I was hoping I'd hear from you."

"You were? Why?"

"Because of the note I left on your car. You did get the note, right?"

"Yes."

"Did you read it?" she asked.

"No, I burned it," I felt a malicious joy in telling her what I did with her precious letter, especially since I learned it held something heartfelt.

Holding her tears back, Preeti mustered the courage to maintain her smile.

"That's understandable."

"Is that what you're here for? To ask me about a note you left on my car months ago?"

"No. I wanted to see you, so we could talk."

"Talk about what?"

"Om, could you please not be so curt? This isn't easy for me."

I was ready to explode! How dare she ask me to contain my animosity after what she had done? Taking a deep breath, I regained my composure.

"I apologise, but can you tell me what isn't easy for you?"

"Coming here! I was worried you'd scream and slam the door in my face. You would be in your right to do so, but I was still scared."

A part of me wanted to move closer and put my arm around her; to bring her head into my chest as I had many times, to inhale her with every breath, to feel her warm, smooth skin next to mine.

"Om, I don't know how to say this. I miss you! You're my one true passion, my one true love," she began to cry, "I fucked up and I'm so sorry for the pain I have put you through. If I could take it away I would Om, I promise you, I would. I've realised so much in the time away from you. I now know how good I had it. I'm sorry I took you for granted. I've been miserable without you and have felt so empty and lost."

Preeti stood up and hesitantly made her way to me before sitting on my lap.

"Give me a chance Om, give me a chance to make it up to you, to make things right," she stroked my cheek, "I'm miserable without you."

I craved to slip my arms around her waist and kiss her. That familiar scent and warmth of her began to arouse me. I had missed her. I *did* want her!

"Preeti," I stood up, taking her off my lap, "I'm sorry, this it a bit too overwhelming for me."

"I understand," she snivelled.

"I am sorry. I understand this took a lot of courage Preeti, but I really need to process all of this."

"Of course, that's fair. Just think about what I said but, before you decide, just read this after I leave," she handed me an envelope from her bag. "Please, don't burn this one," she smiled weakly, "It's valuable."

After giving me a hug, Preeti kissed me on the cheek before walking out the door.

# *Chapter 67*

*Dear Om,*

*I have started this letter a dozen times and each time, I threw it in to the trash. I decided to rummage through your letters and pictures of us when I came across the photos from Orlando. As I flipped through them, I couldn't stop crying. I remembered how happy we were together, how happy you made me. It really was the best part of my life.*

*I know I am the last person you would ever want to see and you're justified in feeling that way, no one can blame you. But you loved me once and I* ***still*** *love you, Om. There isn't and can never be another for me, I realise that now. I'm just sad we had to go through so much for me to appreciate what we shared.*

*I want a chance to have a place in your life again. I may never be able to make it right but I'd like for you to give me a chance to try. If there is a small part of you that feels for me, please give me the opportunity to nurture that feeling and let it blossom. You loved me once before and I believe that I can make you love me again.*

*There is another envelope that accompanies this letter. When you open it, you'll find a round trip ticket to Orlando. I also have a ticket and have confirmed the adjoining seat to yours. I humbly request that you join me and we can begin to mend our love from the point we were the happiest.*

*I don't know what happens next but I've put myself out there for you. I hope you'll be in the seat next to mine and don't worry, this time I've given you the window seat.*

*I Miss you*

*I Love you*

*Preeti*

## Chapter 68

Her incredible smile was warm and welcoming. Reaching out, she brushed her manicured fingers against my hand.

"Thank you sir, and how are you today?"

"Fine, thank you, Miss," I squinted to read her name tag, "Veronica!"

Looking at me from the corner of her eyes, she smiled, appreciating my effort.

I turned around and instinctively scanned the airport until Veronica's question brought my attention back to her, "Sir, have your bags been in your possession at all times?"

As she ran through the customary questions, I nodded robotically till she finished.

"Is the flight on time, Veronica?"

"Yes sir, departure is as scheduled. I see you've already confirmed a window seat. Are you happy with that or would you like to change it?"

"No, that's fine, thank you."

"Going on a well-deserved vacation, are we?"

"Yes, it's somewhat of a special trip."

"Understood!" she said with a broad smile, "Here are your documents. I suggest you make a run for it sir, they've already commenced with boarding. Have a safe trip!"

My mind was still wrapped in confusion as I jogged towards the gate. My heart and mind wrestled with each other, as they swung in opposite directions like a pendulum. I had contemplated calling Jim and Mona but was concerned about their opinions only confusing me further. I knew I needed to arrive at a decision by myself. After days of pondering, there remained one conclusion. The only way I could know for certain would be to take this step and find out.

"May I please have a look at your boarding pass, sir?" asked a member of the cabin crew.

"Have all the passengers boarded?" I panted.

"No sir, we're waiting for a handful more."

"Do I have time to run to the loo?"

"No sir, we'll be closing the gates shortly. I suggest using the lavatory on the flight to prevent any further delay."

Arriving at my row, I discovered the seats next to mine were empty. I fastened my seat belt and started up my iPod. As scripted, the passenger announcement system bellowed.

"Welcome aboard Continental Flight CO 99 on route to Manila via Hong Kong. Our flying time…"

Increasing the volume, I shut my eyes and drowned out the world.

❖❖❖

# *Chapter 69*

***My Dearest Soul Mate,***

***I waited for your smiling face to appear. I pictured running to you and throwing my arms around you and thanking you. As much as I yearned to be with you, I can't say I'm surprised by your decision and nor can I blame you.***

***I'm not quite sure where I go from here but wherever it is, I'll always keep you in my thoughts. If you ever have a change of heart, don't hesitate to reach me. Through my journey I'll still carry the hope of you returning to me.***

***May God guide and bless you, my dearest Om.***
***With all my Love,***

***Preeti***

## *Chapter 70*

With quivering hands, I dabbed the handkerchief on my sweaty brow. As my stomach twisted inside out, I turned to Jim's jolly face for assurance.

"This is it, are you ready?" I asked.

"Oh, I'm prepared, buddy boy, but you don't look too good. Still reeling from the bachelor party, are you?"

"No, it's not that."

"Nervous?"

"Of course, I'm *fucking* nervous, Jim!"

"Dude, we're in a Church," his eyes widened.

"Shit!" I covered my mouth.

"DUDE!"

Putting his hand on my shoulder, Jim leaned in and with a cool confidence whispered, "Don't be, it'll go smoothly."

"Yeah, you're probably right."

"Where are you and Jaymee going after this?" he asked trying to distract me.

"We've booked ourselves at a resort in Hawaii."

"Yeah, I bet you won't even see the island," he nudged.

"Here's hoping."

Scanning the guests sitting on the pews, I noticed one face missing. I hoped Arun would've arrived in the final hours before the wedding but he was nowhere to be seen. I heard about the divorce from the grapevine and when I tried to reach him, he rejected my calls. Rumour was that when he returned from one of his many drinking binges, he had a fight with Rakhi and disclosed the truth about him and Maria. When he woke up in the morning, he had no recollection of the previous night and Rakhi had already left him.

"You can't expect him to be here, Om. Don't worry, he knows where to reach you when he's ready."

"You're right."

The remaining guests filtered into the Church and the ushers prepared them for the start of the ceremony. As we both stared down the aisle at the entrance, Jim took a deep breath and murmured, "So, I was right."

"About?"

"Finding happiness with someone is too big to be restricted by race, creed and culture."

"Yes," I whispered frustrated.

"I've only got one thing to say, '*Om's got jungle fever! Om's got jungle fever!*'" he sang under is breath as he did a little jig.

"Can we please focus?"

"Seriously though, I'm very happy for you, Om."

"Likewise Jim, likewise."

A sudden hush fell on the crowd as the traditional '*Here comes the bride*' bellowed through the giant brass pipes.

"It's show time, Om. No turning back now. We good?" Jim shot me a wink.

"We good!"

"Good luck!" he shook my hand firmly.

"And to you, sir."

The doors gently swung open and we held our breath as our eyes fell on the bride. Draped in a Stephen Yearick halter gown, she treaded softly on the petals that graced the floor.

"That's the most beautiful bride I've ever seen. She looks like an angel," he whispered.

"She truly is one, Jim."

All eyes were transfixed on her as she glided closer to the altar.

"Jim, I have one question for you before she gets here."

"*Now* you have a question? What?"

"Remember how you told me you preferred black women?"

"If you really must know, I like my women like I like my coffee, *Mocha*!" he smiled, "Now shut up and let me enjoy the moment!"

Climbing the steps, she smiled at me before turning to Jim. Mona glowed with joy. The priest commenced the ceremony and instructed the best man to provide the ring for the groom. Jim turned and stretched his hand out towards me and shot me another wink.

"Jim, take care of her," I whispered handing him the wedding ring, "Keep her happy, always."

"I will Om, always!" he replied before turning to Mona and slipping the ring on to her finger.

❖❖❖

# Epilogue

Mona lifted her gown and with Jim in tow, she scurried through the passage of well wishers towards the rented limousine. Pausing at the door, she turned and scanned the numerous faces of the guests, searching for one. Her gaze landed at Om who was smiling at her. Tears began to trickle down her face as she smiled back and waved. She mimed the words 'Thank You' before ducking into the car with her husband.

Om stared at the car as it headed down the street and turned the corner. Overcome with an unexpected heavy feeling, he let out a deep sigh.

"She'll be fine," Jaymee smiled as she wrapped her slender arm around his shoulder.

"I know. They're going to make each other very happy."

Putting her hands his shoulders, Jaymme turned Om towards her and whispered, "And I'm going to make *you* very happy."

Placing her hand on his cheek, she leaned in and kissed him.

"Let's go home."

"Let's," he smiled.

***

Standing in the lobby of the apartment building, Jaymee turned to Om and smiled.

"Babe, I need you to do something for me."

"Sure."

"Can you go to the grocery store and pick up these things for me?" she handed him a list.

"Now?" he scrolled down the list. "I have some of these upstairs though."

"Please babe," she pouted, "I have a surprise in mind."

"If it's a surprise, shouldn't *you* be getting the supplies?" Om laughed.

"Very funny! Please Om," Jaymee began to whine.

"I'm tired, Jay."

"I'll make it worth your while," Jaymee smiled and seductively bit her lip before leaning in and biting Om's earlobe.

"Well," Om chuckled, "If you put it like that."

"Thanks, babe. I promise you won't be disappointed!"

"After that little appetiser, I'm sure I won't be," Om winked.

As she watched Om make his way out of the Lobby, Jaymee repeatedly jabbed the elevator button hoping the doors would open sooner. Throwing open the door to Om's flat, Jaymee rushed to her suitcase and began to anxiously pull out its contents and placed them beside her. Ripping open the bag of potpourri, she sprinkled the dried petals on the floor of the living room. After turning on the special CD she had prepared to set the mood, Jaymee lit the numerous lavender scented candles and placed them around the apartment.

Returning to the suitcase, she reached in for the last remaining item she needed for the ritual. Picking up the small blue suede box, she walked into the bathroom and faced her tanned reflection in the mirror.

"This is it, Jaymee," she whispered as she straightened her lilac halter-neck gown, "This, is, it."

Looking down, she slowly lifted the suede lid, revealing a gleaming platinum ring. A warm smile crept across her face as she began to tear.

Walking down the street toward his building, Om couldn't help but smile. He struggled to recollect the last time he felt as light and free as he did at that very moment. With the wind at his back, a bright sky above, a beautiful and loving woman in his life waiting at home for him and two of his closest friends married, he felt on top of the world. Om realised he was finally content. He was finally at peace. His smile grew into a grin resembling a Cheshire cat. His step had a spring and warm glow grew within. Om's pace slowed to crawl as a sudden shiver passed down his spine. The gentle breeze that was at his back now carried with it an all too familiar scent. Jasmine.

"Om..." the voice chimed from behind halting him in his tracks.

Struck by a sense of fear and shock, his glare fell to the pavement as he tried to process the moment. As much as he wanted to turn around and confront his suspicion, he was too scared. Walking around, she faced him and smiled.

"Preeti," Om whispered.

She wrapped her arms around him and placed her head on his chest.

"I've missed you so much!" she softly said under her breath.

Unable to reciprocate the gesture nor push her away, Om stood frozen. Feeling her warm body next to his and inhaling her scent gave rise to the very emotion he felt when she hugged him for the first time at the Desi party.

"You mean too much to me, Om, and I can't let you go. I just can't."

Om fought the temptation to put his arm around her as he tried to ignore his natural desires. In spite of everything in his mind screaming that she didn't deserve him, his primal instinct felt this was right. This is how it had always been.

Stepping back, she looked him in the eyes as hers welled up.

"What we feel, what we have, is bigger than us, Om."

His instincts urged him to wipe her tears as he did on their first day, but he continued to fight it.

"I know with all my heart that we're meant to be, Om," she placed her hand on his chest, sending a tingling sensation through him.

"I know you feel it, too," she whispered.

He had tried to bury the corner of his heart that he knew Preeti would always have and until this moment, he believed he had succeeded.

"I've thought about this moment for a long time," stepping back again, Preeti wiped her tears and smiled, "And after playing out the scenario hundreds of times, I know that this is as good as any."

Reaching into her back pocket, she brought her hand around. Getting down on one knee, Preeti asked, "Om, my soul mate. Will you marry me?"